Praise for *Rocked in Time*

"*Rocked in Time* offers a great read, beautifully written, and more important, holds true to the flavor and feel of lives lived on the edge, surviving through constant effort and recalibration. Degelman calls out our frailties, indulgences, and errors — including decades of efforts to root out our own ingrained sexism — without denigrating the courage and commitment of men and women whose quest for truth and justice continued forward, utopian anarchists who never forgot how to laugh."

—*Peter Coyote, actor, writer, Zen Buddhist priest*

"I absolutely loved this book! I was attracted by the cover and description and really enjoyed the adventure. After reading it, I went to the author's website and saw this is the third book in a trilogy! The good news is I did not need to read the other two books first to understand and follow the plot of *Rocked in Time*. I will go back and read the other two books because I really liked Degelman's writing style. This book is really a rollicking adventure through the 1960's as seen through the perspective of a member of the San Francisco Mime Troupe. Throughout there are cameos from Shirley Clarke (a filmmaker I really admire), Bread and Puppet theater, Black Panthers, Hell's Angels, Students for a Democratic Society (SDS) and the Diggers. There are also references to Commedia Dell' Arte, and Bertolt Brecht. This book felt autobiographical but it is fiction (though influenced by writer's formative years). I highly recommend this incredible and enjoyable read."

—*Ann M.'s NetGalley Reviews*

ROCKED IN TIME

Confessions of a
Radical Theater Artist

CHARLES DEGELMAN

New York
HARVARD SQUARE EDITIONS
www.harvardsquareeditions.org
2022

ACKNOWLEDGMENTS

Thanks to R.G. Davis and the San Francisco Mime Troupe for helping me fuse the disparate elements of my early years into a lifelong pursuit of art and politics. Thanks to my publisher, Harvard Square Editions, for keeping the fires burning during the long Covid winters. Thanks to the writers at Retrospect Media for reading my resurrected memories, to Laura Kern for her savvy observations and skillful editing, to Susan Underwood for her sharp copy editor's eye, and to Tony Kahn and Savannah Sanfield for their interest and astute outside perspectives. Most of all, I want to express my deep love and gratitude for the patience and persistence of my companion on the road of life. Without her brilliant, good-natured support, I might never have begun, much less completed this journey between the twin pillars of fact and fiction.

—*Los Angeles, 2022*

Whoever wants to fight lies and ignorance must surmount at least five difficulties. They must have the *courage* to speak the truth when it is everywhere stifled; the *intelligence* to recognize it when it is everywhere hidden; the *art* to make it manageable like a weapon; the *judgment* to choose who will know how to make it effective and finally enough *guile* to make them understand it.

— Bertolt Brecht, *In Exile,* 1935

Part 1

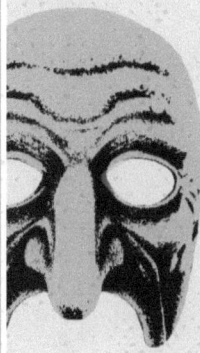

1

RATMAN MEETS
THE 50-FOOT HINDU

The Emeryville flats used to stink of the tide. Dead fish, drying algae, bottles and cans, old tires lay scattered over a landscape of mud and sewage. Stick figures perched on the muddy edges of the East Bay, fanciful driftwood and tin creatures standing stork-legged in the mud, stick-flapping arms, wings, feathers, broken brooms, old flags, weathervanes, hubcaps, rusted saw blades, other detritus. Celebrating America's junk. Resistance. We drove together, my cousin Eric and I, in a VW bus weathered to a chalky blue. Across the flats, the Bay Bridge arched toward Angel Island and beyond, to the summer fog bank of San Francisco. We bounced into the Haight-Ashbury to check out a band my cousin had written to me about the previous winter. He called them the Jefferson Airplane and they were playing at a little club called The Matrix.

1

We were stoned on Mexican weed. I was reciting lines from *Ratman Meets the 50-Foot Hindu*, a play I had recently closed back in Harvard's experimental, black box theater. I played a 50-foot Hindu who had journeyed to America to avenge the murder of the sacred cow. This zealot took his revenge by stomping his burger-munching victims to death with a set of hooves.

I'd picked up the fake Indian accent from the cultural ether without offense. White people had begun to stir, waking to the notion that civil rights were human rights and that racism was alive and well in America. When Ratman and the 50-foot Hindu walked the earth, India still seemed like a distant, overpopulated nation, shaped by British colonialism, its independence two decades old but still imbued with the nonviolence of Gandhi and the meditative power of the spinning wheel. The Maharishi hadn't yet hustled The Beatles, India and Pakistan hadn't yet become nuclear powers, Bangladesh hadn't been flooded out by cyclones, and John and Yoko's meditations hadn't dispatched my generation on a simpleton's goose chase.

So, my Hindu accent was still okay and my character diabolical, a complex being who, beyond his fierce and scheming interior, presented himself as an addled older gentleman whose faith had been defiled by America's hamburger fetish. He was a man with a mission. But the 50-foot Hindu had proven to be no match for Ratman. In the finale, the superhero and his diabolically tragic foe squared off in a revolving restaurant high above the city.

A guy named Mickey Solomon had written the play and created Ratman, a superhero who wore a cape over black tights and jockey shorts. Ratman preceded anyone but the most embryonic underground heroes and antiheroes. Only San Francisco's Rip Off Press and Paul Krassner's heady mix of news and satire, *The Realist* had published anything like Ratman before Mickey wrote his pioneering superhero drama.

The play had been an underground hit spring semester. The culture was still pre-hippie across most of the nation. In San Francisco and parts of lower Manhattan, the beats had begun to emerge from their hiding places in, around, and parallel to the straight world. We were still listening to surf music, but The Kinks and The Rolling Stones were ripping off Chicago and Mississippi bluesmen and generating the bad-boy myth; television had begun sucking Jonathan Winters's straight weirdness into the Twilight Zone.

After the production closed and the spring semester had finalized, I drove west with Mickey, winging it out to California on the Pennsylvania Turnpike in a '57 Ford station wagon. The Ford was a beater, but it had overdrive and a big V8. We were freewheeling through the June heat, me in my accustomed jeans and T-shirt, Mickey in plaid Bermuda shorts, a Hawaiian shirt, and a straw porkpie hat turned up at the front.

A Pennsylvania state trooper pulled us over. He didn't stop us for any reason that I can remember, but the flashing lights in my mirrors set my heart beating. I played it straight, full of "yes, sir"s and "no, sir"s, but the trooper smelled blood. He probably thought he smelled weed, but no. I was headed to the world of weed and could wait to get stoned. Mickey didn't need weed; he was stoned on his own recognizance. Regardless, the trooper made us both get out of the car. Mickey stood in the grass on the turnpike shoulder, hands stuffed into his Bermuda shorts, Hawaiian shirt open to reveal a Cambridge-winter, fish-white student belly, his porkpie hat sitting slightly askew. I stood by the back of the station wagon, mesmerized by the flashing blue dome of the cop mobile.

"Where you comin' from?" the trooper asked.

"Boston, sir," I said, trying to keep things vague.

"Uh, that's Harvard, sir," Mickey said. "We come from the green pastures of Harvard University."

Bob Dylan said that in his first album for Columbia Records, which never seemed like a cop-out, because it was Dylan, and Dylan was exempt. Nothing could touch him, no other songwriter, no other singer, and certainly no corporate authority. Plus, monster straight-world producer John Hammond had recognized Dylan's unique gifts and had taken him on. When he wasn't hanging out in the Village, Dylan hung out in Cambridge to play at places like Café Yana and Club 47 on Mount Auburn Street off Harvard Square. The Cambridge scene was shifting from jazz to folk, from Alan Ginsberg and the wife-killer William Burroughs to Joan Baez and Howlin' Wolf. Folk music, the people's music, was comin' in. I had been exposed to bebop as a kid by the crew-cutted drummer in my high-school band. But jazz was inaccessible to a country boy even with a city background. I didn't play music until the folk thing began when I fell in love with a teenage Joan Baez.

The Pennsylvania state trooper didn't care much about Mississippi blues, bebop, or Bob Dylan. He was busy scoping out Mickey, with the Bermuda shorts and the white belly and the porkpie hat. "Where you two headed," he said. Not asked. Said.

"California, sir," I said.

The cop did a quick take. "What for?"

"Hey." Mickey flashed the cop a casual thumbs-up from the hip. "Surf's up… sir."

I figured we were about to get ticketed or hauled in, but the cop stared at Mickey a little longer, the way a cow stares at humans through a pasture fence. Then, in keeping with his bovine essence, he turned and ambled back to his car. "Just keep drivin'," he said over his shoulder. "You're almost to the Ohio line."

Mickey gave him a second thumbs-up, and I ducked back into the driver's seat.

We made it over the Ohio line and all the way to Berkeley, me ecstatic as we drove into each setting sun, young enough to be caught up in the romance of the road, much of it still two lanes wide with a suicide strip in between, railroad tracks running parallel to us, America slinging freight trains across the plains at 60 miles an hour. The trains were cool, the prairie was cool, the highway was cool, the inside of my head was a scramble of past regrets, anticipatory dread, fears, and fervor; manic, really, the highs and lows sweeping over me three or four times daily while Mickey kept up a rambling string of unanswerable questions and speculative answers. Mickey and I said good-bye in front of an old, brown-shingled craftsman on the flats of Berkeley, and I haven't seen him since. Goodbye, porkpie hat.

Weeks later, Mickey's whacky 50-Foot Hindu still bounced around inside my head as my cousin Eric and I drove into the city to see this new band. I babbled gibberish in the goofy Hindu accent that I had developed for the role.

We crossed into San Francisco, Eric took the Fell Street exit toward the Haight, The Matrix, and the Jefferson Airplane.

"Man, you're funny," Eric said. "You should check out the Mime Troupe."

"Who are they?"

Eric was my California connection. I survived Cambridge winters in part by writing to him and receiving stoned, written drawings in reply. He lived by the bay and drove to class in Berkeley. He ate morning glory seeds and studied Japanese gardening and Chinese feng shui way before feng shui was hip. He launched into a description of the Mime Troupe.

"They're this crazy bunch of radical actors," he said. "They're doing shows but they're all, you know, like, politicos, into class struggle and the revolution, like the WPA used to do. They really kick ass."

"Radical actors?" I said. "Like in the theater? I didn't know about the WPA, Roosevelt's Works Progress Administration that gave money to writers and photographers and painters and theater people right alongside the people who built dams and power plants and monuments and public buildings.

I didn't know about the political theater and agitprop of the 1930s and the new radical stuff hadn't really shaped up yet. There was Dada surrealism and beatnik comedy and the improv satire churned up by the Committee in North Beach, but radical actors? I knew what radical meant, but radical theater? No. Nobody knew about it. Not yet. Not in the overarching Cold War, gray-flannel, apron-and-girdle swamp of the middle class or even in the budding beatnik resistance of the late 1950s.

"They're doing this show, man," my cousin said. "They call it 'Civil Rights in a Cracker Barrel.' It's like a minstrel show, you know, tap dancers in blackface."

"Minstrel show!" I recoiled. The Veterans of Foreign Wars in my Massachusetts town had put on a minstrel show every spring at the high school and it was ugly, even back then, all these old white guys onstage, acting out the racist crap that they had never had to drop in the segregated army.

"No, the Mime Troupe turns it around," my cousin said. "They're all in blackface, even the black guys in the show. And it cuts right to the bone. About how all this racist shit is coming down. Even outside the South."

My cousin had gone to a public school in the East Bay, in Richmond, and Richmond had been a shipbuilding port during the war, its cannery row waterfront converted into one big shipyard, where millions came to work building Victory ships and Liberty ships that carried the tanks and guns, bullets, bombs, and G.I.s to Europe and the Pacific. So many Negro workers had fled the South to work in the war industries out West that Richmond had become ghettoized. My white towhead blond cousins went to school with lots and lots of black kids. Most the time everybody got along fine.

"But last year, after the Watts riots…"

I had been in California when Watts blew up. We crouched around a plastic television set in Eric's bungalow perched on the low-rent side of the hill, watching the LAPD race around with shotguns against the fluorescent glare of burning storefronts. The event was impossible to connect with.

Nobody had ever seen an American city burn like that on television. Below us, the refinery hissed and chuffed in the distance, casting an eerie neon glow on the low cloud cover that hung over the East Bay. Eric, who had seen the tensions grow in high school, had predicted that "someday, man... people are pissed off, man. They're really pissed off and someday it's gonna explode." And it did.

I had read James Baldwin's *The Fire Next Time*. And here it was, the fire this time, baby. Four hundred miles to the south, in Watts, people inhaled the smoke from burning tar and electrical wiring, smarted from tear gas and broken glass. White-skinned mannequins lay raped, denuded, and scattered on the electrocuted streets. The mob, the resistance, the looters, all one spontaneous bunch, first endured the batons of the LAPD, then fell under their shotguns. The governor called in the National Guard to keep the trigger-happy L.A. cops from killing all the black people in Watts.

Baldwin had written about his heightened awareness of the Nazi concentration camps where Jews, gypsies, Catholics, and radicals were registered, stripped of their belongings, enslaved, starved, beaten, worked to death, or gassed. Would we see that happen here? Would anybody care? Or would they look the other way?

During a year off from college, I had sweltered in South Philly, working with an embryonic SDS, Students for a Democratic Society, doing community organizing with my folk-singing Swarthmore friends. They'd been

inspired by their success at forming an interracial movement of the poor in a Philadelphia satellite city, Chester.
They had linked arms with John Lewis and Martin Luther
King, black and white together, not only white college
kids, but poor black people, poor white people. All poor,
all the time.

Working with SDS, I had learned what those neighborhoods were like. On warm Philly nights, kids competed
at street corners they could not cross, Italian and black
kids singing doo-wop across the intersections, much of it
from their own hearts and minds. The Fabulous Fabian had
come from that South Philly neighborhood.

My previous trip to California had culminated in the
March on Washington. I had driven back to Cambridge in
a fellow student's Nash Rambler. I convinced her to detour
from our Boston-bound itinerary and join the massive
confluence of people in buses with banners about income
and equality and jobs and poverty, buses from all over the
nation, flowing past us on the fledgling Interstate as we
plodded East in the little Rambler.

Although we had spoken few words coming across the
country, this young woman and I stuck together through
the March with the swirl of humanity flowing around the
Washington Monument, the Reflecting Pool, and us, our
connection palatable, infectious. We crashed on the couch
of a friend and explored our young bodies, kissing each
other's smiles, buzzing with relaxation but urgent, not
wanting to lose what we had felt with the crowds on the

D.C. Mall, charged with the energy of *black and white together / we shall not be moved*. We moved together, this young stranger and I, in our own microcosm — one mind, one body, one being.

After those early days, the resistance began to grow. Potheads and politicos, hipsters and freaks nodded to each other on the street as the war escalated. The draft intensified. Soon, academia would no longer offer sanctuary. The universities worked in collusion with the war machine as it geared up for profit. Poorly performing classmates were thrown into the Selective Service hopper. We had to do something. So, beyond their liberal arts educations, the universities now offered an adjunct degree in the politics of resistance. I had learned what radical meant in poor neighborhoods and in academia. But in the theater world?

I was still tossing the notion of radical theater around in my cannabis-fired mind when we parked on Fillmore Street's steep incline and tumbled downhill to The Matrix. As a folkie, I had learned the traditional tunes assiduously until Bobby Dylan came along and turned folk music upside-down, stealing lines and snatches from Appalachia, dust-bowl Oklahoma, rock 'n' roll. Dylan came off like a thief, a 20th-century François Villon, composing tunes and lyrics that dug into the furrows of my mind. The Jefferson Airplane promised to offer a different musical trip, more Dylan than rock and roll.

I fought off chills from the pot and the frigid San Francisco summer nights. Inside The Matrix, all went warm. We sat and listened to this strange new music and — although it didn't grab me the way Dylan did — it rocked us into absorbing every sound the Jefferson Airplane cranked out of its Marshall amps. But through it all, I couldn't get this minstrel show "Civil Rights in a Cracker Barrel" thing out of my head. On the way home, I asked my cousin where this group, the Mime Troupe, was playing. "They don't have a theater," Eric told me. "They play outside in the parks. For free."

By day, my cousin Eric and I worked at landscaping a garden. We dug and graded, built redwood retaining walls, and hauled wheelbarrows of excess dirt to the bluffs where we dumped them into the San Francisco Bay without a thought for the environment. And every day, we watched Navy tugs haul another WWII-vintage Liberty ship toward the gray jumble of the Oakland Navy Yard from their mothball moorings in a far reach of the Bay. They were ramping up the war in Vietnam. The navy was re-deploying those heroic old freighters that had hauled war supplies and troops to war in Europe and the Pacific.

Now they were being hauled back into service. The war was building fast, escalation, they called it. We called it the "down escalator," a moving stairway to hell. A reluctant LBJ had gotten his excuse for war, whether he wanted it or not. The Vietnamese had attacked an American airbase just outside of Saigon, wherever that was. Now Johnson's war hawk advisors and a staunch, anti-communist Congress could begin attacking the Vietnamese in earnest.

America, land of democracy, had stopped elections in this little country nobody knew anything about. Our leaders were — once again — afraid the commies would win the election. At least, that's the excuse they used — the domino theory. One nation falls and knocks down the next nation, a dumb analogy to describe poverty-stricken, colonialized countries struggling to manage their economies. It had been getting crazy, with monks setting themselves on fire to protest American intervention.

Operation Rolling Thunder had begun bombing Hanoi and the North Vietnamese countryside after our beleaguered President, like all the others before him, Truman, Eisenhower, Kennedy, all had succumbed to the fear they would appear soft on Communism. What a load of crap. We knew the war was a sham. Every war was a sham. World War Two was supposed to be the good war, but only because we had to beat Hitler. But if you really looked at history, you'd see that our supposed enemies, the Soviet Ruskie Commie Reds had fought the Nazis harder and longer and suffered more loss than anybody else, including our military. Together, as allies, we had fought and beaten down the Nazi threat.

So now, we were supposed to swallow the bullshit that the Soviet Union was the enemy, because they were communists, and communism was a threat to democracy.

It was like in Orwell's *1984,* where the government constantly shifted enemies to sustain an endless war. It was bullshit and we knew it.

They labeled the Vietnamese communists, too. You just had to dig beneath the surface to find out that the Vietnamese were fighting for their independence. They didn't give a damn about communism, but China's Mao Tse Tung was willing to give Ho Chi Minh the help he needed to kick the colonial French out of the tiny country. Now, 10 years later, the only difference was that the French war had become the American war.

So, while we were discovering the Jefferson Airplane and the Mime Troupe, we were also talking about this wicked new war and joining other protestors. We knew we could make big trouble for the Cold War warmongers. Knowing about the Liberty ships, their purpose during WWII and the clear signs of the Vietnam thing escalating, we drove up to Port Chicago where the Navy kept a big ammunition dump.

Antiwar groups in Berkeley had planned an action in Port Chicago to protest the refurbishment of those old Liberty ships. We parked the VW bus and walked down a corridor of sailors and civilians at the munitions docks to the protest staging area. We were going to join the night shift of demonstrators who had swarmed over a trainload of napalm, bound for Vietnam via the same Liberty ships we watched being towed to the navy yard for refurbishing. Refurbish, hell.

The old Liberty ships looked frail. You could see the rust bubble up beneath the slapped-on coats of navy gray. None of us wanted to see American sailors drown while nursing those resurrected buckets across the Pacific. We began to feel a kinship with those sailors, even though, in the Navy, they had enlisted to fight. The draft was another story, that was for G.I.s. The "G" and the "I" stood for Government Issue, men labeled and cataloged just like weapons and clothes and jeeps, only these were people. A big joke if you were into playing ironic with your life. Most G.I.s hadn't been given the choice. They'd been drafted the same way our fathers had been grabbed for The Good War. We marched down the path from the parking lot toward the gates and the wharves where the Liberty ships were docked.

A crowd of locals who worked at Port Chicago had begun to gather. For them, a bunch of pinko commie beatniks had shut down the port, threatening to take away their jobs. A small knot of them had already gathered at the gate, held back by a lackadaisical file of Alameda County Sheriff's officers. My peripheral vision caught a guy about my age tense his upper arm and take a step toward me. Wham! His fist appeared in my face like a Popeye cartoon. I went down, relieved to follow out the non-violent spiral, the gravity-fed arc toward justice. The last thing I wanted to do was fight this guy.

"You okay?" My cousin bent down to lift me by the arm.

"Yeah," I said. I rose to my feet and my jaw began to ache. I could hear the other protestors cheering my recovery. We slept out that night in the sector that "the authorities" had cordoned off for us. The blockade lasted for several weeks, making it difficult to load the ships with enough explosives to vaporize any of the old vessels at sea.

By day, we built redwood retaining walls and brick terraces for some fancy-ass executive at Standard Oil, while over the hill the apocalyptic refinery chuffed out fossil fuel for the American Dream. But with the war building, and the anti-war movement gaining momentum, I couldn't get the Mime Troupe out of my mind.

That Saturday, I found the park where the Mime Troupe had set up under a gray sky, torn ragged blue as the morning fog burned off. The sun warmed the grass. People wandered into the park to lounge on blankets, to sit cross-legged, tipping up green gallon jugs of Zinfandel and Chablis. Nobody brought Gallo. The grape strike was on, and the farm workers would win.

The Mime Troupe stage consisted of wooden platforms and a painted canvas curtain with bright ribbons floating in the breeze off the wood-framed uprights. Across the top, stretched between the uprights, a hand-painted sign in cartoon gothic announced the San Francisco Mime Troupe. Above the company sign, a medieval griffin held a banner in its beak promising "engagement, commitment, and fresh air." The stage, the painted curtain and its flags formed a focal point on the green grass in front of the wedding-cake arches, cornices, and towers of a large gothic cathedral, named after Peter and Paul.

Off to one side, a circle of performers beat tambourines and a primitive drum. One of them played a recorder. They sang a song in Italian and danced, dressed in ragged street versions of Shakespearean garb. This scenario played out years before the tsunami of Ye Olde Renaissance Faires flooded our parks; I'd never seen anything like it. My eye fell first on a tall, gangly actor with straight, long hair, dressed in red-dyed long johns. A second, stocky actor dressed in tights and billowing pantaloons and a ridiculous silk blouse held a mask while he sang. A dark-skinned woman, older but beautiful, ageless to my young eyes, dressed in a peasant skirt and scoop-neck blouse, danced and beat a tambourine. Her eyes were gigantic, and she sang the way she danced — strong and fluid.

This ragged Troupe pranced onto the stage, singing, the crowd clapping out the tempo. The stage floor became a giant drum, their footsteps pounding out the beat. They disappeared behind the curtain and the show began. First came a military general dressed in black with a stubby sword. He moved in gallops, like a child pretending to ride a horse. He introduced the play in a phony Spanish accent. The beautiful servant girl joined him onstage where they performed a hip, updated vaudeville routine full of gags about local politicians, drugs, and the Vietnam War.

I got it. They had brought the 16th century into the present, and they were playing in the marketplace to the peasants. They were crude and funny and very tight, each character taking on specific postures and movements. They spoke in purposely broad Spanish and Italian accents, caricatures of all classes. Another tall guy played a fop and a phony philosopher, a doctor and an imaginary invalid all in one, like in a Molière play. Another woman played the ingénue, and a harlequin clown played a lovestruck servant. Two uniformed characters played grunts in the occupying army, the Italian military. I sat on the grass, leaned back on my elbow and laughed. Everybody wanted to get rich. Of course, they were forced into the narrow confines of their lowly serf and merchant classes so they could only steal from each other. The olive-skinned servant girl was the most powerful in the cast, the only character searching for the truth.

Somebody passed a gallon of Burgundy to me. The neck was covered with saliva. I wiped the neck with my hand and slugged a deep draught from the jug. What unfolded onstage blew my mind. I was used to the classics and restoration comedy, but this was a full-blown dance of grotesquerie and skilled improvisation. The show played like jazz, like bebop, tight but full of improvisation. The masks pushed the characters into high relief, into broad stances, quick gestures. They danced on the stage, the wooden platforms creaking under the footsteps and foot stomps. Their voices carried on the wind, not always audible, but their gestures told you all you needed to know about who leered, lusted, hustled, and who lost to whom.

The beautiful servant girl won out in the end, getting the last word. She carried the moral — You never get rich by ripping each other off, loving and taking care of your brothers and sisters bestowed the only real wealth, love for even the pitiful buffoon who played the cook. Love them all. "And if you want something done…" She bowed deep, her scoop neck revealing her fine figure. "Do it yourself." She stood up, flashing a knowing "gotcha" wink and a white, white smile, while the rest of the Troupe danced back onstage for a raucous curtain call.

The audience rose, cheering, whistling, applauding. The whole company leapt offstage and moved among the crowd, shouting, "We don't take no foundation grants, Bank of America hates us. We give to you, you give to us, brothers and sisters. Give us your money, moolah, smackers, simoleons, shekels, bones, clams, guilt gelt."

People dug in and forked over. The crowd began to break up and drift away. I had come alone. I felt flushed, intimidated by what I had seen. Where did these guys come from? They weren't kids. They had to be trained actors to dance, sing, and move like that. I walked behind the curtain. Soaked with sweat, they were stripping to change back into their street clothes — jeans and jackets, shirts and skirts.

One of the actors was black. That surprised me. After all, it was Italian *commedia dell'arte* and I didn't expect a black guy with a fake Guinea accent. Expect? What was

I talking about? Expect? Expect what? Expect where? Harvard? My all-white high school?

I walked up to the guy who had played the dandy doctor. He was smaller than he looked onstage. His black hair was streaked with a trace of white and he had a moustache. "Hi, uh," I said. "That was… that was…" I shook my head. "… really cool!"

He laughed. "Thanks."

"Who are you?" I asked.

He turned to the rest of the cast. "We are-a da San Fran-cees-co Meeeeeeeem-a-de Troop-a."

The cast turned. They were all charged up and accustomed to each other's schtick. The show went on, even offstage.

I had to laugh.

And the woman who played the servant girl stayed in my view. "You an actor?" she asked.

"Yeah, I guess," I said.

"You guess?" The guy who played the dandy doctor turned around. "Well, are you or aren't you." Not a question. Stated.

"I'm still in school," I said.

"Where," the small dark man with a mustache didn't ask. He demanded.

"Back East," I said. I didn't like to throw Harvard around. People took it one way or another, but they changed after they heard it. I didn't think the Ivy League was going to get me anywhere with this crowd.

"You like the show?" the doctor asked. He walked

to me, wiping sweat and makeup off his face and neck. His eyes danced and he gave off a warm feel beneath the brusque exterior.

"Like it!" I said. "You guys are amazing." My critical facilities weren't all that developed back then; I probably sounded naïve.

"'Amazing,'" he repeated. "What else."

"Just, just… It's about now. I mean, it blows your mind," I said. "You use these old forms and make us feel like you're all peasants and this is the street in some crapped-out Shakespearean village, but you bring it forward. I mean, you're talkin' about today, the economy and maybe even capitalism. The dog-eat-dog nature of it all."

"You got all that?"

"I guess so," I felt stupid, but I pressed on. "So I hear you guys do something like a minstrel show?"

"That's right," he said. "Where'd you hear about that?"

"From my cousin. He got his mind blown…"

"Lot of mind-blowing going on," he said.

"But my cousin, he says you guys use a minstrel show to call out racism. I mean, they used to do minstrel shows for real where I grew up. The VFW…"

He laughed, a light laugh. "Really!" He laughed again. "Where's that?"

"Back East."

"Where?" he asked. I could tell he was checking me out.

"Little Massachusetts town," I said under his sharp eyes. "Only I live in Boston now."

"You're in school you said."

"Yeah…" I could feel him zero in.

"Where?"

"Shit," I said. "Harvard."

"Whoa," he said, laughing. "Hey, we got a Harvard man here!"

I blew off the catcalls and whistles from the cast with a bow. They weren't going to catch me up tight.

"Ease up on the guy," the black actor said. "He can't help it!"

Laughter. I blushed.

"Okay, Harvard man," the mustache guy said. "I'm Vinny. So tell me about your minstrel show."

"Not mine," I said. "I boycotted it. It was racist, all these old fat guys in blackface."

"We use blackface, too," he said.

"But my cousin says your show turns it all around. Uses those doo-dah images to hip people to their own racism."

The tall actor joined us. He had changed out of his droopy long johns for a worn pair of blue jeans and a denim work shirt. Over that he wore a leather vest and a necklace of beads, feathers, and small animal bones. "That's the point," he said. "When you embrace racism, you raise the stakes."

"Either we do it right or we're all fucked!" the black actor said.

"Especially you, Paul."

"Nothing new there," Paul said.

This talk was confusing. Most of the black guys I knew at Harvard worked overtime to sound white. I wanted to know more. About this company.

"Jeez, look, I don't suppose…"

"Come on by the studio," Vinny, the mustache guy said. "We can talk some more."

"Oh wow," I said. "Sure. Do you guys audition people?" Cambridge left my mind.

"Maybe." Vinny handed me a hand-typed mimeographed sheet. "You never know." It was a playbill for the show. They must have passed it out earlier, before I got there. "It might happen to you."

"What might?"

"Who knows?" He pointed to the bottom of the sheet. "That's the address. Come on by." He turned away and rejoined the gang.

The olive-skinned actress waved at me.

I had been a political animal since childhood, rocketed by my parents left-wing take on history, the world, and the long arm of McCarthyism. But my theater experience had been limited to fairy-tale operettas, a few high-school shots at Gilbert & Sullivan and Oscar Wilde, without any mention of his gender proclivities. College carried me over to the naturalists like Shaw or Ibsen and Chekhov, revolutionary in their day but far removed from the growing tensions of mid-'60s America.

But on that hot Saturday in San Francisco, I watched this ragtag theater company with real acting chops mix rowdy comedy with astute political analysis on a stage that stole from the marketplace theater of 16th-century *commedia*, purloined the Marxist expressionism of Weimar Germany's Bertolt Brecht and Kurt Weill, and spat it out into the gathering storm of the Vietnam War, racism, and the romance of the Beats.

My mind was blown. For real. The Mime Troupe had, in one afternoon, synthesized my theater animal and my political beast. My mind shifted into dream gear. What a way to surge into civil conflict, foment cultural crises, and preach laughter and the truth to the clashing communities of wartime America and the New Left resistance. I was ecstatic! If they would take me, I could learn how to make the theater my political work and my political work the theater. I wanted to join that company.

2

THE AUDITION

Holding the Troupe's crumpled program in one hand, I made several passes around the one-way streets south of Market before I found the Mime Troupe studio, crammed in an alley that ran behind the art deco mass of the *San Francisco Chronicle* building. I could hear the presses rolling out the evening edition. Across the alley, the first floor of the Mime Troupe studio housed an auto-repair shop that opened onto Sixth Street. I pulled up to the side of the building in my filthy transcontinental station wagon. Old white bums, alcoholics, the homeless population of a half-century ago, shuffled, stumbled, mumbled, and slept in the shade.

Above the sleeping bums, the studio lurked behind a grid of dirty industrial windows, some pushed out on their metal-framed hinges. On the door, a silk-screened poster featured two men in baggy garments, shapeless hats on their heads. The words ONE PERCENT FREE appeared in bold blue strokes below the figures.

Beneath the poster, a playbill advertised upcoming performances of the Mime Troupe doing the Minstrel Show at Town Hall in New York on the same bill as Dick Gregory, one of the few comedians who ranked up there with Lenny Bruce, comedians who kicked society's ass.

The Troupe was taking the Minstrel Show to New York. *Wow,* I thought. *These people are really doing it!* I knocked. No one appeared. There was no bell. Behind a glass door, a long stairway climbed into the shadows of a distant second floor. I tried the knob. The door opened. Shouting and scuffling rang down the long, narrow stairway. I tried to ascertain if the voices were shouting in anger but, *What the hell,* I thought. *It's a theater company, so maybe it's a rehearsal.* I climbed the stairs, and the shouting repeated itself. Okay. It's a rehearsal.

I stepped inside a large, cluttered loft, like a factory floor without machines. Small-paned industrial windows glared with afternoon light. Against the glare I could make out several lines of old wooden gymnasium assembly chairs. A sofa and a trio of busted-out armchairs punctuated the scratched, varnished rows of seats, and together they roughly defined a rehearsal floor.

I was used to the order and symmetry of the college theater, a full proscenium performance space with swanky, teal-upholstered seats, teak paneling, and a full light grid.

Even the experimental theater in the Loeb, a box painted a uniform flat black, had an order to it, neatly run by tidy Harvard staffers. In contrast, this room shouted chaos. A cluster of gigantic puppet heads leaned in a corner. A cluster of old band instruments, a bass drum, a tuba, and a short stack of parade drums occupied a second corner. I could make out a shop workbench crammed with tools and paint and glue cans. A spread of color-spattered canvas covered one end of the bench, and a jumbled stack of wood scraps leaned into the corner. The open loft space was empty, but voices came from a set of double doors that shed light into the room. I tiptoed to the doorway.

Inside, desks crowded the floor, an office. Guarding the doorway, a sullen teenager lounged across two of the varnished auditorium seats. She wore a faded denim shirt; a long, cotton skirt of indeterminate shape; and a ratty, scuffed-up pair of cowboy boots. A wiry, sharp-faced guy with dirty-blond hair swept straight back European-style leaned forward, elbows on knees, talking to a lanky, good-looking guy with aquiline features and a swashbuckling mane of equally dirty-blond hair. He reclined against the breasts of the sullen girl with the cowboy boots. She played with his hair while he massaged her inner thigh through the cotton skirt.

Behind the front desk, a reserved-looking woman, youngish, in a straight-looking workaday skirt and blouse, spoke on the phone with a Midlands Brit accent. Behind another desk, Vinny, the mustache guy from the park barked into a phone. Now he was dressed in weird burgundy jeans, a black T-shirt, and a dark blue Mao jacket. He slammed down the receiver. "Fuckin' hippies," he growled.

The Brit woman looked up and smiled at me, very warm and relaxed. "Can I help you?"

"I'm here to see him," I said, gesturing toward the mustache guy. "I think."

"Who, Vinny?" The swashbuckler perked up. "I wouldn't recommend it," he said and laughed. "He's trying to get this show on the road."

"With a bunch of lefty students for producers," the Euro-haired guy said. He checked me out with bright black eyes. "How you doin'?" he asked. "I'm Ivan."

"I'm good," I pointed toward the Dottore, now named Vinny. "He said for me to come by the studio one day, so…" I shrugged and grinned. "Here I am."

"Why did he ask you to come by?" Ivan asked. He moved closer, leaned in, watching me intently.

I felt as if I was being X-rayed. "I saw the show the other day in the park, and…"

"The *commedia*."

"Yeah. I guess so." I held up the now-ragged program that had guided me to the studio.

"*Olive Pits*."

"Yeah! That one," I said. "I thought it was cool. Who wrote it?" I asked.

"I did." The swashbuckling guy said. "I'm Erroll."

"No, I did," said Ivan.

"Yeah, he did."

"We all did."

"All of you?" Were they putting me on? They all wrote the play? I was used to being handed a script and learning it, word for word. In *Ratman*, the play I had done that spring, we would work with Mickey the writer to change a few words. Here, I had no idea what they meant when they said they all wrote it.

"Yeah, we all did, only he wrote it." Erroll pointed to Vinny. "I wrote it, we all wrote it."

"And in such a way, we killed the private property of ideas," the Euro-hair guy said.

"Now they belong to everybody."

"For free."

"You guys are full of shit," the sullen girl said. "Judy wrote it."

The woman who had played the servant girl came into the room. "Rebecca's right. She sure as hell did."

"Yeah," said Ivan, the Euro guy. "She adapted it from a dusty old story."

"Like Shakespeare," the actress said.

"Like Marlowe," Erroll said. "All those guys begged and borrowed…"

"And stole from each other," Ivan said.

"But Ivan," the actress said, "you don't believe in the private property of ideas."

Ivan threw her a look, turned back to me. "Just jiving here." He winked, but a smile never reached his lips.

"So where did you hear about us?" Erroll asked.

"My cousin," I said. "He's seen a lot of your…"

"Who's your cousin?" Ivan asked, leaning forward, arms on his knees.

"Hey!" the actress said. "Ease up." She turned to me and held out her hand. "I'm Olivia."

The director came over. He was smaller than he looked onstage. Of course, everybody looks smaller offstage. "He came by the show last weekend. He's not a cop, for chrissakes."

Ivan eased back into the busted-out sofa.

Erroll leaned over, offered his hand. "Sorry. We been getting a few hostile visitors here lately."

"We managed to piss off the city." Ivan took a bow. "They sued us for obscenity."

Vinny came over. He took the program out of my hand and read out loud, stagey, like he was preaching. "In case this is your first Mime Troupe show, we wish to make clear to all." He paused, cleared his throat. "We have never been arrested for obscenity. Troupe director Vinny Miles…" He stopped. "That's me."

"That's him," Erroll said.

Vinny continued, "…was arrested for performing without a permit. We fired a legal blast at the commission. They had set themselves up as censors…"

"Fucking the First Amendment," Ivan said.

"But we will speak out, talk back, and criticize hypocrisy, lies, and the fundamental horror of this society," Vinny continued. "It is our pleasure…"

"And our mission," Erroll said.

"And our destiny," Ivan said.

"To bring some kind of art into everybody's backyard." Vinny slapped the leaflet against my chest. "So that's what we do here," he said.

In rapid-fire, as an ensemble, I heard: "We do theater."

"And we hand people a lotta shit to think about."

I loved it. "Can I join?"

"Can you act?"

"Yeah."

"Can you play an instrument?"

"Yeah."

"Dance?" Olivia stood up. "Can you sing?"

"Yeah," I said. "And yeah. I mean, I can do all that. Well, no, not dance. But I play the guitar like a-ringin' a bell." I had no idea what was going on, but I felt good. Was I auditioning? For the ensemble?

"Go Johnny, go."

"What do you sing?"

"Folk music," I said. "I mean, I listen to rock 'n' roll. I'd play jazz, but I don't know how."

"You got a car?"

"Yeah, I got a station wagon."

"Hmmmmmm."

Was that part of the deal? I thought. *A car?*

"Let's sing. Join us." Olivia began stamping and clapping, heel on the downbeat, clap on the backbeat.

I started clapping. I was pretty sure I could do the

stamping, too. But *is this an audition? Now? Right here? No formal thing? Just… sing?*

Two other guys joined the circle. One wore jeans, a leather vest, a headband, and talismans hung around his neck. He nodded and smiled, and I recognized him. He'd played the old rich guy in the park, with his droopy red long johns and robe and a money bag that hung between his legs like a scrotum. Out of character and out of costume, his baritone voice sounded strong, rich, and obscene.

Paul was with him. He'd played Arlecchino, a comic servant, but I remember watching how well he moved, working against character, precise, acrobatic, athletic. It made no difference that Paul Madison was black. Out of costume, he was stocky, wearing jeans and a San Francisco turtleneck. He tossed a leather jacket onto the back of a chair and joined the circle. "Hiya, kid," he said. "Be careful. You're surrounded by lunatics."

Vinny and Erroll joined in. The rhythm built and tightened, a little Spanish, a little Italian, *commedia dell'flamenco*. The groove felt good. I began stepping.

"Yeah, that's it." Nods and whistles.

Once the stamp-clap thing gathered momentum, they began singing a folky melody that they'd sung in the park. You either learn how to sing in a church or a saloon. I learned in church, and I'd already sung a lot of folk music. I certainly knew what harmony felt like, when it locked. It gives the sum of the voices a power greater than the parts.

Vinny wore flamenco boots, winklepickers with Cuban

heels. He moved with style. Hell, they all looked good. The sullen teenager didn't join them, nor did the Euro-hair guy. I started picking up on the melody. Between the *Olive Pits* program speech and this singing and dancing, I felt great. We stopped. Everybody approved. I had tried to lock eyes with Olivia. She threw me a look of effortless contempt.

I dropped my eyes. I had been summarily dismissed.

"You ever do any improv?" the tall guy asked. Richard was his name, Richard Wolfe.

"Improvisation?" I had done a little, but mostly goofing with all my crazy, alienated motormouth friends who read *The Realist*, and *Mad* magazine. We had done some improv in early rehearsals for the classics we did at Harvard, but you don't really improvise around Shakespeare, and back then Harvard didn't teach a young gentleman the arts. All I had was my stage experience in high school and college, acting straight from the script, and goofing off stage with people. Oh. And *Rat Man Meets the 50-Foot Hindu*.

Everybody sat down and I went to join them.

"No," Vinny said. "Stay up there. Here's the scene."

Okay, so I was going to play a character. I could feel the adrenaline and it felt good, like a warm buzz. I stood in a grid of afternoon sunlight that angled through the studio's grimy industrial windows.

"You're a cop."

Oh man, I thought. *That's weird.* That's about as far away from me as I can imagine, but I'd been around cops plenty already, from the FBI guys who used to check on my parents, to the local, small-town cops I grew up with, to the cops in South Philly, who in the summertime, rode around in red jeeps, four to a vehicle, ready to spring onto the street at any provocation. Cops swarmed around Harvard Square and the off-campus Putnam Avenue neighborhood I'd migrated to. So, I took a spread-legged stance, my picture of a cop, and grasped my belt buckle.

That got a laugh.

Vinny nodded to Richard and Paul. "So these guys, they look like they just finished jacking up some guy and got a bottle of malt liquor off him, some such."

"Racist bastard," Olivia said.

"That's the point," Vinny said.

Richard and Paul got up and began roughhousing off to one side of the stage. They both put on broad black accents. Richard's accent was pretty good; Paul's was the real thing.

I turned and watched them for a minute. *Better do something,* I thought, so I hitched up my jeans again, made it look like I had a beer belly with a gun, handcuffs, a nightstick, probably a flashlight hanging underneath the beer bulge.

Laughter.

"Hey!" I said in a gruff voice. "What are you people doing over there?" I knew that "you people" was code for "those people," the other people, the people different than us. I felt my adrenaline surge again. I was calling these guys "you people," and one of them was black.

I moved on the two black guys, one of them white, the other black. Watts, the cops, the smoke, raced through my senses. What the hell was I gonna do? James Baldwin's voice came into my head. *The Fire Next Time.*

"You two are gonna have to come with me."

They objected. "Aw, come on, man."

"I don't even know this niggah," Paul said.

I had time to wonder if Richard would have used that term. James Baldwin stayed with me. "Now hold on," I pushed between them. It must have looked ridiculous; they loomed over me.

Laughter from Olivia and Vinny.

"But why, officer?" Richard wailed. "We wasn't doin' no harm."

"It don't matter. The new rules are goin' into place."

"What rules?" Paul said. "We don't know nothin' about no new rules."

"They decided." My mind was racing.

"Who decided?"

"The authorities. Instead of killin' you people off one by one, catch as catch can…" Man, I was on shaky ground.

"Catch a nigger by the toe?" Paul said.

"We got orders to round all you people up. We gonna break all the glass in your juke joints and barber shops. We gonna burn down your synagogues. I mean your churches."

Richard Wolfe and Paul froze.

"You gonna have to wear watermelon patches on your clothes."

Nobody laughed. Silence.

I pulled out an imaginary walkie-talkie. "I got two watermelons here. Gonna need backup. And send a wagon. They're ripe and ready to go."

"Go where?" Richard asked.

"We gonna round you all up, put you on trains, and ship you all off to… to…"

"Georgia?" Paul said.

"Mississippi?" Richard said.

"Nope. Some place where nobody cares what happens to y'all anyhow. We finally got us a final solution."

I heard a strained laugh from the audition audience.

Richard, tall though he was, dropped to his knees. "You ain't goin' to send us to the ovens, are you?"

By now they got it.

"I don't want you messin' around my backyard," I drawled. "And I sure don't want your ashes driftin' down on my front lawn."

They lined up, hands behind their backs.

I pantomimed cuffing them and marched them out of the room and down the stairs chanting *"Arbeit macht frei / Work will set you free."*

Silence. Finally, Olivia said, "Wow."

"All right." "Too much." Applause. Laughter.

Ivan, the Euro guy had come in and leaned against the doorway, applauding. So did the woman behind the desk.

"Come and sit down," Vinny said. "All right, well, that was okay. Good."

"Nasty," Rebecca said.

"Nice timing," Erroll said.

"Right on top of it," Richard said.

"The way it should be," Vinny said.

"That sure turned ugly," I said, shaking my head. "I didn't make it up. Not really. James Baldwin, in *The Fire Next Time*, he talked about blacks and the Nazi final solution. It had stuck in my head and heart and surfaced here, as if from nowhere."

"What it should be." Vinny said. "Smart, racist, nasty, and ugly. Nice work."

"Brrrrr," Olivia said. "Cold."

"Has to be," Vinny said.

"I know, I know," Olivia said.

"So why do you want to join the company?" Ivan asked, pushing his Euro hair back. "You heard of us before."

"Ah, not really. My cousin told me…"

"So you stumbled on us," he said.

I didn't know what this guy was all about, but it didn't seem friendly. I decided to ignore that feeling. "Yeah, you could say that. I liked the show. But look, I got no plan here. I didn't even know I was gonna do these scenes and sing that song. I just dropped by."

"What have you done?" Olivia asked.

I told them about starting as a little kid doing operettas, then the comedies, Gilbert & Sullivan, all of that. College theater, mostly small parts, character parts in Shakespeare, George Bernard Shaw. I told them about the

50-foot Hindu, too.

"But no improvisation."

"What about the music?" Olivia asked in a clear voice.

"I sang in church." I felt in control of what they might want to hear. "I could never remember the words, but I could fake it." I sang a fragment of a phony hymn, making up blurred lyrics that parodied the pompous hymnal lyrics.

That brought laughter.

"All that God crap sounded like bullshit to me, but I liked the harmony when we all sang together."

"Then I went to this summer work camp run by the Quakers."

"That had to be on the East Coast," the European guy said.

"Yeah, and I started to play guitar," I explained. "Learning three-chord folk songs, and then at this work camp, I met these guys from New York, and they made that music come alive. And the blues. I've been listening to rock 'n' roll since I was 11, and rock 'n' roll came out of rockabilly and that corny early country, and I knew snatches of jazz from guys like Louie Bellson and Benny Goodman and 'Sing, Sing, Sing' with Gene Krupa playing, but I'd never heard these blues guys."

I didn't notice it, but I was running a second solo routine, and the little company was all ears. "I mean... whoever heard of people with names like Howlin' Wolf, and Muddy Waters, Son House? Man, when I started hearing this music, it moved me. Transported me to another world, very far away from those English murder ballads." I began to sing in an English accent. "'I gave my love a cherry.'"

More laughter. I liked these people. They seemed to understand my ramble, although my biographical monologue surprised even me.

"All this happened even before the March on Washington," I said. "From before Mississippi Freedom summer, before The Beatles, before Dylan came along and blew everything to smithereens…"

"Dylan Thomas?" Ivan asked.

"No man. Bobby Dylan."

They laughed at my cartoon contempt.

"Was that a good thing or a bad thing?" the Euro guy asked.

"Woo! A bad thing?" I said. "Hell, no! My friend Nick — I met him at that Quaker work camp. He came in from Western Mass. We sat up in the woods, in my old man's workshop, and he taught me "Don't Think Twice, It's All Right."

Olivia turned to Richard.

"Dylan," Richard said.

"You put that together with all the Fats Domino, Carl Perkins, Elvis, The Five Satins… all that was cramming into my head even before I was a teenager. And then I was reading Carl Sandburg's Lincoln biography and the history of all these folk songs, John Henry…" I stopped, looked around.

Vinny, Erroll, Ivan, the beautiful Olive lady all looked at me with bemused smiles.

"So you know history," Vinny said.

"I study it." I paused. "I studied it. I started out in anthropology, but some crabbed-out grad student, you know, a full-time professional PhD candidate, told me I was lousy at it, and I believed him. So… history."

Paul burst out with a belly laugh. "You're a trip, kid."

"Is that a good thing or a bad thing," I said, aping Ivan's question.

"What about the Germans?" he asked.

"Like the Nazis?"

"No," Paul said. "The other side. Life. Love. Music. Weimar. Socialism. Theater. Brecht."

I only knew that *Galileo*, one of his plays, had been on Broadway for a while. I didn't know anything about the play or Brecht.

"Do you know what we're trying to do here?" Ivan asked.

What was he asking me? I took a stab. "I saw you guys doing this new kind of theater that used that old kind of theater to say shit about today."

Everybody laughed again. I was beginning to get frustrated. "And all that racist talk we did in the improv?" I said. "Seems like you're acting racist to talk about racism."

"Talk about it?" Ivan asked.

"Face off with it," I said. "Otherwise, it's *Amos 'n' Andy*."

Vinny got up, grabbed me by the elbow, and steered me back into the office. We sat down over coffee from a big aluminum percolator, like in a teacher's room. "So what are you doing now?" he asked.

I didn't say anything about school. Here was this strange, outta sight theater, I was one year away from graduating, but I didn't want to go back. Or did I? I hadn't really given it any thought. I didn't know where I fit in back then. I didn't know where I fit into anything. I didn't have a vision for the future, but I felt armed and dangerous. I was looking for trouble.

I had stood on the main stage at Harvard one night after the audience left. The cooling lights still ticked. The grid and catwalks flew away into the darkness above. The auditorium sat complacent and empty, still warm with the scent of the audience. A door slammed, and a quick laugh reverberated down a hallway. I stood in that quiet space and vowed I would act forever. But the plays had been almost meaningless to me. They reminded me of singing those pompous old hymns in church back home. I loved singing and harmonizing, but the words seemed meaningless. Same with theater. I loved the idea of it, of performing, the romance of the stage and all, but I didn't understand the metaphors that Shaw was exploring with *Major Barbara* and *The Devil's Disciple*. I did understand that I sure as hell didn't want to go back to Cambridge and another slush-filled winter.

3

STANDING AT THE CROSSROADS

My cousin and I finished the landscaping job. I'd made some cash for the school year but returning to Cambridge had no place on my event horizon. The Troupe was performing the Minstrel Show around Berkeley and Oakland. People came, curious, angry, looking for proof that the show was another well-intended honky blunder. I wasn't acting in it, but they put me to work playing banjo and singing on the sidelines with a drummer and a trumpet player. I learned to play old Stephen Foster tunes for the doo-dah racist stuff. We did freedom songs and a tune by Nina Simone called "Mississippi Goddam," with only voices, a banjo, a trumpet, and a snare drum with a high hat.

They put a sketch into the show based on my concentration camp improv. Paul played the white cop. Richard

Wolfe and Erroll played the two street guys. Paul didn't play the cop as a cracker. He played him as stiff, humorless, an executive delivering the news to the two white guys in blackface. "You're not going to be murdered helter-skelter anymore," he'd say. "You children will have the honor of joining your brothers and sisters in the vanguard of Negroes (he enunciated the word carefully) in the labor camps — work will set you free."

Ivan and Erroll began their arcs with jive but pivoted to solemnity, once the reality of this black-in-America final solution sunk in. They were marched off singing "Work will set you free," while we chanted *"Arbeit macht frei"* to banjo and snare drum.

At first, white people came. Then black people showed up, first in mixed crowds of activists. Add a few pioneering black and white couples, gay and straight, and you've got a Mime Troupe Minstrel Show audience. The crowd split in their response. People didn't know whether to laugh or sit in silent shock. Every night, the actors walked a razor's edge. Good satire doesn't reach out to coax you along. It jars you with its sarcasm and cruelty. White people affecting Negro accents and jiving with Negroes onstage caught the audience in a crossfire. They could either stand up and walk out or stay and try to figure it out.

We did a long finale with music by Steve Reich to accompany a film full of watermelons — people eating watermelons, lying on and in watermelons, chasing watermelons down the street. Blowing up watermelons, stabbing watermelons, taking the guts out of watermelons, rubbing them on naked bodies, dropping them from great heights. The plan was to take the icons of racism to their extremes; the watermelon finale delivered the final note, Reich's music writhing in and out of Stephen Foster melodies.

We wanted to deal body blows to the system. I felt the power but also the bone-deep abuse that the Man heaps on us all. This little country boy from white New England felt himself internalize what he was creating onstage, like an adolescent who tries to make it real, but compared to what? In the black-and-white fantasy of the Minstrel Show, the real world closed around me.

Sure, Vinny and Olivia were booking a tour of the Northwest with the Minstrel Show and a *commedia* show. And sure, they were headed for New York to perform at Town Hall with Dick Gregory! Vinny might cast me in the *commedia*. And with my music chops, I was good for the Minstrel Show. But I hadn't told Vinny I still had another year back at the Cambridge brickyard. When he found out, Vinny dragged me into the office.

"Go finish school," he said.

I found it weird that this radical anarchist was so adamant about a college degree. "Isn't this the thing to do?" I said. "You know… turn on, tune in, and drop out?"

"Bullshit," Vinny said. "That's Tim Leary's bullshit. Drop out and you disappear. That's for fucking pop stars, and they don't drop out. They plug in and sell out. Turning on is irrelevant. Get high, don't get high, I don't care, just be on time, know why you're here, and don't forget the ammunition."

He walked me to the bottom of the stairs. Nobody else was around. "We commit," he said. "We engage. We breathe the fresh air of the parks and put on free shows. We take the path. No. We *make* the path of most resistance. We fight the system."

"I know," I said. "That's why I want to work with you guys. Didn't you give me a part in the Minstrel Show? You know I can play the music! You know I can act. What good is a diploma from the belly of the beast? It'll just give me gas."

"It's a weapon," he said. "You run a candy store, you're a part of capitalism. You run a theater company, you run a candy store. We swim in a capitalist sea. Like it or not, we breathe the air of the assholes in power. You learn how to think, you can tell the difference between what is and what can be."

"Even you guys?" I asked. "You're not capitalists, for chrissakes. You're political artists."

"We own the means of production. We don't own the housing, we don't own the food, we don't make clothing, and we drive vehicles and burn gas."

I'd never thought of it that way.

And most important, Vinny said, "We don't own the means of distribution. We've got to hustle our own theater from whatever raggedy-assed network the Left has cobbled together." He paused and grinned. "Got a solution to that?"

"No," I said. "But I'm gonna burn a lot of gas humping it back to Cambridge."

He opened the studio door. "Drop out and you'll be good for nothing but smoking dope and playing guitars. We got plenty of that. We need certified, bona fide smarties with a license to think. You're already a smarty. Bordering on a smart-ass. Get your diploma, and you'll have your papers in order."

Vinny pulled me out the door, past the bums, past the roar of the *Chronicle*'s presses rolling out the evening edition. He shoved me into my station wagon and put an arm on my shoulder. "You're good at this. But for now…" He stepped away from the car. "…beat it. Maybe we'll see you next year."

4

WAY BACK HOME

Driving solo, crawling eastward day and night, I drove against time, moving backward, hypnotized by the flick-flack, flick-flack of the tires on the two-lane concrete highway, buffeted by a thousand westbound semis. One nod, one drift across the double line and I was roadkill.

Night-flying insects spattered my windshield. I drove headlong into each sunrise, each morning taking me further from the rehearsal studio full of laughing actors, the smell of eucalyptus in the parks, the excitement of performance.

What would befall my newfound revolutionary's life once I had returned to the apartment, my room, the cruddy Cambridge street, two blocks away from Harvard's self-satisfied, brick-and-ivy campus?

I drove through Harvard Square, past Club 47 on Mount Auburn Street, and turned onto the familiar dilapidation of Putnam Avenue. The radio was playing "California Dreamin'" by The Mamas & the Papas. I couldn't believe the irony.

All the leaves are brown
And the sky is gray…

I had to laugh out loud. It was ludicrous. The song was too perfect. I'd been back and forth twice between coasts, and I'd grown used to noticing how crappy Boston and Cambridge felt on each return. I landed in the middle of hot, humid August, but autumn would come and with it the gray sky, the bare trees, and the snow, slush, and dog shit of winter. I turned off the car but kept the radio on, drinking in the stillness and the irony of the lyrics.

I'd be safe and warm,
If I was in L.A.

L.A. wasn't the San Francisco Bay, but it was close enough for sarcasm.

California dreamin'
On such a winter's dayyyyy…

California dreamin'… crap. The song ended. Through the grimy windshield, I watched as a squat figure opened the door that led upstairs to my apartment. Two guys in sport jackets and slacks, one with a belly, the other tall and thin, stood on the steps below him. They were both stuffed into heavy black shoes. It was too hot to be wearing a sport jacket and these guys looked uncomfortable standing in the hazy sunlight. My heart clenched. The guy with the keys was my landlord. The other two, I estimated from the brogans, were plainclothes Cambridge cops.

Two uniformed cops sauntered up and paused like city workers leaning on shovels. That's when the landlord saw me. "There's one of 'em now!" he yelled.

The cops spun around. I could either buzz outta there and never come back, or just get out of the car. My head buzzed and my legs had stiffened from the all-night, all-day driving. I didn't have anything to hide — except the one-kilo brick of cured Mexican weed I had taped to the inside of my Gibson, the only guitar I had taken with me to California. I got out of the car to meet them halfway. "What's going on, Mr. Pereyra?" I rounded the back of the road-filthy station wagon.

"That's what I want to know," my landlord said. "Where's the rent?"

Oh boy. I thought I'd left the apartment in good hands with Lucky and Jeffree. I tried to look incredulous, although I knew that Jeffree had planned to split for New Orleans, and Lucky? I should have known better.

The plainclothes cop came down the stairs and took my arm. "Come on upstairs, son," he said. He looked Greek, with heavy brows and a five-o'clock shadow that

51

had already darkened by three, but he had called me "son." I figured I might stand a chance.

We shuffled up the stairway in a parade of butts and feet, me following behind with the Greek cop. "I just got back from California," I said.

The cop kept his grip on my arm. "You know the people stayin' here?" he asked.

"Well, sure," I said. "I left the place with…"

The landlord opened the door to the apartment. "Jesus, Joseph, and Mary," he mumbled.

The place looked like a director had staged a fight. Clothing, newspapers, Chinese takeout boxes, and wine bottles cluttered the hallway toward the kitchen. A broken chair intruded upside down from a bedroom doorway. I heard voices at the far end of the hall.

"Stay here," the Greek said. The two uniforms hustled down the hallway.

A woman screamed.

I heard commands from the cops, the scraping of chairs, plaintive female voices.

My landlord turned toward me. "What the hell's going on here?"

I must have looked genuinely wide-eyed and incredulous. Before I could shrug my shoulders, the landlord twitched his mouth sideways in a snarl. "I know, I know. You just got back from California."

The cops filled the backlit kitchen doorway with two handcuffed female figures, one blonde and tallish, one smaller with short dark hair. I recognized them as two sisters who had come by the apartment with Jeffree. They didn't look like sisters, but they acted like them. They bickered and corrected each other constantly. Now they walked silent and sullen past me, the two uniformed cops pushing them along.

"You can call your parents when we get to the station," the detective said. He stopped as the cops steered the two women out the door. "You know those people?" he asked.

"You know these people?" the landlord parroted. "Jesus, Joseph, and Mary."

"Sort of," I said.

The detective blinked impatiently. "Yes or no. Do you know them?"

"I've seen them before," I said.

"Where?"

"Here."

The landlord groaned. "Nice friends you got," he said.

"They don't live here."

"So you say," the detective said.

"And I don't know their names."

"Good gawd," the landlord said. "What were they doing here?"

"They were shooting up just now," one of the uniforms said. He lifted a small tin box. "This is their works."

"Works?" the landlord said. "What are works?"

"Why don't you go check the kitchen," the detective said to my landlord. "Give me a minute with the kid here."

The landlord glared at me and left us.

The detective pulled me into what was left of my bedroom. He crossed to the table I used as a desk and pulled a roach out of my ashtray. He held it up to my face with stubby fingers. "You know what this is?"

"Yessir," I said. "That's part of a marijuana cigarette."

"That's right, boy. A muggle. A joint. Reefer."

I frowned, as if perplexed. I tried to look shocked and disappointed. "I don't touch the stuff," I said. "I'm a student at the college."

The landlord returned and stood in the doorway, glaring at me.

"So you left for the summer," the detective said.

"Yessir."

"And your apartment filled up with lowlifes," he said.

"I don't know. I left the apartment with people I know."

"Like who?"

"Like my girlfriend."

"Where's she at?"

"I don't know."

"I've seen it happen before," the detective said to the landlord. He turned back to me. "You should have kept a closer watch."

Whew, I thought. *I might make it out of this mess in one piece. Maybe.*

"You should have kept a closer watch," the landlord repeated.

I wanted to belt him. "I'll clean the place up," I said.

"And get the rent to me."

"Yessir." Thanks to my cousin and his landscape work, I probably had enough to cover the back rent. "I can give you a new security deposit. Let me stay. I'll make it right."

The detective started to fidget. "I'm gonna leave this situation for you two to hash out."

The landlord retreated with the cop. He stopped at the door. "I'll think about it," he said.

"Clean the place up," he said. "And we'll see."

"That's what I just said." I wanted to uncoil the whole 3,000-mile trip right through my shoulder, into my forearm, and splatter his face with my fist.

The door closed with a click of the latch. I stood like a stranger in the familiar apartment. The departed detective's Marlboro and coffee breath hung in the air. The wet-heat smell of laundry and pizza ovens rose from the twin storefronts downstairs, returning me to what had been home months earlier. My sheets, torn, crumpled, and stained, lay scattered across the mattress. The August sun oozed through the filthy dormer window, blurring the red-brick lines of the housing project across the street.

I turned to the clutter on my desk. My massive Underwood typewriter had disappeared. I brushed my fingertips along the desk edge; they came away gritty. The velvet curtain hung limp across the now-empty closet where my clothes and guitars had nested. The noise from a solo cross-country road trip, the assault of headlights on tired eyes, the hot wind on my left arm and shoulder, the forlorn blare of country music, all disappeared. Only the incessant moan of tires hung in my ears.

I tossed my duffel bag on the mattress.

"Hey! Are you up there?"

Lucky. The unmistakable timbre of her voice startled me. I crossed to the window. There she stood, all leggy in one of her perennial flower-print Marimekko sundresses, her red-gold hair thick, reflecting the pale sun, straight-featured face turned upward. "Hey!"

I pushed at the top ledge of the windowsill. Stuck. I knocked on the pane and gesticulated toward the door below, centered between the laundry and the pizza joint. *Jeez,* I recall thinking, *two Afghans now,* a second joining Lucille. *Lucky the girl and Lucille the Afghan. Who gives a dog a name that sounds like her own?* I stepped out of the apartment and stood at the head of the stairwell.

Humans often choose animals who resemble them. Lucky's Afghans, long-limbed, winsome creatures with aristocratic features and reddish-blonde hair, looked like her. The two dogs and the girl climbed the stairs, three graceful creatures. I stopped them at the landing. I wasn't sure I wanted to see Lucky, and I wasn't sure I wanted Lucky to see the mess. I felt like a fool. *What kind of idiot leaves his clothes and a guitar in a dump like this?*

"Why were those cops here?" Lucky asked.

"And the landlord," I said.

"Uh-oh."

"You've got two hounds now." I squatted on my heels and hugged Lucille's doggy shoulders.

"Yes. I'm fine, thank you very much," Lucky said, holding the Afghans at bay. "And how are you?"

"Road-burnt."

"You just back now?"

"Sort of. Not all here yet."

"How was San Francisco?" Lucky asked.

"Fine. Where'd you get the other hound?"

"Derek gave her to me," she said.

"Derek," I repeated. *The tall Jamaican.*

"Aren't you going to let us in?"

"Yeah. Sure." I stepped aside, already jealous and suspicious. What the hell had she been doing since I left? *And what right did I have to be jealous?* I thought. *I left her here. What did I expect? That the world would stop because I left? Yeah,* I told myself. *The world shoulda stopped.*

Lucky unleashed the dogs. I stepped aside to let the doggy parade pass. They dashed down the long Pullman hallway to the kitchen, a once-familiar haunt for Lucille. Derek's creature followed.

Lucky turned into the bedroom and stopped. "Wow," she whispered. "What happened?"

I stood there. *Let her figure it out,* I thought. Or maybe she knew what happened.

Lucky's eyes took measure of the bed and its rancid sheets. They fell on the gritty desk, the empty closet, and the shadow of the missing Underwood. Finally, she turned and caressed my shoulder, her fingers falling to grasp my wrist. She smelled like soap. Fresh, despite the grimy Cambridge humidity. "Are you okay?"

"No," I said. "I am not okay." I crossed to the window. "I pulled up just as the fucking landlord and a bunch of cops busted in. The landlord sees me and yells 'There's one of 'em now!' So they drag me up the stairs and presto..." I swept my hand over the chaos. "This is what I found. So, no, Lucky, I am not okay."

The dogs completed their sniff tour of the kitchen and clicked back down the hall, filling the bedroom with curiosity, nosing into scattered shirts, tossed shoes, broken-backed books. Lucky captured the two prancing Afghans. "Aren't you glad to see them?"

I shrugged. I felt the road fatigue beginning to weigh me down. I dropped to the bed, elbows on widespread knees. "When I left, there was just Lucille."

"Where's your stuff?" She crossed to the alcove, empty of hanging garments, kicking aside the detritus of rejected shirts, socks, wire hangers. "Gawd, where're your guitars?"

"I thought you might know."

"Why d'you think I'd know?"

"Because you were going to stick around after I left."

"I had no place else to go. Thanks to you."

"You must have gone somewhere." I recalled the last, painful fight with Lucky, sitting on this same bed, back when it was clean and comfortable.

I had met Lucky in the spring. One warm April night, she had trooped upstairs with Jeffree's friend Marlene, and — as was the custom — the random assemblage cooked pasta, drank wine, and retired to one giant bed to smoke weed and listen to LPs. Lucky and I clicked; we fell into place with each other. One minute we were listening to Jim Kweskin and Maria Muldaur in the incensed murk of Jeffree's room, and the next we were rolling around in another bed, one room away.

Boy, did we have fun.

Nearly every morning, Lucky and Marlene would make the voyage across the Charles from their Back Bay dormitory. Marlene would invade Jeffree's bedroom and Lucky would burst in — Afghan and all — shed one or another of her short, bright sundresses, and pounce, shrouding me in a parasol of reddish-blonde hair. I couldn't believe my life; the clouds had been torn asunder.

But my cousin had lured me to San Francisco with words like Jefferson Airplane, The Family Dog, and the Grateful Dead. Like any young woman aged 19, Lucky was part lunatic. I was a mess. I grew claustrophobic. On the night before I left, I told Lucky she couldn't come to San Francisco with me. I had propped myself against a pillow. Lucky sat sidesaddle on the sheets, a cold sore at the corner of her mouth, dirty hair hanging straight, dress hiked up, not sexy at all, while I refused her pleas to travel with me.

I avoided eye contact, concentrating on my fingers and the Gibson's fretboard, the old Gibson, like the one John Lennon played. Gone now. "I don't know where I'll be," I lied. I knew I was headed to the East Bay to work with my cousin, working outside by the Bay, building gardens. I'd be heading up to a cabin my cousin's family had on the Mendocino coast. I'd be hiking around the Sierras, smoking weed. I'd be hanging out on Telegraph Avenue in Berkeley, drinking coffee at the Café Mediterraneum, home to hipsters and Free Speech politicos. Allen Ginsberg was supposed to have written *Howl* there, and, sure as hell, the best minds of his generation hung out there. Oh, and there were all those California girls to be considered.

"That's okay," Lucky had said. "We don't need to know where we'll be going. It'll be fun."

"I gotta go alone."

"Why?"

"I dunno." I shrugged.

"I do. You think you're gonna get lucky with a bunch of California chicks, don't you."

"Hell, no, babe. I got lucky right here," I grinned. "You're my Lucky."

"Asshole!" Lucky snatched the guitar out of my hands and slid it down the bed. She pounced on me, pinning my arms. She straddled me. I could feel the blood flowing into me. We copulated, hard, not making love, tearing off only essential garments. Lucky seemed to seek both solace and retribution. I tossed her, reversed our position, pinning her arms, the big stud. As we thrust against each other, she broke the skin on my back, leaving stinging crescents on my shoulder blades. We finished quickly.

"There." Lucky had straightened her dress and retreated down the hall to the bathroom. "That'll make you remember me," she shouted. The bathroom door slammed shut. The next morning, I left Lucky with the apartment and headed West.

Now, Lucille the Afghan barked, bringing me back to the present. "Why are you here?" I asked. "Why did you come by?"

"I didn't 'come by,'" Lucky said. "I saw the cops."

I watched Lucky play with the Afghans, her movements like theirs. "I should've taken you," I mumbled.

"I should've made you take me," Lucky said.

"I thought you'd be okay here."

"Jerk. You didn't expect me to stay here alone, did you?" Lucky moved to the window. "I'm sorry about your stuff," she said, her back turned.

I watched her long-limbed form, backlit by the window. I had trouble focusing. Road fatigue was filling in for the adrenaline and shock. "What happened to my stuff, Lucky?"

"I told you, I don't know."

"So where'd you go?"

"Derek got a job bartending in the Village and I wanted to go home."

Oh yeah, I remembered. Derek played congas in the park by the Charles River. He'd also been a Greenwich Village habitué forever. Everybody called him "Bongo." *What a jerk.*

"So, I left with him. I would have been stuck with the rent."

"So, to fix things, you split for New York with Derek?"

"Yes. And don't get all righteous with me, Mister Now I Want You, Now I Don't."

"So, who moved in? My stuff didn't just float out the door. And who were those two girls we found sitting at the kitchen table?"

"What two girls?"

"Yeah, that's what I said, too."

"Oh, that was probably Leslie and Sylvia," Lucky said. "They're sisters. They go to Wheaton."

"They went to Wheaton. Now they're in the back of a police car."

"What?" Lucky looked genuinely astonished. "Why?"

"They were shooting up, that's why. Leslie and Sylvia from Wheaton," I said.

"They were supposed to pay the rent," Lucky said. "I gave them the landlord's address and everything."

The sun fell behind the red-brick projects across the street.

I picked up a shirt from the detritus and snapped it straight.

"I gave you that shirt," Lucky said.

"Did Derek move in here? Did you guys do it in that bed? My bed? Our bed?" I folded the shirt and put it on the duffel bag.

"No. Yes. I mean, sort of."

"And that's how you got the new dog."

"Tafari." Lucky brought him under her wing. "Derek gave him to me."

"So Derek lost a dog and gained a coupla guitars."

"That's not fair," Lucky said. "It wasn't Derek."

"Uh-huh." I mimicked Lucky's tone. "'My new boyfriend didn't steal your guitar. All he stole was me.'"

Lucky spun to face me. "You dumped me, you jerk!" She folded her arms across her chest. "He's not my boyfriend, and I'm not here to be stolen. And I know Derek didn't steal the guitars, because I know who did."

A bus whined away from the corner below.

"Okay." I sat down on the bed and looked up at Lucky. "Then who did?"

"Mario."

"Who?"

"Mario. You know, the short guy with the square jaw and the scar on his mouth."

"Hangs around the Hayes-Bickford, dealing. That guy?"

"Yes."

"And you let him stay here? A junkie?"

"I didn't exactly let him stay."

"So did you sleep with him, too?"

"Lighten up, buster."

"Look around." I swept my arm across the apartment. "Does this look like 'lighten up' time to you?"

"Not my fault, Mister Dump Your Girlfriend. So tell me, did you get laid much this summer?"

"I gotta go check the car. I left my stuff when that homecoming committee dragged me upstairs."

"Go ahead." Lucky pulled the two fidgeting Afghans close. "We're not going anywhere."

"Good." I was glad Lucky was there. I put hands on knees and pushed up, light-headed. My eyes burned. The lint-stinking heat of the downstairs laundry blew across the doorway, pushing me into the hazy-pale light. A small pudgy man walked by, mouthing a harmonica.

I yanked the rest of my junk out of the station wagon and trudged back upstairs.

In the apartment, Lucky looked up at me, tears streaming down her face. "I'm pregnant."

"Oh Jesus." Time stopped. Downstairs, the big laundry fan rattled in and out of syncopation. I needed a place to sit, but not next to her. I dropped to the floor, ankles crossed, clasped my knees, and dropped my head on my forearms. I couldn't look at anything, not anything real. The median strips from the highway strobed in my blind eyes.

Behind me, I heard Lucky collapse on the bed, sobbing.

I needed a glass of water. The road still roared in my head. The hallway and kitchen opened to me with the perspective of a camera eye. The kitchen table still squatted in the center of the room, cluttered with beer bottles, a butt-filled ashtray, and a postal scale. The sink choked on a stack of dirty dishes. An image of tall, laid-back Derek hung over the sink and turned red. I filled with rage and desire. I hated him; wanted her.

I opened the cupboard, found two dusty jelly jars. I turned on the tap, splashed cold water on my face, and stood looking out the window over the low brick tenements to the campus spires, looming distant. I filled the jars, the water swirling cool and clean amid the filthy kitchen. A broom lay on the floor.

I heard the toilet flush, water splashed in the bathroom sink. With an angry sweep of my arm, the mess on the table clattered to the floor. I sat and drank. My anger startled me. Was I jealous? Didn't I leave Lucky behind? What did I care? Why did she abandon the apartment? Who really stole all my stuff? Was I supposed to take over for Derek in this mess? But I mostly felt stricken and sad. For her? Or for me? I couldn't tell.

Lucky stopped in the doorway as if waiting to be invited in, eyes red but face clear now.

I offered her the other jar.

She sat across the table and drank like a child, both hands on the glass. When she finished the water, she set the glass down. "It was us," she said.

"Huh?"

"It was us. You and me. We did it."

"Did what?"

"We knocked me up."

"You've been fucking Derek."

"It happened with you," she said.

That turned me on. The way she said that. But I couldn't believe it. I imagined all the fucking she must have done with Derek. My rage returned. "Oh yeah? How does that work?"

"That last night when you told me you wouldn't let me go with you."

"Oh." Our angry sex that night. No protection. What a way to begin a life.

"And besides," Lucky continued, "I didn't even start 'fucking Derek' as you so delicately put it until he and I got to New York. By that time, I'd already missed my period."

"Okay. What are we gonna do?"

"I'm 19 years old. I can't raise a kid. You'd leave and I'd be…"

"I said, 'What are *we* gonna do.' Not you." It felt crazy to me. We couldn't have a kid together. I reached across and took Lucky's hands. That felt crazy, too. Holding hands with this… girl I barely knew. Imagining us at a kitchen table forever, holding hands. Forced to get married like my poor, sad friends in high school an eon earlier.

"Okay." She pulled my hands close. "What are *we* gonna do?"

5

DOCTOR SUNSHINE

Roe v. Wade lay years in the future. Abortions were illegal, dangerous, and hard to find. I had seen several high-school friends fall victim to the medieval assumption that if you knocked her up, you should marry her. It was worse for her. If she got knocked up, her life as she knew it, or dreamt it, or planned it, was over. The road narrowed. Secretarial school went out the window. Home economics was all she'd need.

Neither Lucky nor I were saddled by that catechism, but we had no money to pay for a visit to Doctor Sunshine, a bona fide doctor on a prescient mission. Lucky was on the outs with her domineering father, her mother didn't breathe without the old man's consent, so the burden fell on us. On me.

How do you reconcile affection, maybe love, with jeopardy, desolation, and the sense that everything is ending? You don't. You feel as if you're covered in a myopic goo like the August humidity outside. Add a trashed domicile, a pressing need for $400 in cash, a felonious trip across state lines, and a heart-wrenching procedure that should have been Lucky's civil right, and you got personal and political hijinks.

But people knew people who knew a guy, and we found ourselves in the lobby of the Copley Square Hotel, talking to a well-dressed gentleman. Through metaphor, simile, and unfinished sentences, the gentleman suggested he might be able to help.

Thomas Wolfe wrote that "you can't go home again." However, the family doctor and his wife had become a sponsor of sorts for me and my sister when my father died, and the household had dissolved. I called upon them for a loan and drove back home, Thomas Wolfe be damned.

The good doctor hadn't arrived home yet, so I sat with his daughter. She was a freshman at Wellesley and was enchanted with her new boyfriend. I listened to her chirp young-love clichés; she read my ennui as a lack of understanding.

"You just haven't been in love yet," she said.

"Okay," I said.

When the doctor arrived, his wife joined us and sent the daughter away. The three of us huddled over coffee at the kitchen table. They asked me about Lucky. My downcast stammering convinced them that Lucky and I deserved a break. They wrote me a check and gave me a hug. Entitlement. I returned to the Copley Square Hotel, cash in hand. There was no receipt.

A week passed. Precious biological time was ticking, doubt laced our bodies with adrenaline, and the well-dressed gentleman had our money. Panicked, Lucky and I returned to the hotel unannounced, raising the ire of our liaison. There had been a delay. He would contact us.

The call came with time, place, and instructions. I don't remember much about the trip. There was a train out of North Station, silence between Lucky and me. I remember the yellow wallpaper on the waiting-room walls in the farmhouse where Doctor Sunshine performed his procedure. There must have been a return trip to Boston. Lucky sat side by side in silence, watching the landscape tick by, numb, confused by the loss of an embryo that would have become a baby, a little kid, then a teenager and a grownup. What would that person become, be like, the living outcome of an angry fuck? Would that make a difference? What would Lucky and I become? Would we stay together? I shuddered, not at the prospect of being with Lucky, but at the awful inevitability of birth and life and destiny. If the tiny speck grew into a person, who would he or she be? Would he or she be anything like me? Or Lucky? Or both of us. Would the child live to grow into an adult? Die? Travel, fight a war, have sex, make other children, become a doctor, a lawyer, an artist, a bum? What if we gave birth to a murderer, a Hitler? I felt a weight, the speculative reckoning of 70 years or more of human existence. We had ended all that with a grim decision. There was no way to rest with our choice. We couldn't stand it, not together. Lucky moved back to New York. I put the apartment back together again. Late September descended into a smoky Indian summer silence and a haze of raked and burnt oak, elm, and maple leaves. I embarked on my final year at the university, recollecting the smell of eucalyptus in the parks of San Francisco.

6

DO YOU, MISTER JONES?

Autumn turned to winter. Lucky returned to school. Neither of us reached out. The trauma of abortion and brutalized affection proved too painful for both of us. Winter turned to spring. I finished my last exam. I would graduate. Now I could return to San Francisco and throw my hard-earned diploma on Vinny's desk. I made no plans for further schooling; there was a war to stop, and I would rejoin the struggle through the Mime Troupe.

Once I graduated, the draft board would slide me into the cannon fodder column quicker than you can move a pawn on the chessboard. The draft was getting desperate as Westmoreland, the U.S. commander in Vietnam — we called him General Waste More Land — demanded more cannon fodder for his "light at the end of the tunnel" in Vietnam. Several of my ne'er-do-well classmates had already been drafted, turned in by Harvard, as did many colleges and universities. The draft board had asked for lists of students who might have one foot over the flunk-out line. I had my diploma but, without plans for shelter in grad school, what would I do to avoid the call?

I bought The Beatles' new album, rolled a joint, lay down on the stained living-room carpet, and put the record on. By the time the music was over, I had decided to take the long shot and apply for conscientious objector's status from my draft board.

Draft resistance. I already knew this territory. As a kid, I had banned the bomb with the Quakers. I had learned to play blues and folk tunes with the people who started Students for a Democratic Society. Three short years later, SDS had become the largest and most influential student organization in U.S. history. I had stumbled into the March on Washington and threw storefront meetings for jobs with SDS in South Philly. In short, I came of age as the big resistance movements of the 1960s were born.

Not everyone had access to these movements. They prepared me for the battles that unfolded as the war escalated and the resistance spread from the farmworkers in California to the anti-apartheid strategists in New York and every college and university in between. I could see that, beneath the horror and the bullshit, the Vietnam War was a class thing and — as the war divided America — it divided us kids. With the escalation of the war and the descending shadow of the draft, life and death could turn on what you knew — or what you didn't.

At demos, I remember standing opposite my enlisted peers, separated only by their helmets, flak vests, and bayonets. Electric storms flashed between national guardsman and protester. Boy soldiers who looked like my high-school friends donned poker faces and glared at us. We would urge them to put down their arms and join us. A few did, but most stood grim and silent, aware of the baton-wielding U.S. Marshals standing behind them, keeping them in line. If you stripped away the uniforms and class differences, they were us, we were them — only not.

The guardsmen who faced us had joined the reserves to help pay for a college education, keep a job, to avoid combat status and stay with their families. During times of civil strife, our working-class contemporaries were called upon to protect the national welfare from our commie-manipulated assaults. Most of those guys didn't want to be there, but once you joined the reserves, if the National Guard called you, you went. Unless you had options. Unless you knew better.

I knew better. What a privilege. I use the word advisedly. At the time, I took my position in life for granted. I had been born into an understanding of the world as a child, and, by the time I was a teenager, I took my knowledge and understanding of the world, limited though it might have been, as a responsibility.

Being a radical in the 1960s was not only about sex, drugs, or rock 'n' roll, although there was plenty of that. The Movement could be terrifying, frustrating, and exhausting, but I became thankful, even exhilarated, to live with such passion, intensity, ingenuity, and joy. Why privilege? Because, even amid the weirdness and chaos, I knew what was happening, at least in the context of politics and history. Or so I thought.

But I didn't really understand how the vague, generalized disparities of class and culture played out until I graduated. The comfortable umbrella of my student-exempt draft status dissolved and zoom! I was out there. I knew I would never fight. They could put me in jail, or I'd split for Canada. *One, two, three four, I won't fight your dirty war.*

Despite my boisterous resolve, I didn't want to go to jail, and I didn't want to split for Canada. But the great river of education, experience, entitlement, and the strength of my conviction afforded me a way out. No, it gave me a strategy that fell somewhere between a maybe and a Hail Mary, but it was a righteous strategy. I knew what I had to do — apply for a 1-O classification as a conscientious objector.

In 1967, few Americans knew what a conscientious objector was. Selective Service defined it as "a firm, fixed, and sincere objection to participation in war by reason of religious training or belief." All that was about to change. As the war escalated, the selective service would tighten the guidelines for conscientious objectors, student deferment, mental defect, all that. I made it under the wire. I had no idea what I would do if the draft board turned me down. All year I had been lost in gleeful anticipation that I was going back to San Francisco to join the wild and radical Mime Troupe, worlds away from my own baggage and the heavy Harvard traditions that hung like a dead Brahmin around my neck. All I had to do was stand before my local draft board.

I appeared one June evening at the New England town hall, where the selective service board kept its chopping block and cleaver. I walked into the musty, austere chamber where the local chapter of the selective service met once a month to review cases and hear appeals. Portraits of wigged and whiskered town fathers gazed down from the dark paneling. Late-afternoon light filtered through high windows. A carpeted aisle catapulted me toward the tribunal. There they sat, high on a dais, my local draft board, three straight-nosed, ruddy-faced Yankees, confident in their integrity, corseted by Brooks Brothers blazers, punctuated with school ties.

I called them the Brooks Brothers, after the clothiers who clad the Ivy League. They personified everything about age, tradition, conformity, boredom, and blue-blazer monotony. I could feel the sweat soaking my collar. My mouth felt stuffed with ash from a genteelly refurbished colonial fireplace. Under my ill-fitting tweed jacket, my armpits ran rivers. I thought of Kafka's Josef K, standing in the docket, pursued by a remote authority in *The Trial*. A grandfather clock ticked ponderously in the corner.

Whistling softly, a crew-cut gent with a bowtie leafed through my selective service record. "Just graduated, eh?"

"Yessir."

"Harvard, right? Which house?"

"Ah, Dudley, sir."

"What?" asked Crew Cut. "What's that?"

"Dudley House. For the students who live off campus, sir."

"Off campus?" he asked. "What'd you move off campus for?"

Damn, I thought. This is weird. *I'm trying to make a life-and-death point here.* I had poured my soul into this argument. While I wrote, my heart had been bursting with the righteous civil disobedience I had learned in Quaker meetings. Thoreau was my guide. All the while, my head said, *This is bullshit, they'll never buy this.* Sure, I'd been raised in the comforting nest of passive resistance to nuclear testing. But now, I felt the silence while I tossed around syllogisms like "war is hell." Nobody knows hell until he or she gets there. Therefore, nobody knows war until they get there, and I'm not going, hell, no. And these guys wanted to know what fucking *house* I lived in?

An age-spotted hand signaled that I should get on with it.

"War is a serious matter," I began, voice quivering, "with

bitter consequences for both the victor and the vanquished…"

"The what? What's that?" A Brooks Brother cupped a hand to his ear.

Oh wow, I realized. *This guy is deaf.* I was further convinced that I had been dropped into a Kafka novel. By the time I finished hollering for passive resistance and conscientious peace, my voice had stopped shaking, but the sheaf of my essay, useless for reference, rattled with my shaking hand. I couldn't read it word for word. I felt flushed, lightheaded. The Bloody Mary I'd chugged earlier to calm my nerves threatened to splatter red bile all over the heavily waxed floor.

I finished and stood, silent and shaking. The three Brooks Brothers leaned in, blue-blazered shoulders hunched, and began to mutter, then argue. The crew cut sat back and folded his arms.

Uh-oh, I thought.

"We're gonna ask you to step outside."

"Now?" I croaked.

"Yes," Crew Cut said. "Now."

Turning their blue-blazered backs, the Brooks Brothers continued to argue.

I walked out the door, my heart pounding.

Outdoors, the afternoon had turned smoky. The oaks and maples on the courthouse lawn cast shadows through the June solstice light. How long would I have to wait out here while they decided? Decided what? What did they think? How did they think? Do they think at all? The numbness had disappeared. I was standing at one of those fateful crossroads where you can't think straight or do right. I could have run, but I knew I wouldn't.

Without the reality of the deliberations going on inside, my mind turned to fearsome scenarios — me dragged, protesting, through the meat machine of the induction center, bent over, spread wide; watching my guts spill through a mortar-torn flak jacket; peering into the eyes of a naked child that I had shot in a thatched farmer's hooch; feeling at one with the scrawny depravity of the boys I fought beside. *Meat is Murder* wrote one kid on his helmet. The television had shown us all so much with its repetitious projections of rotor-blade downdraft tearing up the gentle countryside, the helmeted boys flinching at a nearby mortar explosion, boys in pain, dying helpless. Or not. This event, at the stuffy old building, would decide.

The courthouse door opened, ponderous, big brass doorknob.

Brooks Brother One stepped outside, his ruddy face and striped school tie gleaming in the waning light.

"Looks to be a nice evening," Brooks Brother One said.

"Yessir." My arms and legs felt heavy, my head ached. Weary.

"Good to be alive, nights like this," Brooks Brothers One said.

I nodded.

"You know, I fought in the last one. All the way up

from Africa, landed at Anzio, up the peninsula to Rome. Then Paris." He stared into the sunset. "Gay Paree. Not so gay in 1944."

I braced. War stories. Another time, another war. Nazis, fascism, concentration camps. The Good War, the news anchors liked to call it. Twenty million dead. Victory brought world dominance for the Yanks. God bless America. I'd heard it all. The phony demon. Communists, Reds, the Soviet "regime," twisted to leverage more war. *Not this argument again,* I thought. *Please. Vietnam ain't no Normandy. False fucking equivalence, motherfucker. No comparison.*

"I haven't forgotten. Hard to believe now," he said. "Looking at this green lawn, these trees, this light. Maybe I gained an appreciation of life in the middle of that horror. But I don't think so." Brooks Brother One turned and walked back up the courthouse steps to the great oak doors. He turned back to me. "In the end, I don't think I learned anything in that war that I couldn't have learned at home." He opened the door. "Come on back inside, boy."

I followed the blue blazer up the steps. My skin burnt with crackling static, my nerve endings electrified.

Brooks Brother One strode back across the ancient room, climbed back onto the dais and sat.

Crew Cut sat up, slapped his palms down on the table. He looked huge, elongated up there. He looked down on me and I could feel his body swell with the advantage. "Well, fella," he said. "I can't say I catch your drift, but…"

Brooks Brother One shifted restless in his chair, glared at Crew Cut.

"We decided to grant your peacenik status," Crew Cut growled. "But you damned well better register with the county clerk in the morning."

"Don't he have to do community service?" Deaf Guy asked.

"I'm sure he'll find something suitable," Brooks Brothers One said. "Won't you."

I nodded, neck stiff. *Hell yeah,* I thought. *I'll find something suitable.* Back in San Francisco. Another world awaited me, a continent away, but on that night, I was one of them and the words of Brooks Brother One hung in my mind. *I don't think I learned anything in that war that I couldn't have learned at home.*

The rest was a blur. I felt hollow. My head buzzed with the release of adrenaline. I stumbled down the courthouse steps and drove the familiar New England roads in the soft light of a June evening. I passed kids in junk convertibles, young farmers in pickups, guys with no place to go.

One of these guys will take my place. Several of my old high-school buddies had already gone. I lost track of them after graduation, I was out of here, but they were over there, and our little brothers were about to follow.

On that warm June evening so long ago, a great injustice had been done. I vowed to rail against the inequity of my acquittal and right the wrongs of war, regardless of cost. I felt impotent, reduced by privilege. I tried to convince myself that a return to San Francisco and my place in a guerrilla theater company would recruit me into the gathering storm of the revolution. Together we would conspire to overthrow the government of the United States with theater, music, and satire, but the power of sarcasm felt cheapened by my entitlement.

7

OUTTA THE WEST!

All year long, my cousin Eric and I had written back and forth about our Berkeley and Cambridge experiences. He sent sprawling pen and watercolor drawings inspired by seed-popping Mexican weed and the prodigious ingestion of morning glory seeds. I described my life as an off-campus student, carousing in a crazy Putnam Avenue pad, where music and communal living rubbed elbows with academia. Weeks earlier, Eric had graduated from Berkeley. Via notes, stamps, and envelopes, my cousin and I began to plan a road trip. I would scrape together the bucks to purchase a cross-country vehicle with enough space to include my sparse belongings.

To accommodate our separate new trajectories, I found an old GMC panel truck that I could carry stuff and live in. I had purchased the GMC from a Boston newspaper delivery outfit. Imagine the beating that truck took during its life, delivering heavy newspapers over Boston's twisted, weather-pocked streets. The weary machine popped out of second gear, the floorboards had rusted out from Boston's snow-salted winter pavement, and — as we found out in the first 200 miles of our westward voyage — the used and abused engine consumed oil faster than gasoline.

My friend Gabe, the photographer with a proclivity for painting, swabbed the truck's side panels a sour-apple green and covered the battered red-orange wreck with giant letters in a font known only to Gabe.

T R U C K, Gabe's letters shouted.

T-R-U-C-K!

Day and night, we rolled West with a baggie of weed on the dashboard. At night, we crashed in a field or behind a truck stop. In 1967, the U.S. superhighway system was not yet complete. You'd roll along for miles on a broad, six-lane, median-stripped freeway only to be routed onto an unfinished stretch of two-lane highway with a suicide strip for passing. Oncoming trucks would blind you with their lights, then rock you with their wash as you barreled past each other at a combined speed of 100-plus miles per hour. Crazed motorists would veer into the middle lane to pass, evoking a blare of diesel air horns and flashing lights from oncoming traffic. The cement ridges of the old concrete roadway seduced you into a trance, punctuated only by the flicker of lane markers. It was all so beautiful, and the constant fear of sudden death kept you awake.

In the morning, we'd pull into a truck stop. These weren't chain restaurants. They were mom-and-pop roadhouses that served gargantuan breakfasts: three eggs any style, sausage patties, grits, biscuits, home fries or hash browns, and gallons of coffee, all for about 85 cents. Oh yeah, and gas was 27 cents a gallon.

Those breakfasts always set us up for a day of driving; the road and the weed rendered me ecstatic by the afternoon. By early evening, my cousin and I were both giddy with Americana. As we headed out onto the Great Plains, the railroad often paralleled the highway. I remember pulling over to the side of the road, leaping out of TRUCK, and dashing up to the gleaming tracks to celebrate the passing power of an oncoming Santa Fe freight, the roaring diesels glowing with the orange light of the setting sun. Hell, we were living our own weirded-out version of Kerouac's *On the Road*, Walt Whitman's "I Hear America Singing," and Barry McGuire's "Eve of Destruction."

By the time we hit Boise, the road trip's giddy lunacy had worn thin. We were looking to get to the other coast. It was dusk, I was driving, my cousin was Bogarting a joint. A black Cadillac pulled up beside us and slowed to keep pace. A smiling blonde with a Jackie Onassis flip and a dark-featured driver with a glistening bouffant hairdo honked and waved at us.

The blonde Jackie O motioned me to pull over. Who were these people? Despite our romantic notions of farmers and mechanics and honest folks, my cousin and I imagined that a great cultural divide loomed between us and Middle America. We projected the strong possibility that whoever we might encounter could be hippie-hating, baseball-bat-wielding rednecks for whom all strangers were communists. Nevertheless, I pulled over.

Were we about to be beat up, busted, or seduced? We didn't know.

"Where are you guys going?"

We told them.

"Oh wow! San Francisco. You gotta come with us. We want you to meet our friends and tell us all about it!"

"About what?"

"About peace and love and all that."

"Oh." Eric and I glanced at each other. These gals had great expectations.

The blonde leaned on crutches, a go-go dancer who had broken her leg doing the Frug in a cage at the local lounge. The brunette was a Cherokee Indian princess; her father, chief of the reservation. Hence the Cadillac.

"Will you come with us?" they asked. "To meet our friends?"

Without consulting each other, we knew the answer. "Sure," we said. "Lead the way."

For effect, the princess slapped a red flashing light onto the roof of her daddy's Caddie and away we went into the gathering dusk, blindly following a Cherokee Indian princess and a broke-legged dancer riding shotgun. We were going to a go-go and the devil be damned.

The Caddie pulled into a dusty parking lot before a concrete blockhouse. Lighting up the early evening, a 20-foot neon dancer gyrated on the roof of the lounge.

Inside, our eyes adjusted to the low reds, greens, and purples of the lounge and its dance runway.

"Hey, everybody," the princess called out. "These guys are going to San Francisco."

My cousin and I braced ourselves for a barrage of beer bottles. Instead, we heard murmurs of wonder, then applause and cheers. The lounge's habitués gathered around us, and our escorts led us to a booth. A diminutive denizen in bell-bottoms and a paisley shirt punched the keys of a jukebox.

If you're going to San Francisco,
Be sure to wear some flowers in your hair…

Terrible song. The pop world was trailing the rockers and the hipsters and Stax/Volt and Motown. New people were writing the good tunes and rocking them out, but this copycat crap was still holding down the top of the charts.

That night, we did meet a handful of spunky, mischievous-looking cats who surreptitiously showed us their albums like contraband — Big Brother and the Holding Company, Jefferson Airplane, the Butterfield Blues Band, Buddy Guy and Etta James, the Grateful Dead. Those secret albums were probably considered a gateway drug to the devil weed, marijuana, which would have grown out there like sagebrush anyhow.

They all closed in around us. The girls flirted, but most of them were paired up in old-timey couples, cowboy-style. They asked us questions, some of them smart. And we talked to them. Apparently, our abductors had pre-arranged our seduction. The go-go dancer had tagged Eric, and I belonged to the princess.

She took me to her apartment and showed me photos of her ancestors, serious men and women in traditional dress, posing formally in the beaded buckskin and feathers of the Lakota Sioux. I asked her if she knew of Black Elk, the Sioux shaman who had been kidnapped and taken to Europe where he performed in a circus. Black Elk had learned the ways of this other culture assiduously, but his displacement brought on a psychosis that turned to magic. As with so many medicine healers, illness and near-death had resulted in an ability to see across time and space.

We sat on her bed. "I know about Black Elk," she said. She carefully described the magic in her family. I was entranced and, when she rose and disrobed, her stocky body, soft and round and dark-skinned, she might have

reigned as princess in the low light of a beautifully decorated sweat lodge. She embraced me and, taking me inside,
revealed a smooth, graceful beauty that transcended the
Cadillac, bouffant, cinder-blocked present and took us far
beyond the horror and tragedy that had befallen her ancestors. We lay, almost without moving, feeling the time slip
backward into a primal flow. I felt as if I were floating on
a river, buoyed by her hips and breasts and belly. She felt
young and ancient at the same time.

She woke me. Already fully dressed, she tugged me
out of bed. After I showered and dressed, she thrust a cup
of coffee into my hands. Dawn colored the western walls
and stretched the mundane morning shadows westward.
She drove me back to the pink, asbestos-shingled house in
the center of town. Holding my hand, she took us through
the unlocked door and down the basement stairs to a
pine-paneled rec room. Several of our new friends lay scattered on couches and slumped into easy chairs, the coffee
table was littered with beer bottles and full ashtrays, and
the record changer was stuck on that tune.

If you're going to San Francisco,
You're gonna meet some gentle people there...

My cousin emerged from an adjoining room. The
go-go dancer hobbled from the bedroom door. There had
been no free-love circus at the go-go lounge, but we had
shared an intimacy that carried into the morning. Beneath

the wonder of my night, an eye-aching sadness welled up inside me. All these sleepy kids, so curious about what was happening in these newly mythologized havens, the Haight, Big Sur, Golden Gate Park, about what they might find there, were they ever to leave their jobs, their apartments, their families. They had lost friends and brothers to Vietnam and knew we opposed the war. No matter. Our newfound friends asked questions, nodded, listened, responded. They overwhelmed us with soulful curiosity.

My cousin and I did our best not to discourage our hosts. We knew the truth of what was happening in the Haight. The year before, there had been about two weeks when the great love collective functioned as a free family amid the beauty of fog, blue skies, and eucalyptus. But the media hype burgeoned, tourist buses appeared, the voyeurs remained glassed off behind rolled-up windows gawking at the freaks clustered on the sidewalks, ragged flower children who were beginning to suffer from speed-laced LSD, venereal disease, and Twinkie malnutrition.

By the time I had left San Francisco to finish Harvard, the Haight Free Clinic was drowning in destitute children. The head shops and Free City collectives had begun to shut down. The media was already hyping the turn-on, tune-in, drop-out myth. The funky, down-home ingenuity that had built San Francisco's beautiful anarchy for decades had paled before the flood began the year before. I wasn't heading for peace and love in San Francisco; I was heading into the apocalypse of resistance.

Still dazed, we left our newfound friends and headed for the nearest diner to fuel up on another roadside breakfast. As we staggered through the diner's double-doored foyer, a real, honest-to-gawd Boise cowboy — big hat, boots, jeans, and a longhorn belt buckle the size of Texas — stood in the doorway. "Outta the West, hippies!" he whooped. "Outta the West!"

Part 2

8

THE MILITARY LOVER

While I survived my final year at Harvard, the Mime Troupe had taken a *commedia* and the Minstrel Show on the road to Canada. They made it as far as Calgary, which must have been a little like hitting Boise, Idaho, without the Lakota princess. But instead of two guys passing through in my red TRUCK, Calgary was hit by a troupe of theater freaks with a play, a stage, a curtain, and a band. It was too much for Alberta's cowboy country. It's understandable. Nobody in Calgary had ever met a black person, much less watched people impersonate one.

In response, members of the Royal Canadian Mounted Police planted a baggie of weed on one of the actors and busted the Troupe. The bust did what it was designed to do. The Troupe ground to a halt. Most of the actors sang spirituals in jail over the weekend while Vinny sat on the phone and raised money for bail, for lawyers, for fines. They returned from Canada angry, paranoid, and broke. They never made it to New York for the show with Dick Gregory at Town Hall.

So now I arrived to face a fresh dilemma. The Troupe had shed its old skin — most of its part-time actors and hangers-on dropped out when Vinny axed extraneous projects the way you'd dump ballast off a sinking ship. What could I do? I'd placed all my hopes, fears, and fantasies into a return. I had no choice: I tromped back up the stairs at the studio on Howard Street and argued my way into a second audition.

Here I was at the crossroads again. How would it go this time?

Vinny probably saw me as a little bit crazy. How many actors had he seen disappear for a year into another world and return, filled with as much commitment as when he had banished me? Clearly, I was committed to the cause. Besides, Vinny had plans for me. I would replace a guy named Lee. He'd stepped into the new *commedia*, *L'Amant Militaire*. When I arrived back at the Troupe, I couldn't see the wheels turn in Vinny's head, but turn they did.

Vinny broke me into *commedia dell'arte* in a series of brutal one-on-one up on the floor tutorials. That was rugged. He taught me the basic blocking, stances, gestures, and presentation of *commedia dell'arte*, jammed together in unholy alliance with American vaudeville, slapstick, cartoon physicality, and urban slang. The Troupe was about to launch the new *commedia* into the parks and develop it there, then take off on a tour of radicalized American universities.

I could tell that Lee, this tall, awkward man, was hurt and had no place in the Troupe. He never directly confronted me. I was surprised, having seen how repressed my peers were at Harvard, to see somebody in this free-wheeling environment quietly seethe at the sight of me. I had beat this other guy out for the part. More realistically, Vinny's decision to rehire me was based on the role I would play in the new show, *L'Amant Militaire.* Sure, I felt bad but took the invitation as a good omen. Vinnie knew I would play well against the lanky Erroll, who would play my sidekick.

I would play a sergeant named Brighella, part of the invading Spanish army that served as a dramatic metaphor for the U.S. invasion of Vietnam. Brighella was based on a stock *commedia* character. He was a lascivious little bastard, a sneak and a smooth operator in the military, an opportunist and a climber, but always a varlet, a henchman's bagman. He could be cruel and impulsive, but he had a weak point. He was very sentimental about love. He was, like my 50-foot Hindu, a dark-natured little guy and I loved him. Brighella would teach me all about clever audacity. Back then, I thought I had plenty to learn in that area. Later, I would understand that, in contrast to my self-image as an introverted and insecure young man, I pulsated with audacious rebellion and wise-guy ingenuity.

We began work on the play. I lived in a secular version of heaven. At 10 every morning, we gathered at the studio to warm up and study movement. Vinny led the sessions, very French, very strict, a heavy routine that he conducted seriously. Isolation exercises, dance combinations done in a rotating circle, ballet to stretch limbs, strengthen muscles, develop footwork. The sunlight spread bright squares of light across the dance floor, patterned by the industrial windows. Every minute felt like gold.

After lunch, we discussed the play before getting up on the floor. We would open in Dolores Park in a week. Fresh air and the raucous, lascivious feel of the times would saturate our performance, along with the green grass of the parks, the smell of eucalyptus, and handmade music. We brought theater to the street, where the audiences weren't theatergoers. They were just people. *Commedia* was working-class theater and we aligned with the workers and the marketplace of the street. Not the hippie streets like Haight and Ashbury, but the streets full of workers on lunch breaks from office buildings and commuters on trolley cars, the women who worked for minimum wage and the young men waiting to be drafted for Vietnam.

We put satire in *commedia* to flush out the Man, the gray-flannel, Madison Avenue propagandists, the military-industrial Washington pimps, the occupiers, the System, the Machine, the whole motherfucking wreck we wanted to overthrow with revolutionary theater. It was absurd, but so what?

"Be realistic; demand the impossible," Che Guevara said.

"Change the world; it needs it," Bertolt Brecht said.

Commedia, with its broad archetypes, worked great for the street, the parks, the outdoors. Traffic didn't distract, we made it a part of the act. *Commedia* made characterization quick and easy. You looked the part you had to play with a mask that used basic human distortions and grotesqueries to create archetypes, broad and clear, so that each character could be recognized from afar.

Although the play worked from a script, much of the Mime Troupe's drama developed through physical and verbal improvisation. The body language of *commedia* was designed over centuries to help tell the story in the wide-open spaces and distractions of the marketplace. Verbal improvisation drew great reactions. We could break out of the drama if well-timed and crack wise about the news of the day.

Vinny gave me a book by the Italian linguist and jailed communist thinker, Antonio Gramsci. He'd written about how the ruling class had developed a hegemony that I recognized existed now, in modern form, and how they had reinforced their dominance with art and literature, even music. Hitler and Goebbels also saw the value of culture and had discredited progressive culture as degenerate, or they had co-opted it. We lived in a society where art could be reproduced and disseminated more powerfully than it had in Europe in the 1930s. So every counterculture move we made mattered and brought significance to everyday life. From the top down, of course. Our lofty top. No grassroots sprouting here.

We were figuring out the scope and scale of authoritarian culture, the tools of the hegemony, but we hadn't yet figured out that — to break the form — personal politics had to align with political power. The political would soon begin to be translated through the personal. This new necessity was still impossible to imagine in the real world. This new perspective hadn't yet been realized in the Troupe, and really no one talked personal and political offstage. The first flickering of environmentalism, sure, but a recognition of sexism, even in the midst of our revolutionary fervor? No. Not yet. Everything must change, everything had to change, but sexism? Not so easy. Not so fast… But I'm getting ahead of myself.

In *L'Amant Militaire*, the military lover, the Spaniards had invaded Italy to free the poor, beleaguered nation from its own misguided people. Onstage, I was teamed up with Erroll, who played a dope-smoking private in the Spanish army. We had been given orders to recruit Italian peasants to join Operation Quagmire, a military surge that was supposed to conquer both sides of Italy's boot. Hell, Italy is even shaped like Vietnam. We took orders from

Capitano, a diabolical general who rode a black hobby-horse and spouted bullshit about the Spanish mission in Italy. He, in turn, alternatively hustled and sucked up to by Pantelone, a nervous and gullible Italian businessman with a beautiful daughter. The real hero of the show was the businessman's savvy servant girl, Coralina, played by Olivia. She was in love with Harlequino. Paul played him as a sweet, lovable, but painfully gullible fool. His acrobatic prowess was such that Paul, as Harlequino, replaced spoken lines with physicality, in gymnastic, pratfall *lazzi*. We opened *L'Amant Militaire* in the parks and barreled toward midsummer.

Not to be discouraged by the Calgary bust, Vinny was setting up a national tour for the fall that would end in New York. We would perform at colleges where SDS was ensconced. There were a lot of those. Almost every campus in America, from state colleges to private universities had SDS chapters and they were all turning their heads toward Vietnam. Circumstances were changing quickly. The draft circled around every young male like a vulture. In SDS, our rapidly growing imperial war had taken over for the jobs and income movements, even the anti-apartheid divestment movements. The U.S. used bullshit rhetoric to prevent the Vietnamese from holding an election that would have united the country. The war had become unbearable for those who knew, and that number was increasing fast.

9

THE SWEEP

Now that I had returned to the Mime Troupe, I needed to live in San Francisco. Working with the Troupe was a full-out commitment. If they'd let me, I would have moved into the studio, but clearly the company had had enough of that kind of enthusiasm. So, I crashed at my friend Robin's place on Waller in the Haight.

Every Saturday, the Troupe would bring *L'Amant Militaire*, to the park. Lured by our warm-up music and a *commedia*-costumed parade, a crowd of assorted humans, pigeons, squirrels, and dogs would gather on the grass around our funky portable stage. During shows full of masks and feathers, pratfalls and décolleté, our spectators laughed, lounged, and swapped green gallon jugs of Zinfandel for tokes of weed. After the show, we would pass the hat and hustle spare change.

Robin lived in a gray building in a gray summer, different from the East Bay. The fog closed in daily. In Berkeley, we had seen fingers of fog claw their way over the brown, newly crowded hills of Diamond Heights. Now I lived in it. The fog lent an air of romance to the scene, but the ever-present gray could be a downer. Robin's apartment felt gray with trim painted over so many times that each coat had dulled its multiple layers of life.

San Francisco was Robin's hometown. His father was a big-shot partner in a swanky San Francisco law firm. Robin grew up in Pacific Heights, looking down over the Marina and the blue bay to Alcatraz. Robin had graduated with me and, like me, the years at Harvard had dampened any interest in grad school.

Whereas I wanted to do stuff, Robin liked to appreciate stuff and he did so with great gusto and lack of ego. He played piano, but he was undisciplined about it, put in the time only sporadically, so he bogged down practicing the same Chopin preludes. Besides, Robin was hyper-aware of what other people had done in music. He'd say, "How the hell do you write music in the same world as Coltrane and Beethoven?"

Robin was an enthusiastic voyeur. He'd come out of a film boisterous and explosive over how bad or good it had been, what the director had done, acting out parts, knitting his brows over the darkness of Renoir and all the cinema verité people. He fell in love with all kinds of women, on the screen, on the street, in his apartment building. Not a good-looking guy, Robin, but smart and lovable. I went off to rehearsal with no idea where Robin would go every day. He saw a lot of matinees.

One Sunday, he came to a show in the Panhandle to watch *L'Amant Militaire*. The sun had broken through by the time we began setting up the stage, and by midday showtime, the sky shown blue and the stage radiated hot. I had a great opening speech that set up my character by explaining his position on the war. I'd leap around the curtain and stride downstage right, a cocky little mobster. "Hey," I'd shout out at the audience. *This government I work for, it's crazy. Ten years we been fighting in this stinking country and we gotta stay here till we win. And the way it is now, the generals can't get no satisfaction.*

Backstage, the actors would bang out eight bars of the Stones' "I Can't Get No Satisfaction." I'd do eight bars of a dance then I'd cut them off, bam! *But with the stuff we got now, melt your flesh off, or kill all the trees in the jungle. Pretty soon, somebody's gonna get hurt. But not me. I got a way out.* I'd spin around and shout upstage, "Hey, Espada!"

Erroll, as Espada, built a lanky, rubber cartoon figure in a cape and a beret, big boots, a dull sword. I'd hustle him into chasing after recruits, poor Italian peasants — if he could find any stupid enough. It's a nationwide hustle, Operation Guinea Wrangle. Together, Espada and I hustled Harlequino, the fool, into joining the army. Of course, poor Harlequino is the sad-sack lover of the vivacious Coralina, played by the beautiful Olivia. She acts alone out there. Even when we're working together, she's inside herself, all technique. Her timing is perfect, you gotta move fast to keep up. No time to think about why she doesn't emote.

Robin was sitting out there watching it, a frown on his face, but, after four years at Harvard, I knew him well. He wasn't judging; he was concentrating. I didn't spend much time thinking about him. I was hard at work in the heat onstage and I was new, my timing still not up. I had to think about the next beat, the next line, the next *lazzi*, but I wanted to get it right. Onstage, this broad Spain-buggers-Italy comedy made people laugh while it projected the horror, cruelty, and waste of Vietnam, larger than life.

After the show, Robin rushed backstage. The cast was unabashedly changing in the open, as always. Robin ogled, but he was all over the play, too — how cool it was and why it worked. An ancient theatrical form full of relevance today. Was this satire? It wasn't slapstick, was it? Sure, there were plenty of pratfalls, but the story, characters, and underpinnings were driven by class struggle. Robin got it.

"I guess you guys know that *commedia*'s story lines stretch back to ancient Roman comedies and real-life history?"

"They know," I said. But why not let Robin rock out?

"Two unrequited lovers, a mean old father figure, a corrupt capitalist who consorts with power-hungry generals and phony academics. I mean, it's got everything."

"You're writing a rave review in your head, for chrissakes," Richard said. "Do you work for the *Chronicle?*"

"This is not a call to reform!" He was shouting by now. "This is a call to revolution."

"You should write a review," Vinny told Robin.

"Send it into the *Chronicle*," Olivia said. "They love our work."

Robin guffawed. "Oh no, they don't," he said. "I know all about the *Chronicle* and what they think of you guys. And the busts for obscenity."

"Censorship," Vinny said.

"Its own obscenity," Robin growled back. "The whole paper's an obscenity."

"Right on," Erroll said and gave Robin a simpatico clenched fist.

We left with Robin simultaneously thanking and critiquing the cast. We hopped into his old Peugeot and wove drunkenly between cars on Oak Street, Robin loaded on enthusiasm. "And the servants, the underdogs…" He turned to me. "Who is that servant girl?" He continued before I could answer. "I mean, hubba-hubba. But she knows all, guides the naïve, romantic bourgeois couple to eternal happiness via byzantine hustles and plot twists."

He parked the Peugeot along the Panhandle. The afternoon fog had begun to roll over Diamond Heights and down the hill, a breaking wave of cold and wet. Heads down, we leaned into the fog for the last stretch up Clayton from Haight. We were midway up the block before we noticed that nobody else was on the street, not a person, not a vehicle. Robin and I stopped.

Uphill, squad cars had formed a barrier at the intersection of Waller and Clayton. A mass of San Francisco cops in dark blue coveralls, belts with guns, long batons, helmets, kneepads clustered around the cop cars. *What was going down? Somebody get murdered? Some kinda crime going on here?*

The dark blue wave leapt into motion and came rolling down the hill.

"Fuck," I said.

"Run!" Robin said and turned back downhill.

I stood there like an idiot on a tidal flat, watching a tsunami roll in. I raised my hand like I was in school. After all, I was just heading up to my place.

A six-foot behemoth with his baton held horizontal jammed me in the chest. Hard. I stumbled backward. "You want to be down there," he growled in a broad Okie accent. He hit me in the chest again, jamming me into a doorway. "So get down there."

I spun downhill, away from the baton, ahead of the quick-march phalanx. I heard dull, thudding explosions. I felt the weird energy of law and order putting a practiced tactic into play. Canisters rolled down the street toward the Haight. I rounded the corner into the eddy of the crowd.

Carried on the cold breeze, indistinguishable from the fog, the tear gas hit me.

Tear gas feels and smells like broken glass, ground into an infinity of tiny crystal needles so fine they float and so sharp they lacerate your eyes, nose, and throat. The fog helped distribute the gas. The whole Sunday crowd of out-of-town hippies ran past me, on the way down Haight Street and probably into the park. I ran with the ragtag crowd to the end of the park. I remember one small, very young girl in boots, chartreuse capris, and a tied-up blouse paced in a circle, oblivious to the chaos, chanting, "I must have acid, I must have acid." I doubled back on Stanyan. Still hugging the wall, I worked back up Waller behind the cop cars that barricaded the intersections and filled the street helter-skelter.

Robin had made his way back to the pad from the opposite direction. We climbed up to the roof, half expecting to find snipers positioned up there. The dark pitch of the back stairway opened onto the fog lit by red and blue cop lights flashing below. We scuttled to the edge of the flat roof, vent pipes steaming into the cold air, joining the fog. The tear gas rose to the rooftop in sharp, chemical whiffs. Below, the cops played army. They finished their sweep and regrouped at the top of the street, shouting, laughing, rowdy from the chaos they had created.

What did we do?

Nothing. We had provided workout fodder for the city's new tactical squad — cops with helmets and riot sticks, gas masks strapped to their legs, gloves, and knee-pads — a new gang that the mayor had ordered up to control student uprisings at San Francisco State and the Haight Street circus.

"I bet they're practicing up to kick ass on campus," I said. But it was still summer, so they practiced on the freaks in the Haight.

"Can you imagine if we had guns now," Robin said.

"I'd use them," I said. It was humiliating and scary as hell to get rousted like that — for no reason. The sky darkened with night and the fog ruled. We could hear spits and squawks from the cop radios. Pigs.

"Let's get some bottles to throw down on the fuckers," Robin said.

I turned. "Are you crazy? They'd shoot us."

"From down there?"

"They'd be up here in a split second," I said.

I lay on the roof, mind whirling. The cops had shot up the place with tear gas and made a sweep down the street, the biggest action pigs had perpetrated since the Haight circus had begun. They wanted to see how much they could push us around and how we'd react. They had attacked as the summer afternoon fog descended on the barefoot kids, cold, hungry now. The cops drove the stragglers into the park as night fell, then fell back, leaving the kids to hide in the cold, San Francisco night.

The kids down there were looking for their own version of *ikigai*, a reason for being. I had found what I wanted to do. I was changing the world with theater. Plenty of street kids had a genuine wish to do good, to spread whatever peace and love they carried in their hearts and minds. But few had seen peace or love in others. *There's not a whole lot I can do about the world, they would say. Except be myself,* whatever that meant. There were answers — they just didn't know them.

My answers lay in collective action. As summer ended, *L'Amant Militaire* had grown tight from our weekly shows in the park. The cast meshed into a practiced band of seasoned troubadours. A veteran actress from New York replaced the ingénue. Marilyn played against type, highlighting her offbeat looks with comic turns. Rehearsals continued, improvisation and conversation refined the script and the action. The comic bits grew tighter. The Troupe purchased an unmarked white van to transport the stage, costumes, and props at highway speeds. Vinny had established liaisons with politicos and theater departments at every stop on our planned tour. We were about to depart on a cross-country, kick-ass tour of major campuses from Minnesota to Massachusetts and on to a monthlong booking in Manhattan. We hit the road on a clear autumn morning. I'd never been so excited.

10

OUTSIDE AGITATORS

We arrived in Madison, Wisconsin, on a Friday October afternoon. Madison was stop three on the long-awaited tour after Minneapolis and Iowa City. An SDS kid met us at the gate with a permit and led us along the walkways to the theater. A city motorcycle cop showed up. The kid showed him our permit. The cop gave us a dirty look and left.

"City cops around a lot?" the director asked the SDS kid.

"We been on the streets a lot this fall," the kid said. "Dow Chemical gave the university big grants last year."

"For what?" we asked.

"To make napalm stickier."

"Stickier?"

"Yeah, so it sticks to the skin better and for longer. While it's burning. That's the trick, see? To make it stickier and hotter. Like phosphorous."

"You know a lot about it," we said.

"We all do," the kid said.

We pulled the van up to the loading dock and went inside. The theater tech director met us. He started talking to our techie, bragging about the new light board and grid. It was a swanky theater, around 600 seats, with a grand proscenium and a sprung stage floor. Our funky little *commedia* stage would look great, framed by all that classy theatricality.

We had a routine for unloading and setting up, and it was the first that the students saw of our road company, very together, very boisterous, invading the academic sanctum. We pulled the two uprights and the crossbeam off the top of the truck, shouldered them through the backstage loading dock and laid them upstage.

Next came our outdoor stage platforms, stacked to the side. We set the pylons and the 2 x 6 support beams onstage where our funky little stage-upon-a-stage would sit best, lined up under the light grid. Two actors on each platform, laid the stage floor into place on the frame. Wedges jammed the platforms tight together. We bolted the crossbar to the two uprights and lashed the curtain onto the crossbeam.

The curtain, crude canvas, split in the middle for grand entrances, was painted with a two-dimensional village in a shallow, primitive-styled perspective, no naturalism anywhere. Above that, we stretched a banner with the words "San Francisco Mime Troupe — Engagement,

Commitment, and Fresh Air," carried by a snarling, toothy gothic griffin. When assembled, we lifted the whole rig upright with a big cheer and tied it off to stage weights and cleats. Outdoors, we'd drive stakes into the ground.

I walked up to the back of the theater. Our *commedia* stage looked incongruous against the grandiose stage that surrounded it. The drop curtain was laughable, with its crudely painted village scenario. It destroyed any pretense of proscenium, any expectations of a normal night at the theater.

We dropped our coats — outdoors, the autumn had grown cold in the Midwest — and clambered onstage. The tech guys began to light our little stage from the grid while we tried out the floor. Actors warmed up offstage, out from under the techies and their heavy lights. Play some music, somebody shouted to the techs. Just don't make it "San Francisco (Be Sure to Wear Flowers in Your Hair)" or "San Franciscan Nights," a ridiculous song. There are no warm San Francisco nights. None. Ever.

We executed *lazzi*, falls and leaps on the floor, short physical bits. By now, we had the show down. Although it changed every night in its tempo, details, and audience response, the show had congealed into a funky ballet, at once orchestrated and improvisational. Within limits, you could change beats, insert ad-libs if you didn't break the rhythm. If you ad-libbed and blew it, you'd hear about it. A good ad-lib works well, but only when it's linked to the scene's overall context. There would be no question when it worked, because the audience would explode. Or we could do joke-jokes, laugh catchers where we'd throw in a reference to a hit tune or a San Francisco band, or an irksome professor on campus or insert a reference to dope or a popular villain like General Waste More Land, the commander in charge of the 500,000 U.S. troops in Vietnam. Sex was built into the characters, their relationships, the movement. It was a very bawdy, very political play.

I don't remember when Suzanne showed up. She must have come into the theater during the setup and joined a smattering of kids from the drama department. A loud boho guy with a big mustache established himself as the radical theater expert in residence. Suzanne sat to the side, slouched low in a seat, long legs sticking into the aisle, her angled body crowned with a tangle of thick blonde hair that framed brown eyes, freckles, and a determined mouth. While the boho professor gassed on, Suzanne watched us work.

Once the stage was lit and the techies clambered off the grid above us, we ran a speed through, very fast, very fun, stretching and twisting, staying on cue but whipping through the show. This was a time of invention. The best new work came out of these light, quick run-throughs. Then we'd go to eat and talk strategy with the organizers, all of them SDS members. Suzanne came along.

SDS organizers planned to use our show as a rallying point for the organized protests that were unfolding on every campus — the battle against Dow Chemical, Hewlett-Packard, the napalm brewers and the cluster bomb makers.

In Madison, they also included a protest against ROTC to the anti-Dow action. ROTC. The Reserve Officers' Training Corps. Rot Cee. More 90-day wonders came out of ROTC than anywhere else, the arrogant lieutenants who commanded platoons in battle, often leading with their dicks instead of their heads. College kids getting their young troops killed.

We talked to the SDSers about their politics and strategy, but there was very little ideology to discuss. We were all on the same page. They felt that ROTC created an authoritarian vibe of jingo chauvinism and offered a focal point for the "if you don't like it, go back to Russia" conservatism. The university was supposed to foster academic adventure, not reactionary politics. So SDS demanded the separation between war and academia. They wanted to oust the military recruiters off campus.

After the meeting, we fueled up at the campus student commons and hung out until we gathered backstage for a 7 o'clock call. We'd set our props, repair costumes, do whatever crazy ritual each actor practiced before showtime. Tonight, Vinny, Olivia, and Richard would go to the campus radio station to drum up interest in the show. The Troupe finished eating and began to scatter. Suzanne grabbed my wrist. I waved to my departing comrades.

"Where did you come from?" she asked.

"We were in Minneapolis. At the Firehouse Theater," I said.

"No, no, I mean before that," she said.

"I come from everywhere," I said.

"That's hippie talk," Suzanne replied. "It doesn't really mean anything."

Okay, a discriminating person, I thought. *Maybe she even knows how to argue.* I didn't know it then, but I was fast developing a penchant for girls who didn't take any shit. I hadn't been aware of my underlying desire for equity with another person, but I knew I never lasted long talking with people who couldn't throw ideas around. I'd get bored easily and, despite my desperate need for what I identified as sex back then, I could never last long enough with a sweet or vapid chick to get over. But a girl who would joke and argue, I craved that.

"What will you do once you get back to San Francisco?" she asked.

"Work with this company."

"That's all you do?"

"All we do? Are you kidding me?"

"You just act?"

"It's a full-time job. More than fulltime." I laughed. "Hell, we're overtime!"

She nodded and laughed with me, but I could feel gears working behind the façade.

"So how do you make money?" she asked.

"Petty thievery."

"Ha ha. Very funny. But you gotta make money. Or maybe you're rich."

"Nope. Not rich. And we don't need much money. We live for free."

"How do you live 'for free,' whatever that means?"

"Together. Collectively."

"'Collectively.'" She sat there, smiling slightly, eyeing me.

"What are you thinking?" I asked her.

"I'm thinking, why do you keep saying 'we'? Do you all eat together? Screw together? Think together?"

That stopped me for a moment. "We're a group. We look out for each other. And we're part of a family, bigger than the Troupe."

"What kind of a family?"

"One of our own making. Not like a nuclear family with a mommy and a daddy."

"I get that," she said, "but I'm still wondering what you're doing here."

"A show," I said. "A show about Vietnam. And the war."

"And how it sucks," she said.

"Yup," I said. She smelled good. I raced ahead, imagining Suzanne traveling with us, Suzanne back in San Francisco, Suzanne in bed. Her student status didn't figure into my contemplation. "You gonna be at the show tonight?"

"Of course," she said. "So what's this play of yours?"

"Well, it's about the Vietnam War, only…"

"Tell me the story. I'll figure out what it's about."

"I don't want to blow it. You'll see it tonight."

"Who do you play?"

"I play a wiseass corporal."

She pressed on, wanted to hear more about the play, the acting. Was the corporal a bad guy? Was he more than a bad guy? What were the masks for? Why all the acrobatics in the warm-up — did you bring a circus to town? To talk about the Vietnam War? How does that work?

"It's theater," I said. "It all comes from the same place. If you got something to say, you can make theater talk. Take this *commedia* style…"

"It's old."

"Yeah, but it's been about class struggle, like, forever."

"Forever?"

"Since the middle class came up out of feudal times. Which side are you on? What class are you in? Even a puppet show can tell it like it is. 'Punch and Judy' can make people own violence. A minstrel show can make people own racism."

"How do you 'own' racism? Isn't it something you get taught?"

I felt like she was challenging me. At first I thought, *What the hell, girl, if you don't like what I'm saying…* But I liked her questions. I liked her skepticism. I liked that she didn't accept who we were, what we did. She made me talk, she made me think.

The cafeteria emptied out.

Suzanne rose. "I gotta go."

"Will I see you later?"

"I'll be there," she said. Practiced. One step away from the noncommittal "maybe."

I watched her thread through the tables and disappear into the student union crowd. I felt solid, good, excited.

The tour had brought me a long way from the SDS I had joined three years earlier, when we been trying to collect a dozen local residents for a meeting in a hard-times neighborhood of South Philly. Back then, all we had was a storefront and our politics. Here, in Madison, we had showbiz on our side. I liked this battle better.

By design, we would act as a spark plug to fire up the students with laughter. Every moment felt like a teaching moment, but we didn't see it as a top-down thing. Our show was military-tight and organized, but anarchy ruled our threadbare theater's soul. You could feel the power rolling out ahead of us, leading the way, pulling us along. And we were part of it.

Showtime. We walked onstage. The audience had piled into the classy theater, modern teak panels for acoustics mounted along the walls, well-kept theater seats, unholstered in a rich green. In contrast to the formality of the room, the crowd included preppies in chinos and sport jackets, tweedy, disheveled beatniks, and bushy-haired freaks in jeans, ragged tops, long dresses. Working-class kids mixed in with leather jackets and pipestem pants.

Suzanne returned to the same seat. When I looked up, there she was, wrapped in that fatigue jacket, talking to a cluster of students. The kids were jazzed up. SDS had done a thorough job of prepping for the demonstration tomorrow. The students were savvy about the war and the role the universities played in keeping the war machine going. No dupes here. They radiated energy and noise and they filled the staid hall to overflowing.

Onstage, we formed our warm-up circle. We were on! The *commedia* had not yet begun, but we were singing beside the stage. Unlike proscenium shows, the set was designed to break the fourth wall that stands between actors and their audiences. This rift shattered expectations and gave the warm-up a raucous, funky anarchy. All we had was a recorder, a tambourine, and five sets of hands to accompany our voices, but the audience joined with whistles and shouts. Students ricocheted off the walls. They danced in the seats.

The audience loved the show and left the theater clapping and chanting. They flowed around the campus cops. They weren't prepared for the rowdy, post-show mob that clamored across campus toward the chem building, where the university was conducting weapons research. Everybody danced and cheered and shouted around the chem building entrance, a big crowd, but no one tried to assault the doors. This was no unruly mob. That's what The Man liked to call these protestors, as if they were a large infesting insect. Shortly, "the mob" broke. Groups and couples headed in different directions. Tomorrow, the demo would begin.

Our SDS hosts guided us to an off-campus joint with initials carved deep into the tables. Suzanne floated along with the crowd. She seemed to know them all. Inside, waitresses weaved through the standing-room-only crowd with trays of pizza, burgers, fries, and pitchers of beer carried above their heads.

The SDS kids were full of admiration for the show, how effective it was as a rabble-rouser. There was a lot of smart talk about the points the SDS leaders would make tomorrow. We picked student minds to build jokes and gags about the faculty, the campus, the classes, the local quirks, popular drugs, anything we could drop into the show the following night.

Suzanne sat with us, content to watch and listen. I think she was with me until Vinny started hitting on her. A striking phrase, to "hit on" a person. In elementary school, little girls who were attracted to me would hit me in the playground, always with a bright, malicious gleam in their eyes. As adults, the notion of males "hitting on" females, or other males, or however your gender proclivity rolled, seemed straight out of paleolithic times, when we were all hunters and gatherers. Purportedly, we had hunted and gathered our mates as well as our food.

Vinny and Olivia were a couple at home, but on the road, he pretended to stray in a malicious manner meant to tease her. Later, I would learn that he wasn't always pretending. I leaned into Suzanne. "He does this to make her crazy." I nodded toward Olivia.

Suzanne looked across the table at Olivia, sitting straight-backed, composed, and dark. She had been the centerpiece of the show. Her character turned the whole story from a comedy about a couple of old guys cheating each other into a tale of resistance, a victory for the underdog, and a bawdy celebration of love and trust, guile and intelligence. Now she was sitting alone, silent, pretending not to notice.

"Asshole," Suzanne said. "He's lucky to be with her."

We drank a great deal and stumbled across campus to hang out in the living room of a threadbare, rambling frat house.

Suzanne stuck with me. We ended up alone in the abandoned living room with nothing but candlelight and the LP of a jazz clarinetist playing Zen mantras and improvised modal music with *shakuhachi* flute and ancient Noh theatrical instruments — woodblocks and drums. I left the arm off the record changer. The clarinet and flute wound in and out endlessly as Suzanne and I wound in and out of each other until we fell asleep. At 7 a.m., Vinny and Richard and Olivia tiptoed through the living room on the way back to the radio station. We faked slumber so we could fuck again.

Later that morning, we showed up at the SDS office, our rendezvous point. Everyone hit the mark on time. This was guerrilla theater: we had synchronized our watches, memorized our coordinates, and checked our ammunition. The Friday-night show, and its spontaneous post-show mini demonstration, had left its mark. Fired up by the show, the students were ready to occupy the chem building where the napalm research was going on.

Beyond the morale-building afforded by *L'Amant Militaire*, the Troupe would march the protesters into the chemistry building. But first, students would gather at the administration building. We pulled out our *commedia* instruments: a snare drum, bass drum, a trumpet. We shook tambourines and blew on recorders. We marched across campus as students poured out of the dorms and reached critical mass in front of the chem building.

Two young women draped a hand-painted graphic of a clenched fist over a podium liberated from a lecture hall. A lanky guy with a beard, dressed in jeans, a faded blue work shirt, and a corduroy jacket stepped up. A long-haired student handed him a microphone plugged into a Fender guitar amplifier. An extension cord trailed out of the back of the amp and slithered up the steps to a window in the chem lab.

"We all know what we're doing here," he began. "It's not just because we posted flyers and handed out leaflets about this action today."

Cheers.

"Sure, that was helpful, but we all know that this building is no longer a place of science. It's a weapons lab. And the bosses of this supposedly sheltered academic community, this hallowed ivory tower, they no longer represent our well-being. Now they collaborate with warmongers. They take money from the military and the corporations and tap the brain power of who? Of us! They hold out diplomas like carrots before mules and tell us: 'Do the work. Do THIS work. Use your hard-earned knowledge, your love for science to fulfill our government research grants.' And the people who come to work each day, they use the standards of academia to pressure us — yeah, that's right — 'pressure us' into making the napalm burn hotter, make the cluster bombs tear more flesh."

The crowd booed. It was clear that they — students and organizers — had been meeting frequently. The crowd wanted to hear what this guy had to say. I felt the unity, all these kids understanding the power behind the words, the concepts becoming real, a matter of life and death, even for them.

"And they all know — like I know. Like you know. That those nice people, many so friendly, so sincere in their efforts to help us."

The crowd groaned with sarcasm.

The speaker stopped them. "No! No!" he shouted. "They're sincere. Sincere in their intent to keep the university wheels turning. But now, the wheels have changed direction. They no longer take us toward knowledge and wisdom. Hell, no. Now the wheels turn as gears of the military-industrial complex."

The speaker paused. He looked out over the crowd. No one moved. None had left. He crouched over the microphone, lowering his voice. "They're keeping a list, brothers and sisters. A list of those of us who stumble, who may not be at the top of our academic game. And that list goes to the warmongers."

Boos.

"That list goes to the selective service. To the draft boards. To those who decide who will go and who will stay. To those who can tear us from the halls of the university and drop us in the rice paddies and the blinding jungle. Yeah, the big wheel keeps on turning, brothers and sisters. And the halls of ivy — our halls — glisten with blood and burn with fire.

"They want us, these men at the induction center. The sergeants and the doctors. They want to stamp our asses like pieces of meat. G.I. G.I. Government issue. We are no longer the issue of our parents. We are no longer the issue of our hopes and dreams. We are the issue of the U.S. government. G.I., baby. G.I. Government issue.

"So now we've got to turn our university away from this dark identity as a death factory. We can't let them manipulate our hearts and minds and bodies. We've got to refuse to become the murdered and the murderers — while they make money off our successes and our failures."

The crowd began a chant. The chant began to move, in time, like a single organism. We picked up the tempo on the drums and began to march behind the serpent of protesters that took direction and danced across the campus to the chem building.

One two three four
We won't fight your dirty war
Mao Tse-tung and Uncle Ho
Dow Chemical has got to go!

We formed up at the back of the crowd as we had done so many times in the parks of San Francisco. But this time, we weren't passing the hat, fleecing the audience for spare change and joints. We were serenading the students into a building to sit on the floor in peaceful resistance. But we were no pied pipers.

"Stay outside," Vinny told us. "Don't go in."

"But we can't just march them in there and then leave," I said.

"Oh yeah?" he asked. "And what happens if the cops attack while we're in there?"

"Then we get busted."

"And then what?"

"No show."

"That's right."

"So we drive all the way to Madison, our mission barely begun."

"And we end up here in jail.

Vinny laughed. "Some guerrilla action."

During this exchange, the students knew what to do. One crawled through a window in the chem building. She shoved open the front door. Chanting, the students had rolled into the building. We could see them hunkering down in the front corridors. Others clamored and pushed to get inside. Laughter and nervous excitement. Suzanne waved at me, blew me a kiss, as she floated along with the stream, blonde hair bright against the fatigue jacket. The doors slammed shut.

Minutes later, phalanxes of cops appeared from around the corners of nearby buildings. They were outfitted in coveralls and helmets, gas masks strapped to their legs, gloves, heavy boots, and long nightsticks. Really long nightsticks. Two windowless paddy wagons, shining and new, pulled up to the chem building We retreated to a large statue of Abraham Lincoln. He had been adorned with a gas mask.

Inside, the students jammed the doors with baseball bats thrust under the push bars. Chains rattled through the door handles. They had come equipped.

A bullhorn blared from the police phalanx. The speaker, without identifying himself, declared the students as an unlawful assembly and ordered them to disperse.

Mao Tse-tung and Uncle Ho
Dow Chemical has got to go!

Another bullhorn announcement.

More cheering and singing inside the building.

A shattering sound. Broken glass cut through our drum and bugle tattoo. Unable to force the doors, Madison's shiny new Tac Squad broke through the glass at the entrance. The pigs shot canisters directly into the narrow confines of the chem building hallways. The canisters exploded with dull thuds.

People began to scream, their cries muffled but intense behind the doors and the shouts of the cops. The pigs began to drag students out of the chem building by their arms and legs. Tear gas splintered the clear autumn air with glass shards. They clubbed, kicked, and dragged students toward two large black vans, super-sized paddy wagons.

Shaking off the shock of the attack, the students rallied and counterattacked. They swarmed around the paddy wagons and prevented the pigs from closing the doors. They began rocking the vehicles and punctured the tires on both vans. Fire broke out under first one, then the other of the vehicles. The pigs flung open the doors and the students leapt out, only to be forced to run a gauntlet of pigs and their nightsticks.

For a moment, the scene froze. The cops seemed to come to their senses. Students, beaten and bloody, collapsed on the grass. Only the coughing persisted, as the students convulsed from the tear gas that began to drift away over the autumn-still campus.

The afternoon sun cast weird shadows and an eerie quiet descended. The campus looked like a battlefield. The walkways and grass, the open quads were white with leaflets, a jacket, a lone sneaker, posters on sticks, half of them broken. Stunned students sat back-to-back on the lawn, holding their heads. A table had been set up to sign people up for legal aid. A group with medical skills walked along a cloistered corridor of wounded, kneeling, bandaging head wounds, a broken arm, a swollen ankle. By sundown, we retreated to the theater where a second battle was forming.

Horrified by the Tac Squad attacks on the students, the Chancellor ordered the Madison cops off campus. Then he tried to stop us from performing *L'Amant Militaire* that night. The students regrouped, massing around the theater doors, demanding that the show must go on. We met with SDS at the upturned student union. We wanted to do the show, but we didn't want to instigate another police riot. Although they would have marched into the chem building that day without us, we felt guilty, as if we had ushered these kids to their doom. But the occupation of the chem building had been planned far in advance to coincide with the visit from Dow Chemical's recruiters. The recruiters were nowhere to be seen.

That night, *L'Amant* couldn't have been sharper. The audience radiated anger and sarcasm, they reeked of clear thinking and focused action. The laughs came up like

131

punches, not aimed at us, but at the powers that had brought us to this point, in a Wisconsin theater after a day filled with fury.

Afterward, people hung around the theater and talked. The Man had developed an appetite for brutality, but that night he went hungry. There had been rumor of a curfew, but who would enforce it? The administration and the campus cops stayed out of sight. Neither had bargained for the pummeling the students took in their occupation of the hall. The city cops had tried out their new gear, got their kicks beating the shit out of the kids. They had demonstrated the obscenity of law-and-order violence, gang-banging cops, red-faced white guys in dark blue coveralls, anonymous, shielding their badges from the rage they had perpetrated.

We sat in the theater together, the Mime Troupe and the students. They thanked us and praised the role we had played. Many of the young politicos expressed their newfound conviction that theater could play a tactical role in political struggle. "Who knows?" they proclaimed. "Maybe all art could be powerful." They spoke with the raw energy of discovery that we had begun to share in those times.

Suzanne sat, listening, knees drawn up under her chin, a bleak line to her lips, her eyes staring into the distance. We broke up well after midnight, vowing, performers and audience alike, to regroup for the matinee we had planned for the afternoon. That night, although she rejoined me on the foam mattress, Suzanne withdrew. "Nothing can come of this," she said. "That violence is gonna lead to trouble, and more violence."

"What about the guerrilla war?" I asked her. "What about Ho Chi Minh?" I always turned to the resistance in Vietnam in my case for armed struggle.

"Maybe that works in Vietnam," she said. "It's a different story here."

"The cops rioted. You guys didn't."

"You weren't sitting in there," she said. "I was."

She had struck a chord. I had stood outside, a pied piper leading the mice to slaughter.

"Maybe the cops learned something," I said, although the images of batons and helmets and the Haight sweep hung in my mind like tear gas. I knew the frailty of my position.

"Really?" She laughed a laugh older than her years. "You think those guys learned anything? I saw the look behind those helmets and masks. They got off on it. And they're gonna want revenge. We destroyed their precious cattle trucks."

I sat silent. The two charred paddy wagons had been dragged off campus by tow trucks.

"The war is never won with a single battle," I said.

"Will we win the next battle?" She turned to me. "And where will you be?"

Annoyance crept into my skull. I wanted to repeat the night before, the energy of discovery, the beauty of the low light, the scent of candles and bodies. But the violence of the day had saturated us all. The battle had heightened the libido in some, smothered it in others. I felt unwilling to accept that, but Suzanne pushed me away. I could tell she was near tears. Tears of rage. We fell asleep back-to-back, against each other.

A hand shook me awake from an exhausted sleep. "Come on, man. We gotta blow town." Paul knelt beside me, reaching over the sleeping Suzanne.

"Huh? What about the show this afternoon?"

"Never mind that. The cops are looking for us. They're calling us outside agitators. They want to pin what happened here on us."

I dressed quickly in the morning cold. I knelt and nuzzled Suzanne. This would be our goodbye. She turned away, never opening her eyes. We stole out of the off-campus house we had occupied, started the unmarked white van — no signs, no flowers, nothing to distinguish it from a thousand other white delivery vans.

The tech director unlocked the loading dock, wished us happy trails, 1and said "fuck the pigs anyway." We tore down the portable stage, closed the costume box on rollers, lashed the uprights to the roof, and got out of town in the coming light. I drove the van into the rising sun and conjured Suzanne, how she had turned from open and curious to stunned and distant. How would she change now? I thought of our bodies together, the warm animal scent. I superimposed her on San Francisco, although I knew it was an impossible vision. We fled south and eastward, outside agitators avoiding the pigs, sneaking away at dawn in an unmarked white van and three marginally reliable cars.

II

TRIPTYCH

Suzanne faded into the ribbon of road that unwound in the rearview mirror. The speed of her dissolution saddened me, but my reality had already separated from hers. I had seen the power of resistance coalesce around our theater. We had exposed the stupidity of injustice, the hubris of leadership, the horror of technology unleashed on villages. We had parodied the plight of our dazed and drug-crazed soldiers. We had made a laughingstock of the warmongers who were destroying a tiny agrarian nation and dividing a democracy. The audience responded to *L'Amant Militaire* as we hoped. The next morning, our audience occupied the research building and waited for the cops to attack.

I felt terrible. Suzanne had been the object of tac squad violence not of her making, and I had left her to sort it out with her peers, while we — the outside agitators — drove unscathed into the sunrise. On the road, I had plenty of time to think. An eerie darkness fought with my daylight. I assumed that history and straight thinking could shed light on the war and the rage of black America rising, but the police had won the battle with armored violence. Beyond the campus and our tight little ensemble, the stupefying conformity of television's twilight and a ravening consumerism continued to pave the road for America's cartoon normalcy.

Fedora'd men and beehived women watched the glowing idiot box and suppressed their yearnings while they cluttered their lives with automobiles, appliances, and advertising. It seemed that only the students and thinkers, the freaks and the artists, understood that we had been overrun by the fossil-fuel war machine. Were we the only ones to watch the machine suck the love and livelihood out of people, their hard-earned wages diverted into the pockets of the war traffickers and space-race disciples? Did only we watch public money channeled into private coffers by the great suck of war?

And we lucky few hit the road, flashing mad celebration and fervent desperation from campus to campus, rolling eastward toward our next performance without fatigue or regrets, fired up by the highway and rocked in time to the AM radio, running toward Chicago and the rebellion still bubbling in Detroit.

Chicago has always been a good theater town. Without a film and television industry to dominate the scene, its actors formed companies and developed their own theater culture. Chicago was a labor town; it lived on the chasm between rich and poor, mingling the moneymakers and the men who killed for them, the grunts, the goons, and the casualties, the rapists and the raped. Chicago knew about cold weather and hard work. They still boasted a labor left wing that related to the days of the first big industrial union. Chicago was home to The Industrial Workers of the World, a powerful coalition of miners, loggers, steelworkers, that gained power in the first decade of the 20th Century. The spirt of this "one big union" still permeated the city. Chicago hung out in bars, drank beer with whiskey chasers, growled poetry, and howled the blues. Their drama featured kitchen-sink scenarios with ingénues washing dishes and guys sitting in T-shirts over beers. In us, they recognized fellow travelers. They flipped over our salacious *commedia* and the take we had on the war. We had nailed the machine and encouraged the audience to laugh at it. They dug it.

We weren't surrounded by a campus in Chicago. We performed in a medium-sized theater that seated about 300, down the street from an Irish bar and a Polish restaurant, the El rattling overhead. Sure, there were students there, but that fall, four Chicago gangs had gotten together — the Young Lords, the Young Patriots, the Black Panthers, and the Blackstone Rangers. They found common purpose across race and formed The Rainbow Coalition. Kids of all colors had begun to work together in the poor neighborhoods of Chicago.

At showtime, the Rainbow people surprised us. The audience was filled with brown faces, white faces, black faces, young men and women in leather jackets and berets, all watching the show. They loved *L'Amant Militaire*. They saw the racism we were laying out between the Italians and the Spaniards, they knew the story of imperialism. They laughed, clapped, commented out loud, confirming that our story appealed to anyone who understood class struggle.

Afterward, we went to a party thrown by the Young Lords and black students in a big South Side house. People wanted to know how we learned to act. We wanted to know how they organized themselves so well. They had pressured a church to open its doors during weekdays so they could meet there. They used the kitchen to start a breakfast program, and they were tutoring kids who needed help learning to read, kids who had fallen through the cracks. They were quiet and beautiful and thoughtful, not even drinking.

Outside the umbrella of academia, undercover cops and snitches who play both sides showed up in Chicago. The cops were easy to spot. They really had no idea who we were, but one conversation and we knew they were the Man. They had found fringe people to infiltrate the crowds. There was one white guy there looking very street, who I noticed drifting from group to group, busting into little knots of people with jokes and questions. Most people ignored him. They told me he was always around, and they shut up. I didn't like the guy.

"Why are you asking all these questions?" I asked.

"Who wants to know?" he asked.

"I'm traveling through," I said. "But when people start to ask questions, other people ask why."

"Ask away," he said.

"You know any of these people?" I said.

"What if I do," he said. "What's it to you?"

"Because you don't fit. You stick out."

"You ain't from Chicago."

"No. I'm on the road with this group."

"So where do you get off hassling me?"

"I've seen guys like you before."

"Guys like me?" He raised his voice. "What guys like me?"

Paul turned around. "Come on, man," he grabbed my arm to pull me away.

The guy sucker punched me in the face. My head snapped back and my vision blurred. I shook my head to clear it, and blood splattered across Paul's white shirt.

"Hey, motherfucker!" Paul yelled at the guy who was already leaving, fast.

The pain came on in a wave across my punch-numb

face. I could feel my jaw clench. This time, I wasn't in the mood to go down in homage to passive resistance and non-violence, the way I had months earlier in Port Chicago.

I ran after the guy and grabbed his shoulders. He turned around and I saw a big Masonic ring on his right fist as it expanded at lightning speed between my eyes. I fell backward. Paul and Erroll grabbed me. They dragged me to the bathroom.

"Man, you're a mess," Paul said.

I splashed water on my face and looked in the mirror. My nose looked squashed. *How am I going to wear a mask?* I thought.

"That guy was a cop," I snarled. All I could see was that fat ring coming at my face. *A fucking cop.*

Paul and Erroll pushed me down onto the toilet.

"Nothing new there," Erroll said. He looked at my face and clucked his tongue.

"What are you looking at?" I asked.

"Your face, man," Paul said and chuckled. "You took two in a row." His ease settled me down. "You look like you're ready for a freak show."

Vinny came into the bathroom. He looked at my face, swelling now, I could feel the pressure across my nose. "What happened?" he asked. "How did you manage this?"

"I didn't 'manage' anything," I said. "That guy was a cop."

"So you took him on?"

"I didn't take him on. I just asked him a few questions."

"The guy sucker punched him," Erroll explained. "Twice."

"What kind of questions," Vinny asked. He bent down to check my nose. "He got you good."

"He's probably infiltrated their organization." My rage roamed, looking for a target, a bush to burn.

I wanted revenge. I'd grown up on the TV morality plays of the 1950s, when mythic men turned to action to solve problems. Television problems. Cowboy problems. Good guys, white hats; bad guys, black hats. But their revenge had always been designed to protect others, noble vigilantes. My revenge felt personal, like vengeance, and I wasn't going to get satisfaction from going after that guy. Once again, I had to cop to the reality — we had a show to do.

The mask hurt like hell, and, with my eyes swollen half shut, I could barely see. I did the second night's show blind, depending as much on body memory to tell me where I should be onstage. Later, they told me I had done the whole show with a leaden determination, but that my timing had been perfect. No matter. I wanted to get that guy. After the show, there was another party and, although I was hurting, I showed up.

Marilyn told me I was crazy, that I should rest up, but I didn't want to be alone to ponder my swollen face, and I couldn't turn down another night full of admiration and prospects. Different party, different house, but the Young Lords were there, as were several chicks and cats in leather and berets — Black Panthers. Dylan was on, which seemed crazy to me with so much R&B coming out, Otis Redding, just before he crashed into the lake behind us in Madison. Aretha with "Respect," "Cold Sweat" from James Brown. Somebody tore the needle off Dylan's *Blonde on Blonde*. James Brown came back on, "Cold Sweat"'s funky light snare, the horns, Brown singing "I don't care… I break out in a — bump bump — cold sweat," Maceo Parker's alto sounding like Charlie Parker. I'm dancing with a swollen face — and there was the snitch again.

He didn't see me. His back was turned. He had been the guy who tore the needle off the Dylan album. Made sense. Cops wouldn't like Dylan. Too much resistance. "I don't care / about your past / no no / when you kiss me bay bee…" James Brown, screaming in my ears. I went for the guy, jumped on his back, hooked my arm under his neck, snapping his head back. *I got you, babe.* We went down across a low coffee table loaded with bottles and cans, the crash of glass. I felt his hands trying to pull the crook of my arm out from under his chin. He staggered upright and back. Screams. I punched him landing multiple times on the side of his head until he managed to turn away. He twisted beneath me while I blind punched him, tears of rage blurring my vision. I felt strong hands on my arms pulling me up and away, him standing, blood on his face, blood coming out of his nose.

"Fucking pig," I shouted through tears I didn't understand.

"*Calmate, cabrón!*"

"Fool!"

"My table!" A woman's voice. "You broke my table!"

Me blind for the second time, two men separating us, the party crowd looking at me with shock, laughter, contempt. My face covered with tears and blood and snot, raging, "You fuck." To the men in black sunglasses: "He's a snitch, don't you get it?"

"Aw, man, shut up." Two of the Panthers pulled me out of the room, into the bathroom.

Paul was there, too. "Hey, don't hurt him," he said to the Panthers. He ran water in the sink. "Didn't know you were such a hothead, man."

"That guy — he's a fuckin' pig!"

"S'okay," one of the Panthers said. "We been layin' for him. Tonight was the night, but he's gone, now."

"Fool." The other Panther wasn't so laid-back.

"Hey, I'm sorry," I said. "I didn't know I was blowing your setup."

"Wash up, man," Paul said. "You look like shit."

"S'awright," one Panther said. "Do what the brother says."

"Jeez," I said. "I broke that lady's table."

"The snitch broke it," the other Panther said. They laughed and closed the bathroom door on Paul and me.

My breathing slowed. The water felt cold, clear, tightening up my flesh.

"Sometimes you surprise me, man," Paul said.

I poured water over the top of my head. I could taste blood in my mouth, like iron.

"Sometimes I surprise myself." I ran my fingers through my hair, trying to recognize myself in the mirror. I wanted my identity back, my eyes in my head, my mouth whole.

James Brown funked through the bathroom door, and the party gab had picked up again. *Hell,* I thought, *I feel good.* "Never done anything like that before."

"Nothing wrong with a first time," Paul laughed and exited, closing the bathroom door behind him.

Back then, I could take in the strangest events because every day embraced strange people, distinct places, and happenings, coincidences not coincidental, the significance of every moment sticking to a rolling wheel of mind-blown experience. Whatever had gone down, I had done it, and I was ready to take the rap for whatever might happen next.

I opened the bathroom door and walked back down the hall to the party. A round of applause turned into James Brown playing "I Feel Good."

I found the lady with the table. "I'm sorry," I said. "I got out of control."

"That's okay." She smiled. "It was an old thing any-how. Besides you got him good."

I knelt down to help others pick up the cans and bot-tles off the busted coffee table. Nonviolent resistance had begun to feel like a thing of the past. Two years later, both the young men who had separated me from the snitch were dead, killed by the FBI and the Chicago police. The pigs raided their apartment and shot them, one in his bed, the other who had risen to protect the household. A young woman and her child survived.

The caravan moved on to Detroit. The city felt under siege. A bitter Midwestern cold had settled onto the streets. The uprising of the summer had desolated whole neighborhoods. Even in the cold, we could smell burnt roofing, rubber, and electrical wiring.

Rage reverberated off the blocks of burnt-out ghetto housing and the music of Detroit's notorious rockers, the MC5. You couldn't miss the stark reminders of the summer's uprising where the Detroit cops had arrested partygoers at a "blind pig," a bootlegged nightclub on Detroit's 12th Street. The scene had bred tension all summer, with the Detroit police acting like an invading army. Even now, the neighborhood throbbed from that hot July evening when citizens had gathered to welcome back two black soldiers who had survived Vietnam. Five days later, after the governor mobilized the National Guard to stop the Detroit cops from shooting anything that moved, dozens of Detroit citizens had died and over a thousand buildings had burned.

Now, three months later, we drove through the bombed-out streets looking for our theater. MC5 descended upon us with open arms. MC5 stood for the Motor City Five, and they were Detroit all the way. They smoked more weed than anyone in San Francisco and had teamed up with a revolutionary poet named John Sinclair. The boys of MC5 had advanced from aspiring to screw high-school girls to becoming Maoist revolutionaries, without knowing how to do either.

Everybody had heard of MC5, even in San Francisco. They were like punk rockers before punk rock had been invented. They were all from the street and didn't know *commedia dell'arte*, but our reputation had preceded us from Madison and Chicago. They helped us unload the stage and carry our gear into the theater. They felt the same intense drive we carried: brothers and sisters, poised to tear the roof off the motherfucker. Sinclair had become their political mentor and had taught them that anybody who furthered this endless war in Vietnam, anybody who conspired to turn the wheels of the capitalist machine, anybody who defended the system should be classified as dead meat. The machine had nothing to do with people, with lives, with love, or the sad attempts at happiness that we humans seek. And imperialism? Vietnam? Meat is murder, man. They were hardcore, the MC5. Sinclair didn't need to smoke weed, he needed to talk, and we gabbed, but his lieutenants, loaded up with ready-rolled joints like ammunition clips, would smoke two at a time.

While MC5 signified, we set up for the show. I held off smoking Motor City weed through the setup. We had work to do. The place we were playing in wasn't really a theater. There was no proscenium, no grid, no stage lights. We would have to improvise. We found two big follow spots backstage that we rolled to the hall's downstage corners. The spots threw out a narrow field and cast stark, surreal shadows everywhere. Not what we wanted — surreal we were not. We wanted warm light, our masks, gestures, and costumes bright, our language clear and understandable. We projected reality — of war, racism, the class struggle, gender inequality, preferably well-lit. We would have to live with it.

Before we retreated backstage, I noticed a young woman sitting in the third row. The auditorium was still empty. She was a déjà vu Suzanne, with a head that exploded with frizzy, reddish-blonde hair. Like Suzanne, she had watched us set up. She looked straight at me. I felt as if I was being dissected.

I scribbled my name on an envelope and handed it to her. "Meet me after the show?" She read the note, looked up at me for a long moment, then nodded her head. No words, only a sardonic smile, one corner of her mouth lifted. I scampered up the steps to the stage, not believing my luck.

Several of the Motor City denizens came backstage and crashed our pre-show prep. Vinny, Olivia, and Marilyn had their own dressing rooms, but here came the MC5ers and there we were. And there was that weed. I took a couple of tokes. Never in my showbiz life had I made such a mistake. The moment the show began I realized how stoned I was. I had lost my linear sensibility. What scene happened after the opening? Which lines came first? I walked out onstage and was struck by the stark lighting. I could see my shadow on the walls. Acting is a spooky business. You really need to work into your own zone and suspend disbelief to bring it off. You are not who you really are. You are unrecognizable anywhere except in a dressing-room mirror. Now I was cast in stark two-dimensional shadows on the walls I faced. I oscillated in and out of character like a 60-watt light bulb.

Irrelevant thoughts intruded like chatter in a meditation. A crazy friend at Harvard had once dropped acid and played Bottom in *A Midsummer Night's Dream*. I had thought he was a fool for going onstage loaded. Now I was onstage and loaded. I performed one step behind myself all night long, shirking from the pain of pulling the mask over my punched-out face. I checked to see if anyone else had seen the shadow of my true self, a beat behind my created self, timing off, moves awkward, off-balance, struggling to remember what came next, out of touch with my usual confidence that lines, when memorized, flowed like body movement, without thought, without hindrance.

I made it through the show. And there she was. Sitting as she had before, waiting. *What's wrong with her,* I thought. *Why is she hanging around? Is she waiting for me?*

On the strength of my scribbled note? Two suburban women had accosted Richard. They seemed upset by his character, Pantalone, the greedy old Spanish capitalist with his purse hanging like a scrotum at his crotch. Pantalone spoke with a Yiddish accent. If you look at all the national accents exploited by the cast, he pointed out, we were equal-opportunity racists. We butchered and degraded Spanish, Italian, even black language in *L'Amant Militaire*. Why not Yiddish, too? I watched the women walk away, dissatisfied with Richard's response. It didn't ring true.

We all went out afterward and assembled around a large circular table in a late-night joint. Chop suey, chow mein, fish, sweet and sour pork, chicken with almonds, rice, snow peas, kung pao beef, pots of tea, bottles of beer appeared. We confessed to the chaos of the performance, not only mine, but the effects of the bad lighting, the strange proscenium. A couple of the MC5 crew were there. And she was there, the girl who'd singled me out before the show. She'd come easily, no hesitation. In my arrogance, I assumed she was in the mood for adventure. The table resonated with laughter and a tight, burning energy. The weed had worn off. I felt the familiar ego drive while we dissected the show, others chiming in. Although she was silent — I hadn't even learned her name — I was performing again, this time for her benefit.

The cast spent the last few moments together haggling over the bill and who ate what until Vinny said, "Screw it. Divide it by eight, the money people at the table." My "date" had eaten, but knew she was welcome. Out the door into the early November night, a wind blew down from the north, cold off the lakes, the kind of wind that reminds you that it hurts to be stoned, when you get the shakes. She and I ended up at the apartment I was staying at. Troupers and musicians hung out for a while, then trickled upstairs. We waited patiently, slowing down now. I was sure she wanted me to make a move. So I did. We leaned into each other on the couch, then began to kiss. I felt possession grow like an erection. Mine. My hands roamed under her sweater, owning her, she moving to give me access to her clothes, which I pushed down over her hips, up over her breasts, tugging, kissing, until she was naked, sweater up and off, skirt at first around her waist then down. She sat on the back of the sofa while I stood and thrust into her, jeans down around my ankles, shirt and sweater still on, she nude, me still armored.

She took my thrusts with no sound, and I came quickly.

I stepped away from her. My semen began to cool, wet on both our thighs, a crude by-product of our mean, sudden conclusion. I felt the lust drain out of me. We lay down close on the couch, stuck together. The room grew cold.

"I want to go home," she said.

"Can't you take a cab?"

"No," she said. "You take me home." She stepped off the couch, scooped up her clothes, and found the bathroom.

Grumbling, I dressed, put my layers back on and waited for her with the keys. I felt exhausted, reluctant to move.

She returned, fully dressed. "Let's go," she said, and buried herself in the quilt of her Detroit overcoat.

At first, we drove in silence, her giving me monosyllabic directions. I was still drunk and stoned, my punched-in face hurt, the lights blared in the late night, the streets lay deserted and wet-looking.

"You know," she said. "All I wanted to do was talk to some actors."

"Why didn't you say that?" I asked.

"Would you have invited me?" she asked. "If I didn't flirt?"

"I don't know." I said. Her anger and sudden speech confused me.

"I'm sorry." I said. "You should have said something."

She snorted her derision. We drove through a riot area, ragged and burnt out, store windows still covered with plywood and graffiti. I dropped her at the far edge of the battleground, at the front of an anonymous apartment, three stories with bay windows. She didn't invite me in. She slid out of the van and stood on the empty sidewalk.

"Thanks," she said.

"I'm sorry," I said.

"Asshole." She slammed the door.

I made it back to the strange apartment where I was camped out. I prided myself on my sense of direction. Once I returned to the transient security of the house, I crawled into a pile of blankets stacked on the end of the couch, too wasted to find a toothbrush. At the first gray of dawn, I felt solitude close around my body like November rain, leaving me shivering, empty, and bereft. What had I done?

Growing up male in white America, I'd had no training in subjugation, no need for the sharpened perceptions and strategic skills that most girls learn early and carry forward as women. But what had I done last night to the young woman with no name?

I tracked down our comic ingénue, Marilyn. She had found a bed in a professor's house, a large, well-kept old home on the edge of the Wayne State campus. I didn't know Marilyn well, but she was resourceful. She didn't share our political zeal, but she was a pro, a great comic actress, and easygoing. She'd encountered so much road-company insanity in her professional career that the stakes and high importance of our revolutionary caravan fit fine into her diverse catalog of theater lunacy.

The professor had told Marilyn of a good little place to eat breakfast, close by.

"What's wrong with you?" she asked.

"What do you mean?" I looked up, startled. Another female with a window into my psyche?

She laughed. "Jeez, sweetie, talk about guilty!"

"Of what?" I asked.

"Well, I don't know. Why don't you tell me," she said.

"Nothing."

"Don't give me that crap. First of all, you look like hell."

"I'm probably a little hungover," I said.

"More than that."

"My face probably still looks pretty bad after that fight."

She leaned across her breakfast — poached eggs, dry toast, and cottage cheese. "Sweetie, didn't I see you with a young lady last night?"

"Well, yeah."

"And…?"

"Nothing. I took her home afterward."

"After what?" She gave me a mock-suspicious sideways glance. Marilyn was always onstage. She used schtick as an everyday means of communication.

"Okay, I feel lousy. About what happened."

"You want to tell me what happened? Obviously, she didn't murder you. You didn't murder her, did you?"

"No. Well… sorta."

"Sorta what?"

"It didn't feel right."

Marilyn looked down at her toast and eggs. She dabbled with her cottage cheese. "Sometimes you get with somebody and it doesn't feel right. No blame."

Although I hadn't seen Marilyn go off with anybody, she gave me the sense that she knew what love wasn't.

"I dunno. I think she was mad at me… afterward."

"What… you don't know?"

"I think I was kinda rough with her."

"Uh-oh. You didn't hit her, did you?"

"No!"

"Good." She put down her knife and fork. She ate European-style, fork in her left hand, knife in the right. "You don't have to be in love with the person to have a good time… right?"

I wasn't sure I could answer that. "No, but I…" I had felt an urgent need to talk with someone. Now I wished I could join the home fries on my plate.

"I don't think I cared about her."

"Oh." Marilyn picked up the knife and fork again, working on cutting her toast, using it with the eggs. "Not good. Did she have an orgasm?"

"What?"

Marilyn put on her exasperation mask. "Did she have an orgasm? You know, did she come?"

"I don't know."

"Hmmm. Also not good. Did you come?"

"What?"

She laughed. "What, are you deaf? Did you have an orgasm? Come? Shoot your wad?"

"Oh." I blushed.

Marilyn laughed. "You're blushing! Well, that's a good sign."

"Huh? Why?"

"Because murderers don't blush. Rapists don't blush.

At least I don't think so."

"I guess maybe I feel it was like rape. Jeez, I dunno. I feel like shit. About how I treated her. She felt like a thing to fuck. Kinda like... convenient."

"Oy. You know what the Japanese soldiers called Chinese women during the war?"

"What war?"

"You know, the big one."

"World War II?"

"Never mind. These soldiers called the women they fucked 'convenience women.'"

"Oh."

Marilyn pushed her plate out of the way and leaned on the table. "Look, I don't know what happened with you and this girl."

"Yeah, well," I said. "I don't know either."

"The point is you feel bad about it. Most guys wouldn't know they'd done anything wrong."

"Yeah, I guess."

"So feel bad about it. You may have been a son of a bitch, but at least you know you're a son of a bitch. That's a start, I guess."

"Start to what?" I asked.

She sighed. "I don't know. Let's get a check. I want to take a bath before we go to the theater."

I rose, not feeling any better than I had.

I felt drained. I didn't know what had happened, but I knew I'd better learn. I returned many times to that night with the no-name girl. Maybe I had left apathy behind. I tried to feel her excitement, her anticipation, her fears, her discovery, disappointment, anger, shame, and contempt. In retrospect, I didn't have much to draw on. Now it's nearly impossible to recollect how I felt. The world had not yet progressed toward the liberation of women. I was left to grapple alone with my own cheesy urgency and the damage I had inflicted on her — and myself. I didn't know then that an urgent demand for equality was about to assault the arcane bulwarks of the clueless and dangerous male.

12

ROTC

The students at Lansing had a rawboned determination about them, their lives chafed by the cold winds off the lake and the awareness that the working class always fought the wars. They'd started to hold antiwar teach-ins where hundreds of students and faculty members would seek the true causes and consequences of the Vietnam War. When the Troupe arrived, we found Michigan students had planned an action to confront the military recruiters and ban ROTC from the campus.

They couldn't single-handedly stop the war, but they could mess with it. The strategy was a tough call. Some kids depended on ROTC to pay part of their tuition. They owed the Man war time. SDS demanded that students who had received ROTC scholarships be given university scholarships instead. That's when the shit hit the fan. It was okay to talk about peace and love and rail against imperialism, but when the students called out the university on grant money, the whole serenade changed key. Now, the kids were ready to rock and the action was timed to our arrival.

We put together the marching band as we had at Madison, when we had led the students off to slaughter by the Tac Squad. This time, the students were in control. Despite the Michigan cold, we stood outside the ROTC building and played, while the students sang, danced, shouted slogans. One of the students spoke.

"We're in touch, all of us, everywhere. We got phones and mimeograph machines and we get all the underground papers. We can see the big picture, right? And we're not only talking about students. Freaks everywhere, even a few workin' guys now, hard hats, dragging on The Man, pricking at him, a dick for a dick, making it harder for these guys..." He swept his arm over the Rot Cee recruiters and the uniformed students. The recruiters stood ramrod still. A squad of Rot Cee kids showed up in uniform to counter demonstrate.

"And we got something right here to deal with, part of the big picture, right on our campus, right in the middle of Michigan. Rot Cee. Reserve Officers' Training Corps, where they pick the guys who like this macho, military, hup hup hup. Gung ho. Gung ho guys."

The student soldiers stood at parade rest, hands behind backs.

"Did you know that Rot Cee kids become second lieutenants in Vietnam? They take command of whole platoons. Anybody here want to be led into battle by one of us? Are you kidding me? I wouldn't. Shit, people, most of us don't want to go."

He faced the uniformed counter protesters. "Do you guys want to go?"

Silence. The ROTC students stood stock-still, implacable, kids' faces masked in manly military deadpan. The speaker continued.

"Even the Chancellor's survey found out that 90 percent of us think we should get out of Vietnam. We don't need the whole history of the world to know this war is fucked up."

Back then, we still took for granted that the boys had to go war and the girls could not. The girls thought that sucked. Their brothers and boyfriends were on the chopping block. And they were supposed to stay home, study art history, and learn how to cook?

After the ROTC demo and before the show, we sat around the student union, drinking hot chocolate, a big staple for these Michigan students.

"Look," one woman said, "the Vietnamese women fight right alongside the men."

"Yeah," another responded. "And I bet no Vietnam army guys go around calling their comrades 'chicks.'"

"It's the same with Cuba," a third woman said. "Some of the SDS people in Chicago are in touch with people there. They're gonna go to Cuba in solidarity with the cane cutters. They're gonna call themselves the Venceremos Brigade — meaning 'we will win,' and they won't be no tourists. They're gonna go to into the countryside to cut sugar cane."

"It's really hard work. But they're inviting everybody — guys and girls because that's the way they work down there. Everybody pitches in."

"And it's hot." That was greeted with a chorus of "yeah"s, "right on"s, and "sign me up"s.

"The women don't just cut cane in Cuba. They train as combat soldiers in the Cuban army."

"So do Vietnamese women. So if Cuba can do it, we can do it."

"I think I'd rather cut cane than shoot people."

"No kidding!"

The women didn't want to go to war because they wanted to fight. But they had a sense of fairness, of equity that was being violated by the draft. We hadn't yet updated our vocabulary from "girl" to "woman," and we had assumed from America's television, movies, and comics that girls don't fight wars. But they had. Women had died in every war, some of them collateral damage, but many as snipers and pilots and medics. Still, the women remained girls, regardless of age, and the boys muddled on with the ubiquitous and noncommittal "guys." We had a way to go — from Lansing, Michigan, to New York City; from girls to women.

13

VERITAS

November brought the cold and the gray. The tour wound through Ohio, Pennsylvania, Western Massachusetts, and on to Harvard. It was sweet to play at Harvard. We did the show at the Sanders Theatre, where years earlier I had seen Hal Holbrook play Mark Twain, my literary hero. Sanders Theatre is located north of Harvard Yard, in Memorial Hall, a lugubrious gothic monstrosity. At one end, Sanders Theatre offers a warm interior with a wooden stage and pews for the old Calvinist bastards to grind their bony butts on. It resembles an Elizabethan theater, with a steep rise to balconies, and a center space for the groundlings to gather and grumble.

At the other end of this red-brick and sandstone monument to gloom looms a large, cold auditorium with a vaulted ceiling and tall, murky stained-glass windows. I took final exams there, starting at 8 a.m., when you can see your breath in the air and your fingers are numb. Here, you assemble with your exam-mates at long, narrow tables. You sit on hard benches right out of *Harry Potter* without J.K. Rowling to remind you that you're dreaming, which you are not. A proctor, equally frozen and therefore mean and grumpy, slings a blue book at you. You then commence thinking, writing, and freezing for three hours with one break and no talking.

So imagine re-entering that terrible building one year later. You stand in the wings, mask in hand, about to jump-start a recurring dream only this time for real, using the art form you pursued — past your father's disapproval, past a college where young gentlemen do not aspire to the stage, past all obstacles — to land in this platoon of anti-war activists and artists. In that warm, wooden theater, you don your mask and leap onto the stage, banishing the cobwebs and mold of academic misery with the light of resistance, rebellion, and theater.

The show ran its ragged course, punctuated by a raucous appreciation of our unholiness that rocked the old haunt. Afterward, I sat on the edge of our funky, splintered, roped-and-wedged, pennant-bedecked stage-upon-a-stage and watched our audience disperse. I knew no one. I felt as far away from Harvard as I did from the small public school and the New England farms I had labored on as a kid, picking corn in July, apples in September, and potatoes in November.

During the day, I walked down Mount Auburn Street past Club 47, its doors and bulletin board plastered with the names of new folk singers. I turned toward the Charles River and walked to my former home on Putnam Avenue in a November drizzle. The pizzeria had folded but the laundry survived. Upstairs, clean, cheerful curtains announced a better class of tenant for the landlord. Jeffree had left for New Orleans and I hadn't seen Lucky since we returned from the visit to Doctor Sunshine and she split for New York. She hadn't asked to go to California a second time.

Opening night, Tommy Dillon showed up. Tommy and I had acted together at Harvard. The university had given him a scholarship when they were awarding what they called "diamond in the rough" scholarships. Tommy was a scrappy working-class kid from Philadelphia, tugboat tough with a strong sense of irony. He was the first to laugh about his Harvard tenure.

LSD had landed at Harvard — Timothy Leary and Richard Alpert, later known as Baba Ram Dass, had conducted their psychedelic experiments until the spring of my freshman year. I recall the leaflets that made their way around the campus announcing the founding of their extra-curricular organization, IFIF, the International Foundation for Internal Freedom, an outfit devoted to fostering the use of consciousness-expanding drugs outside the university's aegis. I thought an expanded consciousness might make me study better, so I applied, but Leary and Alpert were only accepting grad students as their lysergic acid guinea pigs. Within months, the university busted them.

Tommy once took acid while we were performing *A Midsummer Night's Dream* on the Loeb Theater's main stage. We both played rude mechanicals, but Tommy had been cast as Bottom, the character who falls in love with the queen of the faeries. Bottom awakens and delivers a soliloquy.

In Shakespeare's faerie tale, Tommy's character, Bottom, wakes up from his midsummer dream and delivers a soliloquy that bears an eerie resemblance to a commonly held admission — it's impossible to describe an acid trip. In the play, Bottom wakes onstage to deliver Shakespeare's midsummer's dream. But Tommy had submerged himself in a lysergic-acidified version of Shakespeare's dream and didn't deliver the opening line of his soliloquy. The deathly silence of a dropped line stretched into a dramatic eternity. I knew that Tommy had dropped acid before the show and could see he had evaporated. I dashed onstage and shouted in my best rude mechanical accent, "Bottom! Your cue has come! You have been called!" With that, Tommy awoke and launched into his lines, too good not to repeat here: *Methought I was — there is no man can tell what. Methought I was, and methought I had — but man is but a patched fool if he will offer to say what methought I had. The eye of man hath not heard, the ear of man hath not seen, man's hand is not able to taste, his tongue to conceive, nor his heart to report what my dream was.*

Tommy made it through the lines without blowing them. Talk about method acting. He was tripping on acid and simultaneously acting out Shakespeare's pre-psychedelic version of an acid dream. Centuries later, anthropologists found clay smoking pipes in the Bard's backyard, but on that night, no one knew that the actor was tripping on — and tripping over — the bard's fantastical poetry. The incident made me wary of Tommy.

When the review of *L'Amant Militaire* came out in *The Harvard Crimson*, Tommy insisted that we meet — he wanted to read it to me, to get my thoughts. We met at a coffee shop in Harvard Square. He carried yesterday's *Harvard Crimson* folded under his arm.

"You gotta hear this," he said. "The guy couldn't have seen the same show I saw," he said. "But he sure is a snotty son of a bitch."

"I don't want to hear a bad review," I said. Cambridge was already beginning to give me claustrophobia.

Tommy looked disappointed.

"Read it," I said. "It'll probably present a perfect cartoon of academia." So I sat and listened.

> *"The San Francisco Mime Troupe is one of the world's great things. It brings joy in hysterics to all who behold it not just those whose narrow preconceptions drive them into unflinching hatred for all authority..."*

"Did you hear that?" I asked. "Read that again, will ya?"

Tommy read it again. *"…those whose narrow precon-ceptions drive them into unflinching hatred for all authority dot dot dot."*

"What a mouthful," I said. "What does that even mean?"

"He's trying to show us he's bigger than your revolu-tion, I guess," Tommy said.

Then the reviewer got clever. He speculated that the CIA had hijacked the cast and put on a performance to blacken the Mime Troupe's reputation. The CIA's ver-sion of *L'Amant Militaire* was nothing like the Troupe's, he claimed. It was vulgar, unfunny. "In its cruel ruse," Tommy read, "the CIA team of writers resorted to such timeworn tricks as the formless plot, the dialect joke, and the dead-president slur. But again, the audience refused to see its vision dashed, and the CIA's most basic weapon, mimicability, carried the show."

"Get this," Tommy said. "First he says it has a form-less plot." He rattled the paper open at the fold. "Then he says 'the plot was based on an 18th-century *commedia* by Goldoni.' Shit, man, all those old plays had a plot, for chrissakes." Tommy seemed pleased with his critique of the review.

The review jolted me. I saw the show and our efforts as part of a movement to trash imperialism. *L'Amant Militaire* was supposed to be broad and joltingly crude, an obscene extravaganza, purposely over-the-top plot, not melodramatic, but authentic, with strong acting and skillful movement. And we moved well, all of us. But like any cruel review — especially written by some guy who thinks he's a radical — it hurt. We'd always been on the move before, so we never got to see what anybody wrote in the school papers. And of course, *The Harvard Crimson* was the *sine qua non* of university newspapers.

"Ouch," I said.

"Oh, fuck him," Tommy said. "Some English major trying to make his bones by bein' a prick. I'm sick of this place."

"Stick around," I said. "You've only got a year to go."

"I know," Tommy said. "But I saw you come back last year. You didn't seem all that happy to survive another Cambridge winter for the privilege of wearing a gown to commencement."

"The director made me come back and finish up."

"I'm not gonna make it," Tommy said. The waitress filled our cups. "Not after seeing what you guys are doing out there. This place sucks. The theater sucks — Shaw, Shakespeare, dusty old classics. I gotta get outta here, join the Troupe, do what you guys are doing."

Back in *A Midsummer Night's Dream*, Tommy had shortcut the same outcomes we had worked so hard to create with *L'Amant Militaire*. You worked hard to understand your character, the scenes, and the meaning of the play. As Bottom, Tommy had shot his acid trip into the play, screwed up his cues, and had come away intolerant of and impatient with his offstage reality.

I couldn't get into Tommy and his complaints. Performing *L'Amant* had hauled me full circle to teach me life lessons — about a different way of living, a different style of acting. Tommy wanted to take the short cut to the political stage. But there were no short cuts and I didn't like Tommy's whining braggadocio. I said goodbye, paid the bill for both of us, and dashed to the theater and the shelter of performance.

14

MANHATTAN

After three days in Cambridge, I was relieved to be back in the welcoming blasphemy of the Troupe. To hell with Cambridge and the Putnam Avenue apartment. Screw Harvard Yard and *The Harvard Crimson*. I was trucking down to New York City with the Mime Troupe. We had blown Dow Chemical and their napalm recruiters off a dozen campuses. We had agitated students' passions from San Francisco to Boston. Now we would put on *L'Amant Militaire* in Greenwich Village, right down the block from *The Fantasticks*.

We contrasted in every way with New York's standard theater fare. And we hit big! The downtown, off-off-Broadway scene landed right in our laps. The little theater filled up with hip, curious, enthusiastic people — poets, painters, musicians, actors, beatniks, and anarchists. The whole

NYU theater department showed up. The Living Theatre came with people from La MaMa. The cast of *Hair* made the scene just before it opened at The Public Theater.

At 24 in '67, you think you're right and everybody else has missed the target, fallen through a counterrevolutionary mirror, or been sucked into co-option. To my young mind, we were at odds with all of them. We took direct aim at the war, at the military-industrial complex, at capital greed and corporate conspiracy. Everything else was bullshit. We weren't compromised by academia. We weren't hippies, aesthetes, mystics, or anarchists. We were revolutionary artists in the spirit of Brecht, alive in post-Weimar, pre-Hitler Berlin.

We were invited to a rehearsal of *Hair*. It felt like a hippie capitalist rip-off of the already tired mantra — turn on, tune in, and cop out, a bootlegged amalgam of *Peter Pan*, *Lord of the Flies*, and Timothy Leary with Christian overtones.

We watched the Living Theatre perform. The Living Theatre had been around since right after WWII, and they watched the off-off-Broadway scene grow around them like a magic-mushroom ring. They did Shakespeare, they produced an antiwar play at Café La MaMa. They had a long history of producing European stuff, Brecht's *In the Jungle of Cities*, Cocteau, Pirandello. They even worked around T.S. Eliot and Gertrude Stein's poetry. We watched them perform a big, onstage group grope called *Paradise Now*.

Paradise Now felt to me like the theater of grievance. Not protest. Complaint. "I'm not allowed to travel without a passport. I am not allowed to walk naked," they shouted. To me, the obvious response could only be "so what," "who cares," or "get your papers in order." But the Living Theatre did live their theater. Wholeheartedly. And they were good at it. It was full of choral work and the writing was precise and powerful. People came, they watched, they laughed, gasped, and cried. And I learned a valuable lesson watching them work. It's always easier to dump on the comrade next to you than to grapple with the enemy.

And there we were, right next to them, the self-described radical players, infiltrating the downtown theater scene, which, in turn, lay at the center of New York's art scene. Everything in the world seemed to happen in the Village. But we'd been on the road for months. We were tired of each other, worn out by the tour.

Conflicts began to surface between Olivia and the Troupe's leading men. She was the centerpiece of the show. She portrayed a smart, funny, and powerful woman who knew how to affect change. People in the audience loved her, but in the Troupe, the life lessons we learned from our characters seemed to stop at Olivia.

Onstage, the men destroyed the world and broke hearts. Onstage, Olivia as Coralina cared for her bungling lover, pitted her bosses against each other, and maneuvered to reunite the foolish lovers. Coralina operated between entitled-male power and its predictable idiocy. But the men behind the masks weren't ready to explore the real-world realm that Olivia as Coralina occupied.

Offstage, she remained, above all else, a woman, not a comrade. No one seemed willing to accept Olivia as a strong woman. From World War II through the 1950s and into the '60s, Rosie the Riveter, with her own paycheck had been puréed into a blend of Barbie doll and June Cleaver from *Leave It to Beaver*. Olivia fit neither role.

Marilyn presented a different story. She had conspired willingly with Vinny to develop a comic rendition of an ingénue. Onstage, she cast her character as a self-deprecating female who dashed standard notions of an ingénue in love, an iconoclast but not a revolutionary. Offstage, Marilyn identified herself as a hired gun and had no stake in shaping the Troupe's trajectory.

Olivia wanted to be heard as an active part of the company. When she put out ideas, she had to fight for them in private. She and Vinny would finish up the theater day, and the next morning Olivia's ideas might or might not appear. As important as her political mission, Olivia lived deep inside the personal world of the Troupe and the show, but she had no allies except the other actresses who served more as consorts than sisters. Millions had read Betty Friedan's work on the fiction of happy homemakers, content with housework, kids, and their husband's version of sex. But if you lived outside of that, with or without Friedan, you took your chances as a kook, a loner, or a libertine.

Olivia had grown tired of watching Vinny hustle one young thing after another in the name of an "open" relationship. In Madison, he had tried to hustle Suzanne out from under me. "Under me?" She wasn't "mine," but for a minute we were each other's person of interest. Because she was beautiful, but more important, because she was "mine," Vinny made a pass at her, winking at me while he flirted, watching her respond to him. I knew her already as a badass, but here she was acting like a high school girl. Confused. Disappointed. "Vinny," I said, "lay off, she's with me."

He laughed his absurd laugh and said "okay" in the same breath. The whole interchange was painful and ridiculous. Suzanne wasn't anybody's badass or high-school girl or anybody's anything except her own. She wasn't an object or an orifice. She had instincts as an independent woman, but that reality lay beyond the moment.

Olivia didn't confront Vinny directly in our company; she was too proud for that. Vinny tended toward female faculty members he could seduce with iconoclasm. He would stalk whatever notions — usually theatrical, sometimes political — a targeted female held sacred and dash them. It seemed to work for him as a hustle to dissemble their thinking on whatever — the theater, the war, peace, Marxism, their love for academia, the university that we were at, whatever worked for Vinny to deconstruct them into bed.

Olivia was reduced to watching her partner prance through this travesty. I tried to imagine what their arguments must have been like. They were caught in the relationship through their love for the theater and the dedication to the Troupe. They were both smart, but Vinny argued like a machine gun; he would mow you down with rapid fire. Olivia possessed her own mojo. Hers began with her role onstage, where she was bright, funny, compassionate, and strategic. Vinny modeled his behavior one-on-one with his character, a cynical, invading general. Male entitlement still carried radicals, beatniks, actors, painters, and the New Left everyman.

One of the most persuasive raps that Richard and Vinny used in public maintained that our individual personae were shaped by what we advocated onstage. The art, the politics of the drama would shape the actor who portrayed those ideas. So, all of us, by this way of thinking, could live by the principles expounded in *L'Amant* — that love, ingenuity, and a war against imperialism, against inequity — could overcome all power abuse.

Although Vinny could preach that principle, he couldn't live it with Olivia. He had to be in charge, the boss, the ruler. I don't know whether Vinny made her cry, but I do know they were stuck in this juxtaposition on tour, in the company, at universities, before the students. Everything settled on their shoulders. He could be a son of a bitch, Vinny.

Olivia did not retaliate. I never saw her step out after a party or show up at the theater with anybody except Vinny or Marilyn. She expressed her strength through artistic control; she was flawless onstage. Her character demanded mirth, a flashing beauty, and a precisely effervescent energy that she always managed to muster, onstage and — usually

— off. But toward the end of the tour, the composure wore off, and Olivia oscillated between sad lady and bitch.

Greenwich Village nightlife began about the time we finished the show. Curtain was at 8, 8:15. By 10, the show was over. A Q&A about the play would follow, where ubiquitous, white-bearded white guys did most of the talking. All these people were older than me. I could hardly believe they took the time, but they wanted to know how the Troupe had come together; how we learned to act in masks; the classic origins of *commedia* character archetypes; how we liked being on the road; how did we think the war would end; and come on, did we really think we were part of a revolution, for chrissakes.

We called out the cynics. The old white guys, gray beards in their 50s and 60s, confident that they knew everything about life, who explained to us who we were, how we could think that a theater piece could stop a war. I loved getting back at them by playing outside their box. "Didn't we just levitate the Pentagon?" I'd ask. "And yeah, we come from California, but we're not about peace and love. We ain't no fucking hippies. We're about art, political art. All art is political, and art is a political tool. We're political and we're free city, creators and stewards of liberated zones."

I loved to argue with these obsolete dinosaurs. I had no compassion, no feeling of respect for them. Most of them hailed from academia, NYU professors on tenure track. I saw them as sheltered, self-hating, trapped by salaries. They sought no adventure and answered to everyone. They preferred to bully students with their concretized points of view. Oh, I knew them. The rule of the penis heads. After four years of university subservience to guys with beards in tweed jackets, I reveled in playing proud and arrogant. I threw options at them that I knew they could not make. Look at me, I'd boast. I live on $25 a week and answer to no one. Nobody. I never mentioned Harvard in these testosterone-driven, intellectual jousts.

Greenwich Village can be provincial. Villagers believe they live at the center of the universe. And in a way they do. There's nothing you can't find in the Village. At least nothing that wouldn't interest a 24-year-old actor and self-described revolutionary, alive and free and on fire with the possibility of change. Greenwich Village is a very exciting place to live, but be careful that you don't let the Village voice engulf your head. I had grown fond of arguing with these guys, but I had no idea I was killing the father, killing the king. Many of them were probably single or estranged. They couldn't accept women; they suffered for that. Later, as I recalled those arguments I so eagerly leapt into, I realized that those old guys, cast in concrete, had been tattooed by their misogyny and the bright, lit hothouse that was Greenwich Village. If you could be provincial in the middle of the world's greatest city, they had done it.

Me, I would be out of the theater by 11, ramped up from the performance and ragging with these old guys. I'd be ready to roll down the street to a restaurant, bar, or coffee house. I could drop into the White Horse Tavern to drink Irish whiskey and listen to Dave Van Ronk play blues, ballads, and ragtime. I could walk over to Seventh Avenue and descend into the Village Vanguard to listen to John Coltrane play everything from bebop to modal music far, far above my head. I could fall into the Figaro, order a beer and talk to Bob Dorough, a great Village pianist, original hipster, and songwriter.

One night, Jackie de J, a jazz drummer of some repute came to the show. He was blown away by what we were doing and saying with the show. We took a liking to each other, and he invited us up to the Palladium on Broadway and 53rd to listen to the music. The Palladium was a dance club, and when we got there, a super-hot band was playing, all horns, congas, and maracas, two bright drums called timbales, a killer piano player who set up what Jackie explained were *montunas*, rhythmic and harmonic rifts that would lead the band wordlessly into the next tune.

Everyone was welcome, and the rhythms felt ancient and gut shaking, like they were coming from some mystic party in the bowels of the earth. I'd never seen people dance like that, close and fast with so much passion, it was like they were fucking standing up. As a kid, I had worn the grooves off a record by Art Blakey and The Jazz Messengers. The record featured carved African masks on the cover and was called *Drum Suite*. Drummer Blakey had invited some heavyweight Yoruban musicians from Nigeria to play and record the hottest rhythms I'd heard anywhere.

The rhythm and the horns beat against my body like hands on my lungs, heart, and head. In the breaks, a piano player and some horns, a rhythm section, bass and Jackie on drums. They were playing bebop, but with a battery of congas and a tight drum set called timbales. The bebop and the Afro-Cuban music and rhythms fit together like the sun and the moon, like light and dark, like sex. I fell in love with every woman in the place. After too much rum, I floated out of the Palladium with my ears and body full of the tempos, the melodies, the thunder of the congas and the flare of the horns.

One night, people from the Living Theatre invited us to a party thrown by a filmmaker at the Chelsea Hotel. Earlier, the filmmaker had made *The Connection*, which had started out as a play about junkies and had been done by the Living Theatre. Maybe that was how we got invited.

The Chelsea Hotel was a huge, red-brick monster, built a little like the Sanders Theatre and Memorial Hall in Cambridge. A million famous people had lived there, and the filmmaker was one of them. Her name was Shirley, and she was small, dark, and good-looking. She was older than me, maybe even older than Vinny. She had short hair and wore a bowler hat that looked just right. Her face was slightly pockmarked but she came on classy and she moved like a dancer. She had beautiful legs and her feet always seemed to be in second position, not like in a pose, but automatic, like falling into a *commedia* zero.

She'd come to see *L'Amant Militaire*. I hadn't seen *The Connection* and she was busy now, finishing a documentary about a gay hustler. Both films embraced the camera and crew as cast and content. Shirley identified herself as a dancer and she wasn't putting us on. She had studied, performed, and created dance, which meant she had discipline at her core, but she had become a filmmaker. She had seen a similarity between her work and the way we made the play say something. She was also vehemently antiwar and had finished working with her daughter on an abstract piece that carried the violence through this pretty girl. I thought her mom was hot, and she liked to touch people.

The party was jammed with hipsters, but Shirley was solid. She didn't mind talking to me. I asked her how she had made *The Connection*. She had seen the stage version and it had grabbed her, not because of the junkies but because of the elephant in the room. The playwright and director had turned the junkie story into a play within a play about making a play. Shirley had thought she could turn *The Connection* into a play being filmed, with the larger story being the intrusion of the filmmaking.

"You went beyond the play," I said. "I mean, it sure as hell isn't only about the characters."

"I wanted to use the camera to push people away from the story."

"They had to know the camera was there."

"That's right! The same way you guys show us that your play is on a stage."

"Our crummy little wooden stage."

"Yeah, if you want to call it that." She lit a cigarette.

"We're talking about the war with a play. We want people to remember that, to stay on the outside, to feel on the outside looking in."

"Yes." She grabbed my arm. "Same with *The Connection*," she said. "I didn't want to film a bunch of junkies shooting up. It was the conflict between the junkies and the filmmakers who — no matter how hip they think they are — are dissecting the personal lives of drug addicts like they're bugs on a microscope slide."

"Outsiders."

"Yeah. Like what you do with your play." She got up and crossed to a table and poured herself a martini out of a shaker she had hidden behind a cluster of spent wine bottles. "I had to do it that way," she said. She came back and sat next to me, her knees pressing against my leg. "The camera's an elephant in the room. I wanted people to see the elephant, how present it was, how intrusive it was.

Otherwise, there's nothing to do but feel bad for a bunch of junkies. How far does that go?"

"And the elephant was all these guys with their lights and their cameras."

"That's right," she said, looking at me over the martini glass.

"Only this time it was you and your cameras."

"Filmmaking isn't a woman's thing," she said.

"It is for you."

"Yeah," she lit another cigarette. "I try to break down that wall. We're half the world, but we're invisible."

"Whoo." I had to shake my head.

"You don't believe me."

"No, I do. I do. That makes a lotta sense."

"Either we get recognized for the usual crap — the kids, the marriage, looking pretty…" She blinked at me. She was pretty. She barely missed a beat. "When I did *The Connection*, I didn't use heroin, I didn't know anything about the dope world, and I cared less. But the camera eye became a symbol of people on the outside. Like me."

"Okay, but wasn't it your film? You made it, right?"

"Right."

"And isn't this your place? Your party?"

"Yeah. But so what? I'm still on the outside — a crazy lady. A one-off. A black sheep, a kook. Women still don't run things."

"But you're running things, aren't you? When you do a film?"

"Fuckin' right, kid." She stubbed out the cigarette.

I sat there listening to the rising chatter of the party. The booze was taking hold. I thought that if I waited long enough, I might be able to go to bed with her. But that was a long way off, and the things Shirley said made me think of Olivia and the chasm between her role on the stage and who she was when she sat alone at a party, pushing people away. "There's somebody I want you to talk to," I said.

"Oh yeah?" Shirley asked. "Who?" She looked at me with mock alarm. I don't think anything scared this woman.

Olivia was sitting alone, watching the party go by. Vinny was leaning on a doorjamb, arm above the head of a comely NYU grad student. That would make a face-to-face between Shirley and Olivia difficult. *What the hell,* I thought. *Let's try to make it work.* I introduced them. Vinny and Shirley had already met of course, but Olivia had not. "I wanted you to meet each other," I said to them both.

Shirley jumped in to be obliging, I suppose. "I saw your performance," she said. "I loved the play — especially your work. You were the closet captain!"

"Oh?" Olivia said. "Closet captain?"

"Yeah," Shirley said. "Running the ship — and nobody on board ever knew!"

"How so?"

"You know… You pulled the whole story together. Stuck it to the moneymakers, paired up those clueless lovers…"

Olivia laughed at that. "The dashing Spanish lieutenant."

"Thanks to your strategy."

"That's written into the character."

"But you give her life."

"Thanks." Olivia seemed to need bumping down the log and Shirley had no idea why I had introduced them, but I wanted Olivia to meet a woman who knew she was on the outside and still got things done. "Shirley is a filmmaker."

"Oh. That's exciting," Olivia said.

"She does it on her own," I said.

"No, I don't," Shirley said. "It takes a whole crew to get the job done."

"And all of them men," I said.

Shirley and Olivia both looked at me as if to say, "What's your point?"

"Like our company, like *L'Amant*."

Olivia leveled her gaze at me. "So now you're going to tell me it's like life," she said.

Shirley joined Olivia with a look to say I was telling them both that the sun rose in the east and set in the west.

"And Shirley told me she's used to working on the outside, feeling like an outsider. You know, kind of like when you…"

"When I what," Olivia asked me, piercing my chest with her eyes.

"Yeah," Shirley added. "When she…" she mimed — when she what?

CHARLES DEGELMAN

"You told me it was always uphill because the whole industry is male-dominated and…"

"What's your film about?" Olivia asked.

I decided it was time to step back and shut up.

"I just finished a piece about a man I know, a gay black man."

"An outsider," Olivia said.

"That's right," Shirley said.

"And are you like him?"

"In certain respects," Shirley said.

Olivia turned to me. "You think I should make a film about a gay black man?" she asked.

"No, no, I just thought…"

"You thought what?"

Shirley interrupted. "Look, Olivia, we don't have to talk. I enjoyed your performance." She shot a few darts at me. "Thanks for introducing us." She bowed out, knifing through the crowd. She immediately became engaged talking with a tall man with blondish-white hair, almost like an albino.

"What was that all about?" Olivia asked me.

"I thought she was interesting. She works on her own, calls her own shots."

"And I don't?"

"Sure you do. I was thinking that…"

"I'm calling my own shots now," she said. "Shut up, go away, and leave me alone."

"Okay," I said. "Sorry."

"Me, too," she said.

The party volume seemed to increase. It was time for me to leave.

15

FIFTY-FOUR HOURS

Richard owned a Volvo, one of those 1950s jobs with a rounded back that looked like a '48 Ford, only smaller. When the tour was over, people scattered. Richard and I teamed up to drive the Volvo back to San Francisco. I was thrilled. Richard had become a model for me, colorful, articulate, in charge of his destiny. We climbed in that car with our battered luggage, guitars, a box of contraband Cuban cigars, and a bottle full of black beauties. We threaded our way through uptown traffic on the West Side Highway and under the Hudson to the Jersey Turnpike.

Two hitchhikers were walking through the trafficked slush toward the entrance to the tunnel. It was a stupid place to hitch from and we knew nobody would pick them up, so we stopped. They were young and grateful and had no idea what they were facing. We let them crawl into the back seat, where they arranged themselves around our jackets and discarded coffee cups. The trunk was full of gear and musical instruments, so they had to hold their suitcases on their laps. And that was how they rode across the country, crammed into the back seat of that Volvo. The enthusiasm rose and fell, and the exhausted boys grew silent as Richard and I careened westward, cranked on speed, gasoline, chocolate, and coffee.

We'd made it out of Jersey and crossed most of Pennsylvania before we had to stop for gas. Richard disappeared into a phone booth. The two hitchhikers stretched their cramped limbs while the attendant filled the tank, checked the oil, and cleaned the salt off the windshield. Up to then, the trip had been a tour de force. The weather was for shit — rain, snow, and sleet slathered across much of the East and Midwest, the highway flicking from Eisenhower's broad asphalt interstate to the narrow two-way ribbon with a suicide lane, but the Volvo was humming smooth and we were making wicked-good time. The hitchhikers lapsed into forced hibernation, Richard and I were rocking to the radio and chewing through the cigars.

In Iowa, Richard began to get antsy. "Look for the Ames exit," he kept repeating. "The Ames exit. Did we miss it?"

We'd done a show in Ames, at the University of Iowa, but I saw no reason to sightsee. The speed had worn off and it felt like we'd been on the road forever.

"We're gonna stop here for a little while," Richard said.

"What? Here? Why?"

The hitchhikers stirred.

"There's somebody I gotta see."

"Who?" I was annoyed. We were on a roll.

"Remember Kim?"

"No. Who's Kim?"

"When we did the show."

"Here?"

"Yeah. Where else?"

"How the hell would I know, Richard? Maybe there's somebody you could see back home instead."

"I want to say 'hello.'"

"Uh-huh. Or, hey, I got a good idea."

"What."

"Maybe you've fucked somebody in Texas. We could hang a left and head south to ol' El Paso, eat some barbecue, learn a couple of cowboy songs…"

I heard a groan from our back-seat captives.

"I was kidding, guys. Come on, Richard," I said. "It's cold and dark out here. Cut the crap."

"I won't be long. I promised her I'd stop."

"And she'll die if you don't."

Richard drove on, silent, determined, preoccupied. We zigged and zagged, looking for an address on Maple Avenue or Elm Street. One of those tree boulevards.

"There it is!" He shut off the car and reached for the keys.

I grabbed his wrist. "Oh no, you don't," I said. "You want us to freeze to death?"

"Hey, I won't be long."

"Asshole!"

"Honest."

The way I said "asshole" reminded me of that night in Detroit when I'd fucked the curious girl with no name and unceremoniously dropped her off outside her apartment. "Asshole" was all she had said. Was this karma? Payback for my cavalier indifference toward that Detroit girl?

I started the Volvo. "Sorry, guys," I said. "His car. His fucking world."

"His *fucking* world," one of the back-seat boys said.

"Yeah," I said. "His fucking world." I pulled my jacket over my chest and shoulders and put my feet on the driver's seat.

The stopover did nothing for our hitchhikers. Their suitcases remained on their laps, their knees had become frozen into 90-degree elbows of galvanized pipe that ensured that no blood reached their feet or returned to the warmth and comfort of hearts and lungs.

I endured the humiliation of waiting outside while my brother in art and politics indulged himself. We had not been invited in. When I could stand the mortification no longer, I left our whimpering hitchhikers to stretch in the cold night air and went to fetch Richard.

An irritated young woman in bunny slippers and fuzzy pajamas opened the door. She was incredulous that Richard had left people freezing in the car. "They're in there," she said, jerking a thumb toward the bathroom. "I can't believe he did that," she muttered as she shuffled back to her bedroom.

I rapped on the door. "Come on, Richard," I hollered. "Let's get outta here. We're freezing to death out there."

He was actually angry. Son of a bitch.

"Hi, I'm Kim." She held out her hand. Small, dark, round, bright brown eyes snapping. She, too, was incredulous. "You actually left people out there in the cold? So we could do this?"

I looked past them. They had been fucking on a bath towel in a narrow corridor between the bathtub and a toilet.

What an idiot, I thought later, after I stopped bragging about the near-record-breaking 3,000-mile marathon. On and off the partially constructed freeway, it took us 54 hours coast-to-coast. With a stopover so Richard — or should I call him Dick — could get laid. I was scattered for weeks afterward. Everybody took the holidays off, but I had nowhere to go so I crashed with my cousin in Berkeley. I had gotten rid of the truck before the tour. Sold it for junk. I let it fade into the wrecking yard, its apple-green TRUCK shouting to the world, even as death approached in the gleaming jaws of a wrecking-yard metal press.

Part 3

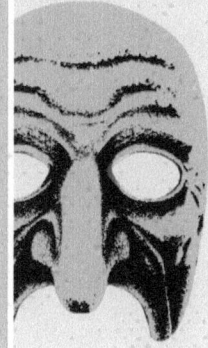

16

TURANDOT AND
THE BULL DYKE EXPLOSION

A new year. The Troupe began to gear up for the coming season. Life would resume its frenetic pace. Driving back and forth over the Bay Bridge was impossible. I needed a place in the city. Erroll told me there was room in a Digger household above Market and Castro. That suited me fine. The room was on the third floor of an old frame house built room by room up the hillside. I borrowed my cousin's crooked VW bus, grabbed my clothes, guitar, and the pinewood trunk that held my personal belongings, and set out to build a home base.

I unpacked everything I could hang in the closet. I set up a lamp on an upright orange crate by the box spring and mattress. I tacked up political posters from antiwar demos and a portrait of Che Guevara with a quote: *"At the risk of sounding ridiculous, the true revolutionary is guided by great feelings of love."*

I made the bed with sheets and a quilt my cousin gave me and unzipped my down bag. I closed the door and settled onto the bed feeling lonely but relaxed. The lamp cast a low, warm light on the room, largely bare but clean. The upper floors lay quiet, the traffic whooshed blocks below at 18th and Castro. Muffled by the fog, a trolley rang on Market Street.

Murmurs and muffled laughter wafted upstairs from a small group of people including Erroll and his girlfriend. I'd passed them coming in. Erroll had introduced me with grins, friendly nods, and a "Hey, brother" but nobody rose. He helped me haul the trunk up the stairs, opened the door to the room. "All yours, man," he said. "Knock yourself out."

Two floors down, the front door opened and slammed shut several times. Lively words interspersed with laughter, loud chatter, and a final slam. Heavy shoes clumped up the stairs. I recognized Erroll's clear voice and bawdy laugh. He and Rebecca talked for a while. Rebecca's soft laughter cooed around his declaratives, a woodwind to his French horn.

They grew quiet and I dozed off. I woke to the sound of heavy breathing and a groan, followed by a breathy oh! The groan morphed into a moan and a second, lighter breath joined the first. The sounds built in speed and intensity, their rhythm first punctuated by, then drowned out by growls as they ascended their erotic massif. After a cadenza of bed squeaks and pounding, the two love doves bellowed in coordinated climax and fell back into murmured coos, syllables, and low laughter.

I woke to a second movement. They built to a crescendo that prompted me to consider intervening to save a life, but I wasn't sure whose life I would be saving. The wave subsided and I slipped back into sleep. At dawn, they began the third movement of their duet, complete with its own ode to joy. *Maybe I'll get used to it,* I thought.

I hopped on the trolley and, after a short descent down Market, sat back down in the Mime Troupe studio, comfortable with my place among the tour-surviving actors who were about to plunge into the future. Vinny was there. Olivia was there. Erroll and Richard joined the circle. Marilyn had stayed in New York. She had bowed out after we closed the show. She loved us all but didn't live for the Troupe. I suspect that Vinny and Olivia had paid her equity wages. She had been one helluva hired gun. All's well that ends well.

Paul had moved on to work with a black playwright and director in the Fillmore. His departure made me uneasy. We had gotten close — he tolerated my brash, white-boy rebellion with a mixture of humor and impatience; he knew how to set me straight without bringing me down. I would miss him, but I understood the move. In the Minstrel Show, he could strike at racism, forcing it to the surface of the audience's self-awareness. We made the audience squirm with the long discomfort over blackness. In *L'Amant Militaire*, Paul was satisfied with the statement we all made — that the war in Vietnam constituted the rape of a nation. Beyond that, Paul had settled for playing the paradox of a black Harlequino. "What the hell," he said. "Othello was black. Shakespeare was white. I've even played Iago for the Man, reinforcing all kinds of black and evil stereotypes."

Black power was making its way into the theater. The move toward blacks running black outfits had started the year before when Stokely Carmichael, the former head of the Student Nonviolent Coordinating Committee left the biracial organization. He called for blacks to organize blacks, to build black power. Stokely's separatist call was powerful, but Paul and the people they were working with didn't spend much time talking about it — they lived it. The playwright and his company were doing black plays featuring black people. They didn't have to work hard to guilt trip any white people who came to the shows, but that wasn't their objective — they wanted to explore black life.

After we caught up with the tour, we began to look ahead. Outside, a winter rain slanted across the studio windows. A trio of empty paint buckets stood in the corner of the shop catching leaks from the first rain.

"The landlord's gonna get right on it," Spider said. That brought an easy laugh.

The little troupe felt loose, excited. Vinny was full of ideas about different dramatic forms. He wanted to woo a broader audience. He saw limits to a theatergoing crowd, even outdoors. His thinking came more out of politics than art. In the same way black theater didn't bother with distinctions between black and white — you did black —Vinny didn't bother with distinctions between politics and art. You did politics and let the content define the art, using the alchemy of the theater. To participate in that process blew my mind. If alchemists worked with mind, body, spirit, music, magic, and the stars, we did the same with history, dialogue, gesture, time, place — and mind, body, spirit, music, magic, and laughter. Hell, we didn't pull any punches from alchemy. We were the stars.

The politics of war and class conflict shaped *commedia dell'arte*. *L'Amant Militaire* had used Spain's 16th-century domination of Italy to represent our 20th-century domination in Vietnam. *L'Amant* lit up the sharply drawn class distinctions in *commedia* against the blurred class structure of the American dream. But now, Vinny wanted to move beyond the parallels *commedia* provided. He wanted to explore different issues with different forms.

On the third day, Richard and Erroll came in late.

The first two days, the sessions had started early with focus and energy. But now, planning took an abstract turn. What were we going to create? Why? For what audience? Juris, a tweedy professor of dramatic literature with a thick Scandinavian accent came in to join the discussion. I couldn't tell why he was there.

Vinny began to talk about a Brecht play he'd found, Brecht's last — *Turandot or The Congress of the Whitewashers*. It was about gaslighting and doublespeak and the power of lies. Vinny wanted to explore propaganda. Marshall McLuhan had brought out his latest work on information — decades before the Information Age began.

Congress was set in China, Brecht's favorite playground for imperialism and parable. The Scandinavian guy knew a lot about Brecht. And Orwell. They seemed to go together in this guy's head along with McLuhan, whose already overused phrase "the medium is the message" resonated in the room like Leary's nowhere advice to "turn on, tune in, and drop out." The Scandinavian guy made me restless. I thought we were looking for engagement and commitment, not intellectual constructs.

Richard looked distracted. He stood up and paced while the Scandinavian guy went on about Brecht and Orwell and McLuhan and Thelonious Monk. I figured we'd all benefit more from a table reading of the *Whitewashers* script, to get the play out into the air, to see if it worked at all. Richard kept pacing; Erroll fidgeted. Watching Erroll twitch, I couldn't get the sound of his orgasmic bellowing out of my ears. I wondered how I'd deal with more wild nights at my new home, the Digger pad.

After Juris left, we were about to break for the day.

"Hey, before we go," Richard said. "I want to talk about the truck." Around the city, the Troupe relied on an old flatbed GMC to carry the stage platforms, costumes, and props to the parks for performance. He wanted to use the truck to make runs to the produce market, to hustle the big distributors into donating free fruit and vegetables. Erroll tossed in anecdotes about how much free produce they'd scored from the farmers' market.

Richard and Erroll were talking from their place as Diggers. The Diggers were a loose collection of artists, wanderers, free spirits, and anarchists who took their name from a movement in Cromwellian England. The English Diggers had believed in economic justice, an egalitarian contract between human life and the flora and fauna of the planet, and open sexuality. They had lived in rural communes and developed a self-sustaining livelihood. But the landed aristocracy felt challenged by the success of these communal ruffians and fornicators. The moral objection to the Digger lifestyle gave an adequate smoke screen for the real complaint — they'd challenged the property rights of the aristocracy.

The landed gentry descended on the Diggers for liberating English common land originally been granted to the underclass for grazing and gardening. The local aristocrats had gradually taken it back. They attacked the Diggers, citing their libertine behavior, but the Diggers persisted. Three hundred years before the Summer of Love, the English Diggers had laid the groundwork for my brothers and sisters to liberate San Francisco.

So now the Diggers reappeared in urban communes on New York's Lower East Side and here, in the Haight-Ashbury. They had taken the name, spirit, and philosophy from their British forebears. The latter-day Diggers launched a contemporary assault on the bastions of private property, the sanctity of the family, and repressed libidos. I'd already been witness to the contemporary Diggers celebration of the libido with Rebecca and Erroll's triumphant orgasms. Armed with the slogan "one percent free," they set out to create alternatives to the rules, regulations, and expectations of a big American city at the pinnacle of its postwar wealth and hegemony.

In resistance to the still-expanding consumer culture, the Diggers maintained they could create an alternative society that would depend on neither profit nor war. They had set up Free Stores East and West to distribute contributed clothing, blankets, appliances, and abandoned furniture. They set up a Free Clinic, launched a Free Bakery and a coterie of Free Presses. Although they hadn't been a Digger invention, the Mime Troupe's free shows in the parks operated with the Digger spirit.

Armed with the Diggers' revolutionary history and their contemporary zeal, Richard stood righteous. The Troupe was part of the "one percent free" spirit that motivated the Digger collective. As members of the same community he argued, the Troupe should share the wealth — in this case, the flatbed truck.

Vinny was silent, but Olivia spoke up. "So who drives?"

"I don't know," Richard said. "What does it matter?"

"So what if you guys wreck the truck?" Olivia asked. "Or get hit? How do we do the shows?"

"We'll repair the truck," Richard said. "Look, this is ridiculous. We're not going to have an accident."

"You don't know that."

"We're all part of this community, right?"

"I don't know," Olivia said. "Am I?"

"Sure," Erroll said. "We're all a part of it. You're welcome to the food we collect."

Vinny got up and disappeared into the office.

Olivia continued. "And cook, right? The food has to be cooked."

"Sure. And Digger bread has to be baked."

"So who cooks the food?"

"We do."

"Yeah, but who makes it? Who cooks the Digger stew you guys like to give away?"

"All of us."

"No," Olivia said. "Not true. Rebecca, Carol, Helen, Sierra, Diana, they cook it."

"What are you getting at?"

"The women cook the food. You hunter gatherers, you go out and forage. You bring it back and drop it in the kitchen."

"We help out."

"Help out?"

"We're urban diggers. We gather food instead of farming it. Then we invite any and all who want or need to eat to join us. For free. In the park."

"Cool," Olivia said. "Like our free shows."

"For free," I said.

"In the park," Olivia said.

"Yeah, and…" Richard said.

"And we need the truck to do free shows," she said.

"And we need the truck to hustle free food."

"We only have one truck."

Vinny returned with a mug of coffee. "This is bullshit," he said. "You guys like to brag about your ingenuity. Find your own truck."

Richard leapt up, yelling about how much he had given to the Troupe.

"Yes, you have," Olivia said. "But we're looking for the common good here."

"That's right," Richard said. "The most good for the most people."

"And who decides that?" she said.

"Goddammit," Richard shouted. He began to pace. "Y'know what?" he said. "You're acting like a fucking bull dyke."

Olivia laughed. "That's where you go with this conversation? That I'm a bull dyke?"

"You're acting like one," he said.

"Okay," Olivia said. "What is a bull dyke? According to you, of course."

"You're pushing your agenda on me," Richard said.

"No," she said. "I'm pushing the Troupe's agenda on you — we need the truck. That makes me a bull dyke? How does that work?"

"You're intractable." He was sputtering. "You can't see beyond the narrow interests of your little niche in the theater."

Olivia laughed. "Oh, so now we're 'narrow?' Now we're 'little'? Why all the diminutives all of a sudden?" she said.

"Look, if you're just going to analyze this…"

Vinny laughed. "Of course we're gonna analyze it. How the hell else do we make decisions?"

"Fuck it," Richard said. "You've already decided." He yanked Erroll out of his chair. "Let's go." He stopped at the door. "You know," he said, "I've never had a day in my life when I didn't have a schedule. Maybe now's the time."

"Carpe diem, baby," Vinny said.

"Who knows," Olivia said. "Maybe it's the first time in your life you didn't get what you wanted."

And with that, Richard Wolfe stomped out of the room. On the way out, Wolfe's tall sidekick and my housemate turned and shouted, "One percent free, brothers and sisters! One percent free!"

When I first landed at the Troupe, I considered Richard to be one of the coolest, most charismatic men I had ever met. Throughout the tour, we had been friendly, and I looked to him for guidance and advice. But since that night on the road when he had left me and our two hitchhikers out in the cold while he got laid, I had begun to see Richard in a different light. Or maybe my lens had changed.

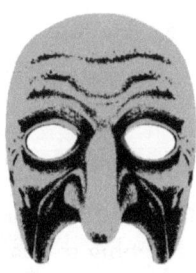

17

WON TON BY GASLIGHT

The three of us sat in the empty studio. How could this have happened? Over a few days, the company had gone from a busy troupe of 12 down to the three of us. Beyond Vinny and Olivia, I was now the senior member. I felt abandoned by Richard and Erroll, Paul had split. Olivia looked as if she was ready to either disappear or kill somebody. Vinny, not in need of introspection, wanted to get going.

"To hell with this," he said. "Let's go eat Chinese."

We walked down Market and grabbed the Muni into North Beach. Me in a navy pea jacket against the fog, Olivia in a trench coat. Vinny wore his usual Mao jacket, layers of shirts and sweaters, a goofy black watch cap, talking into the neon-lit glow of Chinatown. It felt cool, romantic, talking theater in the misty fog. We clustered around a back seat on the bus.

"Auditions," Vinny said.

"Who?" Olivia said. "For what?"

"For a production," he said. "A big production. Of *Turandot*."

"The opera?" she asked. "Are you kidding me?

"No. A Brecht version. *The Congress of the Whitewashers*."

"Brecht?" I asked. I didn't know much about Brecht, but he hadn't been a Broadway hitmaker, I knew that. "And you want to get with the people? How does that work?"

"I've been reading the papers," Vinny said.

"Yeah, so? We all do." I was surprised. I had found a voice.

"They love to think they're doing a great job of bringing the war into people's homes. They're all whitewashing the war."

"Blood and guts and TV dinners," Olivia said.

"And it's bullshit," Vinny said. "Watching people shoot at each other in the jungle, napalm explosions, body counts — that's not covering the war. And Congress. Jesus! Send more troops. Bring the troops home. Nuke 'em all. Train more Vietnamese. Let 'em fight their own battles."

"We all know they lie," I said.

"Or avoid the discussion. How many gooks did we kill this week? What does that tell us? They all give me a headache."

"This is it," Olivia said.

We stepped off the bus and walked down the steep sidewalk to basement steps that led into the steamy warmth of the restaurant. My glasses fogged. A waiter in a long white apron grabbed menus and led the way to a row of high dark wood booths. Without a word, he tossed the menus on the table and disappeared.

"The only real question is…" Vinny peeled off his jacket. "What we're doing there in the first place?"

"They gotta know we're losing," Olivia said.

"And they gotta know we know they're losing," I said. "Ask any G.I. He knows. Most of them figured it out after a few days in-country. The papers, do they think we're all stupid?"

"I don't think they care," she said. "They need a good cover story to keep the machine going."

"They lie."

The waiter returned with a pot of tea, snatched the extra setups off the table. "What you want?" he demanded.

Olivia laughed. "We just got here."

"We been talking," I said.

"Stop talking and order," waiter said.

"Three Tsingtaos," Vinny said.

"That all?" the waiter asked. "You come here for Chinese beer only?"

"No, no, we'll look at the menu," I said.

He disappeared.

"It's like this," Vinny said. "Repeat after me. If Vietnam falls to the commies, it will knock over Cambodia."

"And Thailand. And Laos. And Australia. And Peru. And the Bronx," I said.

"The Chinese have been kicking their ass for millennia."

"The Chinese are kicking our ass right here," Olivia said. "What do you want to eat? I'm starving."

"Never mind that. Repeat after me. If Vietnam falls to the commies…"

"But they're using Soviet tanks and guns," Olivia said.

"Repeat after me," Vinny said. "Vietnam wants to be communist. And the commies stole the election."

"But we stopped the election," Olivia said. "Didn't we?"

"No, the commies stole the election," Vinny said.

"I get it," I said.

"Bingo. You been gaslit. And that's where Brecht comes in."

The waiter reappeared with three beers and three glasses. He slammed them on the table. "So what you want?"

"We don't know," I said. "We'll look now."

"No, no," he said. "Too late. You talk too much, you know dat?"

"Sure we do!" Vinny said. "We gotta make the world go 'round."

"World goes 'round plenty good already," the waiter said. "I make you a deal. How much you wanna spend?"

"Wait a minute…," Olivia said.

"Waited long enough," the waiter said. "I fix you up good. You see. How much?"

"Ten bucks," Vinny said.

"Twelve bucks for everything, you pay for da beers."

"Deal," Vinny said.

"Okay. Deal. Drink the tea. I didn't bring you tea for nothing." The waiter disappeared.

"This is gonna be good," I said.

"We'll see," Olivia said. "And Turandot? What's she like?"

"She's a princess. Her father, the emperor, he needs to explain to the people why there's no cotton. But there's lots of cotton. Too much cotton. He needs to raise the price of cotton to pay off his debts and continue to enjoy life's little pleasures. Now, in this dynasty, intellectuals get paid to mess with information. To manufacture reality."

The waiter brought soup, floating with wontons. He tossed three porcelain spoons on the table and vanished.

The broth was hot, rich, and salty. "Oh man," I said. "Taste this!"

Between spoonfuls, Vinny continued. "These thinkers, Brecht calls them Tuis, they live by warping thought. They get paid to make up excuses, deflect blame, normalize the abnormal."

"Sounds like the news."

"Exactly. But there's another wrinkle," he said. "Turandot is a sapiosexual."

"A what?" I asked.

"She gets off on intellectuals. She thinks smart is sexy, but she doesn't really know who's smart and who isn't. She can't find a Tui who turns her on. She's getting pissed off. She's used to having her way."

"Jeez. Brecht and his women," Olivia said.

"You like da wonton?" The waiter slid large round plates in front of each of us. He turned and took plates from a young busboy. "Vegeble egg rolls. Shrimp wit' lobster sauce. Subgum chicken chow mein. Beef wit' broccoli. Sweet and sour fish. Shrimp wit' mushroom." He turned again and set down two covered lacquer bowls with white rice. Steamed fragrance filled the crowded dining room. Everything smelled delicious. The kitchen clanked and rattled downstairs, people laughed over the booth partitions. "You want more beers?"

"Yeah," I said. "Puh-leeze."

"Don't forget you gotta pay for da beers, full price."

"Got it," Olivia said.

"Okay, now stop all da talk talk and eat. Crazy people. No more talk. Eat da food. Enjoy it. Let's go," he said to the busboy and disappeared.

We scooped out portions onto our dishes, inhaling. We ate in silence for a short time. Each dish tasted and smelled like flowers, and the cold beer chased it all into a steamy, fat-belly, buddha-like sense of well-being.

"Turandot wants an intellectual for a husband, the emperor needs an intellectual who can bullshit away the bumper crop of cotton."

We ate. The cold beer and hot tea washed the good food down with a heady buzz.

"But in the end, the people rise up. The emperor freaks out. The intellectuals can lie, but they can't change the fact that people are walkin' around the streets naked and starving and the warehouses are full of cotton."

"So how does it end?"

"The end needs work. Brecht didn't finish it."

"I mean, the way Brecht has it, Turandot runs off with a good-looking crook."

"What if Turandot was a man?" Olivia asked.

"That won't work. Besides, we need tits and ass. Tits and ass. This is the theater, lady." Vinny laughed his maniacal laugh.

"Another cold, manipulative princess," Olivia said. "That sucks. Why do the women always get stuck with the shitty roles?"

"It's the emperor who gets fucked in the end," Vinny said.

"Yeah," Olivia said. "And did you notice? Brecht makes Turandot beautiful? His only beautiful female character. All the Brecht women I know are solid, stolid. Working woman on their own. And they drive the story."

"Oh, she'll drive the story," Vinny said. "You'll be doing the part."

Olivia ate silently.

"Besides, she's a period piece. Part of an earlier time," Vinny said.

"Yeah, but aren't we bringing it up to date?" I asked. I wanted to see where Olivia was taking this.

"No. Maybe. I don't know," Vinny said. "Brecht didn't seem to care much about the battle of the sexes."

"Except when he wanted to get laid," Olivia said. "Or when he wanted somebody to do the dirty work."

Olivia turned to me. "Did you know that Brecht didn't write his own scripts? His women wrote them."

"You don't know that," Vinny said.

"There's new scholarship on it," Olivia said. "Sure as hell wouldn't surprise me."

The waiter brought the check. "Good deal, huh?"

It was a great deal. I nodded, mouth still full.

"Yeah, good deal," Vinny said. "How come no pork?" Vinny asked. "You kosher?"

The waiter cracked up. "Kosher! That's good one." He turned to Olivia. "He's funny man, comedian, right?"

"Right," Olivia said. "A real comedian."

"No pig here," the waiter said. "We don't serve pig. Pigs good people."

"Pigs *are* good people," Vinny said.

"Good people," the waiter said. "You got dessert coming. Ice cream. Green tea, lychee nut."

I'd never had green tea ice cream.

"Try it." Olivia ordered the ice cream.

"And we're gonna need actors who can play instruments," Vinny said.

"We can handle that. We had musicians for the Minstrel Show."

"This will be different," Vinny said. "The music should

be like a character. A voice. Integral. Like Noh."

"Like Chinese opera."

The story made sense. The gaslighting made sense. We could use it to talk about the media and the war. I liked it. The television news, especially about the war and the protests was driving me crazy. I wouldn't watch it.

Vinny paid up and we walked back out into the foggy night.

"Night, kid," Vinny said. They crossed the street to grab a cab and I walked down to Columbus Avenue where I could grab a bus through downtown and back up Market Street to Castro. The fog had thickened, turning the lights myopic and deadening the night sounds of the city. I felt as if I was walking through a scene from *The Maltese Falcon* and that Sam Spade would come around the corner in a fedora and trench coat.

On the bus, we passed City Lights, the iconic bookstore, started by the King Lear of all beat poets, Lawrence Ferlinghetti. *Jeez, what a city,* I thought. *This is where all those guys, Ginsberg, Kerouac, Ferlinghetti, hung out.* The conversation at the Chinese restaurant played through my head. Vinny had made a really good case for adapting this Brecht play to modern times and the media. But Olivia had sounded off about the Turandot character. I hadn't heard her do that, go up against Vinny, not even on tour. I wasn't surprised, she was a strong woman, but I wondered how that stuff about the princess character Turandot was going to play out.

18

THE NIGHT TRIPPER

The next morning, I was back at the studio bleary-eyed. Erroll and his lover had serenaded me again and were both snoring blearily through the thin walls when I rose, showered, and split. At the studio, a full-sized school bus crowded the narrow alley. The bus was covered in dust so thick it was impossible to determine its color. On the back door, someone had wiped off the dust layers and scrawled "Dr. John the Night Tripper" in chalk. Who was Dr. John? What was a night tripper? Who belonged to the bus? I was curious. Friends of Vinny and Olivia's? Diggers? Theater people? I was curious. Had people arrived to fill the void?

I hiked up the long flight of stairs. Vinny greeted me from behind the desk. "I want you to meet some people," he said.

A man and a woman rose. He was short and slight of build, but he looked strong — carpenter, mechanic strong.

A beret covered sandy hair and a moustache. A goatee rose out of a week's worth of stubble. He was dressed in a denim shirt and jeans and wore a short leather welder's coat. She was lean-faced with high cheekbones, dark-haired with a wide smile and calm blue eyes. She wore a tie-dyed T-shirt under paint-spattered farmer's overalls tucked into worn cowboy boots. They both held out their hands. He felt jumpy, while she seemed comfortable and at ease in our peculiar settings. But maybe not. The paint spatters and work clothes gave me a hint. Theater. Tech.

"I'm Donna." She held out her hand. "And this is Peter."

"Call me Spider," the Peter guy said.

"We've been talking about what's happening around here," Vinny said.

"Design-wise," Donna said.

"Aha!" I said. "New blood."

"Fresh meat," Spider said.

"We're hungry," I said. "We've been losing actors left and right."

"Puppets are always an option." Donna grinned.

We all laughed. They felt familiar, as if I knew them from another place. "Where from?"

"We're both Manhattan refugees by way of Vermont."

They had worked at Bread and Puppet Theater. I'd heard of this company in New York. They had been founded by a German painter and baker and his wife, a dancer. They worked out of a studio on Delancey Street in the Bowery and had been building strange, ghostly masks and gargantuan puppets and marching them in demonstrations. I'd seen a film of them and their puppets, tall beings, movements exaggerated by their size and height, otherworldly, powerful.

"Building puppets?"

"Building all kinds of stuff. Puppets, crankies…"

"What?"

"Paper movies. You'll see."

"So you guys do theater?"

They laughed. "A little," Spider said.

"Donna's a designer."

"And I build what she thinks up," Spider said.

"Got to make it real," Donna said.

"A package deal," Vinny said.

"You got it." They answered in unison. They felt united by hours, days, months, years, by projects designed and built and miles traveled in tandem.

"To work with us?"

"We've been talking for a while now," Vinny said. "Long distance."

"From New York?" I turned to Vinny. "Is that where you guys met?" I hadn't remembered them from the tour, and I would have. They stuck out.

"We've been talking from Mexico," Donna said.

"Where I was in prison."

"Back-to-back busts," Vinny said. "Calgary and Mexico."

"Yeah," Spider said. "But your bust was righteous. Mine was stupid."

"He bought weed from a cop," Donna said, and cuffed him on the shoulder. Playful.

"In Mexico?"

"Yeah." Together again.

Not a good place to land in prison.

"For how long?"

"Forever works for now," Donna said.

I laughed. "That's good." I liked them. They felt authentic. "Guess that's your land yacht downstairs."

"The Night Tripper," Spider said. "Yeah."

"Cool," I said. "I got a question."

"Okay," Spider said. "Shoot."

"Who is Dr. John the Night Tripper?"

"You don't know?"

"No."

"He's the New Orleans patron saint of jazz, the steward of gris-gris, a crossover from the world of Santeria."

"He inherited the role from a long line of Dr. Johns, all New Orleans musicians, back from the beginning of slavery."

"Jeez," I said. "What a legacy."

"What's Santeria?"

"Voodoo. But more for real —

"It's a mix of religions from slavery. Most of the slaves practiced vodoun, from the Yoruba tribes in West Africa."

"And had Christianity forced on them…"

"… but they twisted and turned around it to keep their gods and goddesses."

"That makes 'em a lot more beautiful and useful than God."

"They sound like rebels," I said.

"They are rebels," Donna and Spider said together.

"Enough with the gods and goddesses," Vinny said. "This god and goddess are gonna start right away."

"All right!" Donna said.

"Okay, boss," Spider said.

"First, we build a new stage for the parks."

"What's wrong with the old one?" I asked.

"It's heavy," Donna said.

"It's falling apart," Spider said.

"It's full of splinters," Olivia walked into the office.

"We can build a lighter one," Donna said.

By the time we finished the tour, the old stage had fallen apart. I knew they'd do it right. It didn't feel like credentials. It felt like family. I took Donna and David into the shop at the far end of the studio. "I know it's a mess."

"They always are," Donna said.

"The cost of creativity," Spider said.

"Only it never is," Donna said. "Order and balance is the mother of creativity."

"And the old man messes it up," Spider said.

"Always," Donna said. "Jailbird."

They kissed. Spider grinned and said, "This is gonna be good."

This was gonna be good, I thought.

I returned to the Digger house. I had jumped so fast into the Troupe and the tour that I hadn't met anybody outside the company. My cousin was in the East Bay, Robin was good when he was available, but he had found a girlfriend, and they had turned into a double-backed hermit.

I brought a loaf of bread and a bottle of wine back to the house after the long day at the studio. The house was empty, so I opened a can of soup I found in a kitchen cabinet, heated it, and ate it out of the pan with the bread and wine. I found a slab of cheese in the refrigerator. We hadn't talked about house rules, but I figured what the hell, and cut off chunks of cheese to eat with the bread and wine.

While I ate, I ran over what had transpired during the day. Vinny had spent most of the day on the phone. I had spent my time with Donna and Spider, cleaning up the shop. They had ideas for tools they needed but they also knew how to scrounge. They intrigued me. They had come across country in the bus, hanging with various friends, checking on the theater scenes here and there, but they had their sights set on the Mime Troupe after seeing us in New York. They had talked to Vinny after one of the shows and he gave them a tacet nod. Like me, that had been enough for them, that and their take on *L'Amant Militaire*. They had come West to join the Troupe on a nod and a surfeit of enthusiasm.

They had come up from Sonora where Spider got himself busted. Donna spent her time hanging around the prison town, getting him sprung. Not a smart idea in Mexico and it gave me a hint that Donna might be the together one in the house, but they didn't show any friction about it. I liked them both. They both had a sense of humor and they seemed to know how to land on their feet. The lawyer who sprung them was lending them a house in the Oakland hills while they got oriented.

"You should come over to Oakland and visit us," Donna said. "The house he lent us sits in a eucalyptus grove. It really smells good."

Wow, I thought. *Good karma. How else does a lawyer lend you a house?*

The silence of the empty Castro Street house closed in around me. *Is this what life is gonna be like?* I thought. The lonely days on Putnam Avenue returned, when I had often found myself eating alone. I decided to take in a movie and rolled back down the hill to the Castro Theatre. *Wild in the Streets* was playing and I lost myself in the darkness. The film was a stretch — a teen rock star used his charisma to turn his band into a confused political organization whose only agenda was to kick everybody over 30 out of politics and throw them into concentration camps. It was ridiculous and not surreal enough to be funny or weird. Hollywood was trying to catch up with the Haight-Ashbury. They were failing miserably.

When I returned to the Digger house, a small cluster of

people turned to regard me from around the table. Erroll's girlfriend Rebecca motioned me over to sit. I wasn't ready to settle in yet. I might as easily have climbed the stairs to my room, I was glad for the company. The bottle of wine sat empty on the table and they were halfway through a gallon of Zinfandel. A wedge of sourdough left scattered crumbs across the table. Ivan, the sharp-faced guy with the swept-back European hair sliced a chunk of bread off the loaf and handed it to me. I'd met him at the Troupe when I first auditioned. Now he was here with a pretty, dark-haired woman.

"Home from the wars, eh, my lad?" Ivan leaned into me, black eyes sharp.

"Yep. Good to be back home, though."

"Home San Francisco? Or home here?"

"Both, I guess," I said.

"I guess we'll see, won't we?" Ivan oozed with innuendo.

I took the opportunity to break up whatever web was building here. I walked around the table and held out my hand to the dark-haired woman. "Hi," I said. "I don't think we've met."

She took my hand. "Helen," she said. "Nice to meet you."

I nodded and grinned.

Helen pulled out a chair next to her. "So you just got back from the Mime Troupe tour?"

"Back home and ready for more," I said.

"More what?" Ivan asked.

"More theater, more politics, more political theater."

Helen rose, washed out a jelly jar in the sink and set it on the table. She poured me wine from the big jug of Zinfandel. "So you like working with the Troupe."

"We hear you people kicked ass all the way cross-country," Ivan said.

"I guess we did," I said. "Did we make that big a splash?"

"We keep in touch," Ivan said, glancing at Erroll, who twitched and inhaled to clear his nasal passages.

"And that student organization, they got people out to the shows," Rebecca said.

"SDS," I said. "We were mobbed, right?" I looked to Erroll.

"Right on," he said and nodded his head. Usually wordy and articulate, he had sat silent since I returned from the film.

"So what did you think about the discussion the other day?" Ivan asked.

"We covered a lot of ground," I said, laughing.

"And the truck. What do you think about that?"

"Yeah, that got pretty heated." I turned to Erroll. "Jeez, you guys aren't really leaving the Troupe, are you?"

"Changes," Erroll said. Rebecca shook her head.

"And the truck?" Ivan continued. "I hear Olivia got uptight about it."

"Yeah," I said. "She was pretty clear."

"About ownership."

"I'd say so." I looked to Erroll.

"She laid it out all right," Erroll said. "We'll figure out another way to go."

"And what's your take on it?" Ivan pushed again. "The ownership thing. My land. My house. My truck." He made me uneasy. So far, this wasn't feeling much like home.

"Haven't thought about it much," I said. "I notice my wine was your wine," I laughed and pointed at the empty bottle on the table.

"Let's stick with the truck," Ivan said. "If you actually had a say in how things go with the Troupe…" He took a sip of wine. "Whose truck would it be?"

I shrugged. I really couldn't see what the issue was. "What do you need the truck for?" I knew, but I was beginning to feel bristly.

"To feed the people."

"Oh right," I said. "And we need it to carry the stage to the parks. We feed the people, too."

"Good one," Ivan said. "Right. Art. Nourishment for the soul."

"Are they in competition here?" I asked. "I woulda said we're on the same page."

"You know what we need the truck for."

"Sure."

"And the truck is just an object, right?"

"Right." I was tired. I took a shot of the Zinfandel; it tasted sour.

"Use value," he said.

"Right," I repeated. "Just like the man said."

"What man?"

"Karl Marx."

Rebecca got up and began to clear the table.

"Oh boy," Ivan laughed. "And let's not forget Engels. *The Origin of the Family, Private Property and the State.*" He laid the emphasis on "private property."

"Oh wow," Rebecca said, standing at the sink. "Aren't we into it? How the family robbed women of their witch power."

Erroll laughed. "Right on!"

"But the Troupe's truck is private property, right?" Ivan persisted. "Part of the patriarchy, right Rebecca?"

Ivan ignored Rebecca's sarcastic laugh. "So why is Olivia standing up for it?"

"Wow," I said. "What is the problem here? The truck? Or Olivia?"

"Neither!" Ivan said. "Just trying to get acquainted." He grinned.

Helen stood up. It seemed as if she had been at this place before with Ivan. "I'm going to bed," she said.

"I'm with you." Ivan pushed back his chair and held out his hand. "Nice talking to you."

Ah, I thought, shaking his limp hand. *So this Ivan guy lives here, too. My housemate.*

The kitchen gathering folded. I sat for a while, looking out the window at the lights and traffic, dwindling now at the intersection of Market and Castro. A streetcar passed beneath the labyrinth of high-voltage wires, its pole sparking ozone blue through the fog. That night, while I listened to another erotic symphony next door, I thought about a magic bus parked in a eucalyptus grove, high in the hills of Berkeley.

19

GORILLA GUERRILLAS

Vinny began to run studio workouts again. He started each morning with isolation exercises. This was a favorite time of day for me. I worked hard; Vinny was full of movement tasks to master. He'd studied with Étienne Decroux in New York after the French mime had given up on Parisian actors who didn't want to follow the strict discipline and training that Decroux's mime demanded. Decroux considered himself a body sculptor, like Rodin — very passionate, abstract, and impressionistic. We're not talking French striped jerseys and whiteface here. That was pantomime. This was not about creating a glass wall with the hands, drinking a glass of water that didn't exist, or playing a pretend guitar.

In Decroux's mime, you *became* the guitar. You analyzed the construct and function of a guitar, its resonant body, the neck on which to fret the strings, and how it created sound. Then you turned your body into a guitar. Your chest and lungs would become the guitar's resonant body. Your left arm would become the guitar neck and your voice, through lips and tongue plucked by the fingers, would create the sound of a guitar.

As a young man, Vinny had absorbed Decroux's method and studied ballet. His morning workouts drew upon all the ecstatic, precise sadism of the French mime and centuries of ballet masters. The workout was rigorous and progressed from isolation exercises to circular walks using different ballet leg positions. He might as well have walked round with a long cane like a ballet master, correcting us, but Vinny was too anti-authoritarian for old-school crap like that.

The new year came. Vietnam raged on over the networks and in the establishment papers, always with body counts and film clips of battles in places most people didn't know and rarely looked up. They called it a war of attrition. The commander in Southeast Asia, a stiff named William Westmoreland — we called him General Waste More Land — invented the term to describe his strategy, a cruel euphemism for slaughtering the Vietnamese people into submission.

The establishment news focused on a hilltop marine base in a place called Khe Sanh. The North Vietnamese Army — NVA for short — surrounded the Marine base with infantry troops and occupied the high ground on hills like the bald, bulldozed, bunkered bump the Marines doggedly defended in the center.

During the day, the NVA shelled Khe Sanh from the surrounding hills. At night, the shelling stopped, and the NVA infantry attacked the perimeter. The NVA had been fighting forever, against the French, then the Japanese, and then the French again. They knew how to fight and — most important — they knew why they were fighting. This knowledge, shared by every boy and girl, man and woman in the North Vietnamese Army, along with the decades of battleground experience they had accumulated, made them tougher and smarter than all our people put together.

For the Americans, the only way in or out of Khe Sanh was by helicopter. The news guys must have decided it was a test of bravery to get dropped from a chopper onto this thrashed and futile hilltop. A series of feature stories began to appear in the media from reporters in flak vests and helmets talking with officers and grunts alike while artillery rounds rained down around them. Before nightfall, they'd board an outgoing helicopter and two hours later they'd be back at the hotel in Saigon, eating, drinking, and telling their stories. Then they'd write them up and ship them off to the States. The war flashed in America's living rooms while the poor guys on Khe Sanh's hilltop fought off the NVA in the darkness.

Then, while our commanders swallowed the bait, thinking that Khe Sanh was the target of a major attack, divisions of the NVA filtered into south Vietnam to join forces with the Viet Cong, the southern resistance. Together they launched an offensive on South Vietnamese cities, taking the American commanders off guard. General Waste More Land and the other hawks tried to defend their stupidity, but word was out. Plenty of Americans knew how hollow and useless this war had been from the beginning. But now, a broad swath of Americans and even the arrogant hawks in LBJ's White House began to challenge General Waste More Land's brutal attrition strategy. No one could separate the Vietnamese army from the Vietnamese people. And Waste More Land's ludicrous ability to see "the light at the end of the tunnel" became a bad joke — not only in the antiwar movement, but in Middle America as well.

Whether or not there was a connection, a coincidence, or a manifest destiny, actors, actresses, and even a few musicians began showing up at the Mime Troupe studio. They'd seen *L'Amant Militaire* on tour, or they'd dug the Minstrel Show, or smoked and drank through the shows in the parks. Regardless of the prompt, they came. Vinny invited them to show up in workout clothes to participate in his rigorous morning workouts. Whether they knew it or not, the new prospects were being auditioned. Not everybody made it through Vinny's two-hour workouts, but by the spring, the Mime Troupe had rejuvenated itself.

Emmett, a lanky, straight-looking guy from Southern California turned out to be a strong piano player with college-bred acting experience. He could sing with loud, in-tune exuberance, and he broadcast a wry, self-effacing sense of humor that stalked laughter.

Lenore, a winsome actress from Connecticut had made the pilgrimage after seeing *L'Amant Militaire* in New York. Where I had been born into a political family and developed a hunger for theater, Lenore had been born into a theater family and grew an appetite for social justice. She had joined an SDS project like the one I had worked on in South Philly. When she saw the Mime Troupe perform, her politics and art mated as they had for me.

Nikki had crossed paths with Paul after he left the Troupe. He had seen her frustration and told her of the Troupe and its work. She was an accomplished dancer who breezed through Vinny's workout and asked what was next. She raised an eyebrow as if to say, "Is that all you've got?"

What was she looking for here, among a bunch of white anarchists? Whatever, she was a wonderful actress, full of emotion, and she wasn't afraid to show her anger. She was learning. Black men had run the theater companies she had worked in, and she had had enough of that. I wasn't sure that she would find much respite or get much traction here in the Troupe, but I wasn't going to try to explain it. I knew I couldn't.

Olivia was delighted. Both women were younger, but she hardly felt competitive. Instead, I could see a kinship developing among the trio of actresses.

Then came the surprise. As the child man who sat in the tight circle of the Mime Troupe survivors, I was about to receive people into the company, people I knew. Jeffree came first. After the house on Putnam Avenue had fallen apart, I lost track of him. He lived for a while in New Orleans, and other places, avoiding the draft. He would never tell me, and I wouldn't ask. He had come and gone from my life, but he always showed up again with his remarkable brain and his books. He thought William Burroughs was hot shit. *Junkie. Naked Lunch.* Burroughs always seemed like a privileged rich kid trying to be a badass. Such a badass that he killed his wife in a game of William Tell. He was supposed to shoot the glass off his wife's head. She was drunk; he was drunk. He blew her brains out. He got away with it; he was a rich kid.

But Jeffree had a wild, non-sequitous way of talking that belied his origins as the son of a psychiatrist. The children of shrinks make the craziest people. He had attended Cornell for a year but couldn't stand the pretense. We had long, tangled conversations about ancient civilizations and animal behavior and bebop and doo-wop. He showed up at my cousin's place first. I don't remember how we reunited, but I had told him about the Mime Troupe when I returned to Cambridge. He was good with tools and always carried his keys on a brass rigging clip.

So here he was, as anti-intellectual as he was intelligent, just as the company began to move. We had to leave the South of Market studio, and Jeffree was there to help. Even then, the developers were moving in. Soon, they would attack the large Mexican population that had there since the 1930s. That was the beginning of Jeffree in the Mime Troupe, the company that spun beneath its many feet, like jugglers on a circus ball.

But did we begin work on Brecht's *Congress of the Whitewashers* as planned? No. One day after the morning workout, Vinny pulled me aside. "You remember what we did at Madison? During that protest they staged?"

"Sure," I said. "We marched them into the chem building with a drum, a trumpet, and a couple of recorders."

"And left them there to be slaughtered by the cops," Olivia said.

Nikki and Lenore stared at us. "Really?"

Olivia laughed. "No, it wasn't like that. They had planned the action for weeks, after they were already protesting Dow Chemical."

"Ahhhh, right," Lenore said. "Dow makes napalm, right?"

"And some kinda chemical that kills all the leaves on the trees," Emmett said.

"Agent Orange," Jeffree said.

"The Madison students planned to occupy the chem building."

"Timed for the weekend we did the show on campus."

"It felt weird," I said. "Guiding them in there like lambs to the slaughter."

"Lambs, hell," Vinny said. "They knew exactly what they were doing. But we didn't. That's why it felt so conflicted."

He was right. I addressed the new Troupers. "We wanted to join the students, but we couldn't occupy the building. We would have been busted. If we'd been busted, we couldn't have done the show. Simple tactical reasoning.

"So now we need to build a band for future demos," Vinny said. "A marching band."

Oh crap, I thought. All I could picture was the kind of boring outfit that I had drummed street beats in our small-town Memorial Day Parade — military stuff.

"Do you guys know who the Mummers are?" Lenore asked.

"Oh yeah," Olivia said. "They hold a parade every New Year. In Philadelphia, right?"

"Been around forever," Lenore said. "They go from door to door, doing their thing and telling stories. They'd get paid in bread and whiskey."

"I bet the whiskey-drinking beat out the bread-eating."

"They sprung up over here, right after the Revolution. Stuffy Philadelphia got tired of them."

"It was a class thing…"

"As old as *commedia*. Same street origins."

"They sound like the Diggers."

"I don't think they had any other purpose than to party."

"That sounds like the Diggers, too," Olivia said.

"Who are the Diggers?" Nikki wanted to know.

"You'll meet them," I said. "Stick around."

"I plan to," Nikki said.

"Their costumes got more and more elaborate, like Mardi Gras in New Orleans," Lenore continued.

"And racist," Vinny said. "Right?"

"Oh yeah," Lenore said.

"Great," Nikki said. "They sound like a perfect group to imitate."

"We'll co-opt the racism," Vinny said. "Like we did the Minstrel Show."

"Wait a minute…" Nikki said. "You guys did a minstrel show? That sucks."

"You didn't see the Minstrel Show?" I asked.

"This was a different kind of minstrel show," Olivia said.

"Uh-huh," Nikki said. Skeptical.

"I'll explain later," Olivia said.

"We'll put together our own Mummers company," Vinny said.

"A marching band. The storytelling will be simple. We'll use banners."

"No racism and U.S. out of Vietnam."

People built on the idea.

"Costumes," Donna said. "We can cover that. I'll work off Mummers parade photos."

"Ragbag, ragtag. One size fits all," Spider added.

"Woo-hoo!"

I had played drums as a kid. I had a fundamental attraction to rhythm and carried a metronomic sense of time. Syncopation bounced through my brain from a deeper zone. My first introduction to jazz came through drums. All the old street beats I had learned since I could join the band in fourth grade came back to me.

Emmett, Jeffree, and I went instrument scrounging.

"You know your friend, what's-his-name, is gonna show up," Jeffree said.

"What's-his-name," I said. "Can you be a little more specific?"

"You know, the guy you used to act with. He did that Shakespeare play with you." Jeffree didn't give a damn about what he knew and what he didn't know.

"*A Midsummer Night's Dream*," I said. "Oh! You mean Tommy?"

"Yeah. That's the guy. With the long hair. He played the other fool."

"That's Tommy," I said. "The other fool."

We found an old wooden bass drum at a pawn shop in the Tenderloin. One head had been kicked in, so the owner gave us the drum for nothing. "What the hell," he said, "it's just takin' up space. Who beats a broken drum anyway?" We promised to put it to good use and hoisted the drum into the back of the Mime Troupe truck.

I couldn't teach people to play reeds or brass. Guitars were useless on the street. But I could teach people to play drums. As with any foraging effort, once you start looking, stuff comes to you. Within a week, we had a bass drum and two snare drums. We needed volume and a percussive timbre to cut through the omnipresent street sounds of boulevard and park. We also cadged a set of cymbals and a glockenspiel! We also found a pile of parade drums, tom toms, good for marching.

I developed rock and R&B street beats by splitting the elements of a rhythm on a trap set — bass drum on the downbeat, the snap of the snare drum on the backbeats. I also developed a two-person technique to play the cymbals like a hi-hat that could be struck by a drumstick-wielding second drummer. When the two players, cymbal holder and stick-wielder coordinated, they produced a hip hi-hat sound.

People who don't play instruments are usually delighted when they can make good sounds. Olivia took the glockenspiel home with a set of marching melodies she could pick out. She tackled the instrument the way she did everything — with concentration and hard work. Vinny had played the trumpet and often used the instrument in the parks. He was undisciplined, but he did have an embouchure.

Donna found a huge stack of old Civil Defense helmets, the kind used in WWI. She also found a bale of cut ends from a shirt factory, all different colors and sewed them onto panels with armholes. When you put them on, you looked like a walking bale of rags.

We dubbed our outfit the Gorilla Marching Band, and Donna painted a cartoon gorilla on both drumheads with "SF MIME TROUPE / GORILLA BAND surrounding the crouching ape. There had already been enough talk

about guerrilla warfare, armies. We often described ourselves as guerrilla theater — it was apt. We worked off the
beaten path.

Then, Tommy showed up. He'd hitchhiked across
the country but looked as if he'd been dragged here from
Cambridge behind a pickup truck. Despite my misgivings,
it was good to see him. I introduced him to Vinny.

Vinny took one look at him, turned to me. "Friend of
yours?"

"We went to Harvard together," Tommy grinned.

"Did you finish?" Vinny asked.

"Hell, no," Tommy said. "That place was killing me.
A bastion of imperialism, old money, backward thinking,
and dead professors."

"How do you really feel?" I asked.

"In other words, you're a dropout."

"Yeah," Tommy shouted. "Damned straight!"

"Can you act?" Vinny didn't wait for an answer. He
turned to me. "Can he act?"

"He's acted," I said.

"Go meet Donna and Spider. They need somebody to
help with tech."

"Great!"

"You willing to go on the road?"

"I'll go anywhere with you guys," he said. "Anytime."

I set Tommy loose on Donna and Spider.

Jeffree became the lead drummer, but Lenore and Nikki
set to work learning how to play drum rudiments — flams,

paradiddles, single- and double-stroke rolls. Tommy had played drums in a high-school marching band and made a good addition to the ensemble. Vinny still hadn't auditioned him.

Springtime brought San Francisco rain, but we had the studio to work in. With work, we could march around the studio in a rough semblance of a cadence and parade rhythm.

The San Francisco St. Patrick's Day Parade was a straight affair, full of high-school marching bands, drum and bugle corps, and various social societies like the Knights of Columbus and the Pioneer Daughters. There was a reviewing stand set up in Union Square for the dignitaries including, of course, the mayor, the chief of police, and local politicians, including a congressman or two. We thought it might make an opportune time to lay down a little "good trouble."

By now, everybody in the Troupe could play something, even if they were just blowing into plastic horns and abusing tin penny whistles. Donna painted a gorilla on the bass-drum heads, encircled by the words:

San Francisco Mime Troupe
GORILLA MARCHING BAND.

We worked up a small repertoire of parade standards including "When the Saints Go Marching In," "Yankee Doodle Dandy," and "The Battle Hymn of the Republic." We also played a terrifying version of "The Star-Spangled Banner." Our street beats began to sound snappy enough, so the slouching non musicians couldn't blur the edges. We perfected our rock 'n' roll beat between snare and bass drum, with the cymbals clashing out eighth notes on the upbeat, a real wrist-breaker. Our R&B beat was based on Martha and the Vandellas' "Dancing in the Street," a real groove when we broke it down. We would use the tune as a call to protest.

We applied for a slot in the parade. This was part of Vinny's plan to bring our work to a broader audience than the hippies, freaks, and bohos who watched our park performances. Like the Mummers, we wanted to comment on the icons of straight society by mimicking them. Our best efforts at reproduction would, of course, look and sound ridiculous. We would perform our marching songs and maneuvers with — as one reporter wrote later — our most "earnest, radical, Marxist, clown-ragged efforts."

The whole band wore Donna's outrageous Mummers' costumes —sandwich-board tunics we draped from our shoulders, cutting-room cloth remnants glued on the tunics in a shapeless tatter, with more remnants glued to the old army helmets. In addition to their drums, tin whistles, horns, and tambourines, three bandmembers each carried a sign fragment that — when assembled — read:

GET — OUT OF — VIETNAM.

The parade committee accepted our application and assigned us a slot. Lucky for us, they didn't request footage or photos and there was no videotape. We were in! On the day of the parade, we picked up a parade marshal, a tall man who wore a long, thrift-shop cape over a tartan kilt. He carried a long staff like the drum major of a bagpipe corps. He resembled Moondog, the eccentric, aristocratic composer who performed on the Manhattan streets.

Moondog wrote unique, technically sophisticated music that he performed on instruments he crafted himself. Our version of Moondog stood proud and imposing in tartan kilt and sash. He carried a long, ornate concert-master's staff, and comported himself with great pomp and impeccable dignity. No one knew how he found us; he materialized. He called himself William Wallace, after the Highlander who led Scotland in its rebellion against England. He saw the current unrest in America as a people's war against our own ruling kingdom. He expressed great admiration for our resistance and called it "a battle from the belly of the beast."

The parade marshals were too busy lining up the bands in sequence and had little time to notice our bizarre presence in the blurred lineup of purple and gold, red and black, white patent-leather boots, palomino horse brigades, and fez-adorned Shriners. So away we went, Mime Troupe drums tattooing, brass blowing, and ragged uniforms flapping.

Along the way, when it seemed as if we had the audience's attention, I would blow a whistle. William Wallace would stop, turn, and, with great authority, signal the band. The Gorilla Band would march in place and three Troupers would unfurl three separate sign flags shouting GET — OUT OF —VIETNAM. We drew about 50 percent cheers, 30 percent catcalls from construction workers above us — in 1968, the working guy and most labor unions hadn't yet grasped that they'd been fucked by the war — and 20 percent boos, a cross section of American opinion on the Vietnam War.

On the way back to the studio, we picked up quarts of Rainier Ale, a gallon of Zinfandel, and pizza from Sal and Carmine's. We sat around the studio, ate, drank, and listened to the articulate and insane commentary of William Wallace, our own Moondog grand marshal. It had been a good day. We felt bonded by our experiment. Marching through straight America with a GET — OUT OF — VIETNAM message had juiced us all. Nikki, Lenore, Jeffree, and Tommy had all stepped up to the task. Donna and Spider had never participated in such an audacious caper. "Now *that* was guerrilla theater," Donna kept saying. "Damn!" Olivia and Vinny were delighted, and so was I. I hadn't been hot to build a marching band, but the Gorilla guerrillas bore no resemblance to the small-town, out-of-tune ensembles I toiled through in my youth.

We all split. Vinny and Olivia disappeared. I didn't know where Nikki and Lenore were crashing, but they left together. Donna and Spyder embraced me before they took off with Tommy for their new home in the Berkeley hills, leaving me and William Wallace to wander off into the night. I took the Muni up the hill to Castro and climbed the long stairway to the Digger house.

20

THE BREAK

The remains of a meal cluttered the kitchen table with soup bowls, torn bread, jelly jars empty of wine, and a few spent bottles of Anchor Steam beer. A vat of Digger stew sat coagulating on the stove. I heard murmuring from the next room. I walked into the living room. The light was low and the room unfamiliar. I had spent no time there since I moved in. My eyes adjusted to the light. Richard lounged in a busted-out armchair. A small, dark, big-eyed woman huddled on the chair next to him. She looked familiar. Richard smiled at me like the Cheshire Cat. "You remember Kim, right? Iowa?"

She looked up at me, embarrassed.

"Sure," I said. "We met."

"Briefly," she said and tossed a withering look at Richard.

Erroll and Ivan sat on the floor. Their "women," Helen

and Rebecca, sat together on a couch.

A bent spoon, a Zippo, and a small tin case with Chinese lettering lay on an old cable spool liberated from PG&E. *Shit,* I thought. *Works.* Somebody was shooting up. I hadn't seen works since the bust at Putnam Avenue, a continent away and an eon passed.

Richard slid off the chair and knelt at the coffee table. He raised the metal case that held the works and pulled a little vial of clear liquid toward him. "You want to do some of this?" he asked. "It's clean. Pharmaceutical."

"What is that stuff?" I asked.

I heard a chuckle. "It ain't LSD," Ivan said.

Rebecca and Helen shifted on the couch. They were both watching me. Whatever it was, I didn't want any. I was full of beer, pizza, and bonhomie from our St. Patrick's Day adventure and wanted to go to bed. But here I was and there they were — Richard, Erroll, and Ivan with assorted female consorts. They felt like the old guard, ancient, something from a past that I hadn't recognized as obsolete. "I made a promise to myself," I said, improvising. "Nothing under the skin."

"Got it," Richard nodded. "A man who knows himself," he said. "Good on you."

"Smart choice," Rebecca said. "Not like some other people I know." She got off the couch and stomped barefoot out of the room. Her curly red hair seemed to flame under the high, bare kitchen light. Clattering dishes reverberated from the sink.

"We've been abandoned," Ivan said.

Richard rose. "I've got to split," he said. He looked down with faux tenderness at Kim, who glared up at him, half in terror and half in anger.

"I'll be by tomorrow," he said. "You'll be in good hands here."

Kim looked away.

Richard stood over me. "Good to see you again, brother. That was some drive, huh?"

"Sure was," I said, although our return from New York seemed to have happened in another lifetime. Except for the one link to the present — the small, dark woman curled in the easy chair. "The whole tour was a trip."

I felt a silent shriek from the dark-haired hurricane that crouched in the chair.

"Right on!" Richard sailed out of the room. "Good night, ladies," he boomed to Helen and Rebecca.

I heard mumbling, and Richard's basso tone, a couple of snapping female retorts. "Uh-oh," Erroll said and rose. "Time to help with the dishes," he said.

Ivan rose as well. He reached down and stroked Kim's hair. She recoiled. "You're welcome to stay here," he said. "I think we have a quilt or two we can spare, right?" He turned to me.

"Oh sure," I said. I hadn't the foggiest where any extra blankets might be hanging out.

"Good," Ivan said, and strolled into the kitchen.

I turned to Kim. "What are they high on?"

"I don't know," Kim said.

"Yeah." I sat down on the sofa opposite her. "Welcome to San Francisco," I said.

"He didn't tell me he was married," she said.

"He isn't."

"Married enough."

"Yeah." Richard had a girlfriend named Blue who lived with him in a little cabin on the uphill edge of Dolores Park, although he rarely mentioned her. "I don't really know what their relationship is like," I said.

"He tries to make it sound like it isn't important," Kim said. "He had the nerve to tell me that nobody is private property, including his 'old lady.'" She snorted. "Old lady. What bullshit."

"Like I said, 'Welcome to San Francisco.'"

Helen came into the darkened room with a blanket and a quilt. "You can crash here," she said to Kim. "I'm sorry about the mix-up."

Kim shrugged. "Thanks."

"He can be like that sometimes," Helen said.

"Like what?" Kim asked.

"Like… that," Helen said.

"Like, not here?" I said.

"Yeah, I guess." Helen laughed. "Anyway, here, these should keep you warm."

"Thanks," Kim said.

Helen looked from Kim to me. "Good night, you two." She turned and padded out of the room. We heard her climb the stairs.

"You know, he never mentioned that he left people sitting outside in his car when he stopped at my place that night."

"I didn't think so."

"He was gonna leave you out there in the cold?"

"That seemed to be the plan."

"What a dick."

"They don't call him Richard for nothin'," I said.

"You're funny," Kim said. "Who were you in the show?"

"I was Brighella. The bossy sergeant in the green mask."

"Oh right. You were a dick, too."

"Yeah, but that was a play."

"Not real life."

"No." I thought about that night in Detroit when I had been a dick — a real dick, and a premature ejaculator at that. I mustered up enough conviction to say, "I hope not. Well, I guess I'm gonna turn in. It's been a big day. There's a bathroom down here," I said, realizing I hadn't yet explored half the Digger house rooms.

"I know," Kim looked up at me from the chair.

I turned to go.

"I was wondering…"

"Wonder away," I said.

"I don't really want to stay alone down here. This room gives me the creeps, with all the needles and drugs…"

"Not exactly grad school, is it?"

"Can I stay with you tonight?" she asked. "We don't have to do anything…"

I hesitated. Richard. Would he find out? So what? Did I owe him anything? Owe him? For what? The exchange of chattel property? Did this person in the chair belong to him? Loyalty? He came and went as he wanted. This person sitting in the chair told me what she wanted.

"That's okay," Kim said. "I understand."

"No, no, no, please," I said. "Come on up." I reached out my hand. She stood and we walked through the clean and empty kitchen. "I gotta warn you though," I said. "My neighbors can get kind of loud."

"Okay," she laughed. "I've been warned." In the hallway, she picked up her bag.

"You travel light," I said.

"Just as well, isn't it," she said. Together, we tiptoed up the stairs.

21

PANTHERS AND PUPPETS

Kim and I showed up at the studio in time for Vinny's workout. She wanted to escape the orb that might include Richard whenever he felt like dropping by. I had come away with a sour taste in my mouth, not from the night before but from the peculiar loneliness I felt at the end of a week's stay at the Digger house. If Richard or Erroll had still been working with the Troupe, there might have been a common thread, but without that connection, any camaraderie had faded fast. The drug use hadn't thrown me as much as Richard's cavalier abandonment of Kim.

Once she felt safe in the studio, Kim revealed an independent spirit. She watched the beginning of the workout, caught my eye, waved goodbye, and disappeared. She left her suitcase with a note — GONE TO NORTH BEACH. The suitcase told me she'd be back.

"Friend of yours?" Jeffree asked. We were changing into our workout clothes, which for Jeffree meant a sweatshirt and paint-spattered G.I. paratrooper pants full of pockets and holes.

"Happenstance," I said. "Her name's Kim. She saw *L'Amant Militaire* in Iowa."

"I saw it in Cambridge," Tommy said.

"Wow," Emmett said. "That tour seems to have bagged a netful of fish."

"Me included," Jeffree said.

"And Lenore."

"And Nikki."

"Nikki didn't find us on tour," I said. "Paul told her about us when he joined Ed Bullins's company."

"She quit Bullins's company to join ours?"

Lenore stuck her curly blonde rag mop in the door. She looked like Little Orphan Annie with eyes. "Whose company?" Lenore said.

"Ed Bullins's," Vinny said. "He's a playwright and producer at Black House. When the black theater community split, some wanted to form liaisons with the white community. Others wanted to use their art to strengthen black identity. Nikki said she wants to make connections, not break 'em."

"This Kim girl," Emmett asked. "Is she staying?"

"I don't know. She didn't come to see me."

"I think she came out to see one of the other guys in the cast," Tommy said.

"Who?"

"Richard," I said.

"Oh yeah," Lenore said. "Pantalone. Tall, dark, and handsome. Why did he leave?"

"He wanted to put more time into the Diggers."

"The who?"

"Is there an owl in the room?"

Lenore had recently arrived from back East and was full of questions about San Francisco's theater scene. I missed Richard, despite his crappy behavior. He and Paul had been my beacons. It reminded me of how much the Troupe had changed.

Sweaty and full of energy after the workout, we bounced into the office. Two black men in leather jackets and slacks with straight-line creases sat facing Ann. They both wore sunglasses and looked out of place amid the broken-backed furniture and office clutter. One man was older, with a goatee and moustache. He wore a beret. The other, sporting a stingy brim fedora, looked young, in his teens or early 20s.

"Ah, gentlemen, welcome, welcome," Vinny said.

I was getting used to Vinny's surprises.

"This is Bobby Seale. He's co-founder and head of the Black Panther Party. We've been talking about puppets."

"You mean like running-dog lackey puppets?" Jeffree asked.

"Portable puppets," Vinny said.

"Guerrilla puppets," the older man said. "Hit-and-run puppets."

"Far out!" Tommy said.

I looked at Donna. Donna looked at Spider, who raised his eyebrows. Emmett and Lenore kept straight faces, while Nikki directed a skeptical squint at the two men. She had left a theater company due to what she called "an excess of testosterone."

"Mister Seale," Olivia said, "would you explain to the company what we've been talking about?"

The older man put an arm around his younger compatriot. "First, I want you to meet Little Bobby Hutton, treasurer of the Black Panther Party. Bobby was the first man to join."

Little Bobby nodded and smiled, a proud young man.

"Little Bobby and I saw you march in that parade," Seale said. "We went because I wanted to see white power on display. In the culture. The straight culture. In a concentrated form. And we saw that."

"They didn't need no military bands," the young Panther said. "They don't have to do that. They already got the power."

I was struck by how differently Seale and his young colleague saw the world. I knew they were right, but I was unused to seeing through that lens. I thought about the quiet, polite power, the easy, unkempt, low-profile wealth that I had experienced at Harvard. Nobody in that old-money crowd paraded their wealth; it existed beneath the surface, hidden, homespun out of whole cloth. And nobody needed to parade their power; it just *was*.

"We watched your band come up the street," Seale said.

"You caught my eye," young Bobby said. "You people looked so damned funky."

"No gold braid on the uniforms," Vinny said.

"You all flapped in the breeze like rags on a clothesline." Young Bobby grinned.

"We caught your political intent," Bobby Seale said. "You carry a message in your work, and we have a common purpose. You went there armed with words. And words matter. Words have consequences. And I saw you people do that thing with those signs: GET — OUT OF — VIETNAM.

"We saw your Cracker Barrel show, too. That Minstrel Show. You almost got it right," Little Bobby said.

"White people don't want black people to have power. White folks are like kids, raised by people who told them there's not enough to go around. Not enough love, not enough money, not enough power. Racism is a power tool. When you hold it in your hand, you don't want to give it to anybody else. Black people been denied access to those power tools. All you got to do is look at the vote to see that. When I sat down with Huey Newton, we decided — if we want to exercise power, we have to back it up with guns. Guns treated like tools. Tools to deliver the message — stop killing black people. Stop murdering us. We want whitey to pay attention. And there's nothing that gets whitey's attention like black people with guns."

"So we call ourselves the Black Panther Party for Self-Defense," Little Bobby said. "We have a program, a ten-point program." He waved a sheaf of leaflets. "We got copies for you all here."

"In our situation," Seale said, "we rely on our legal right to self-defense. For us, self-defense means protection from the police. Protection requires us to know the utility of weapons, how to use them safely and within the law. We studied up on this. Our brother Huey Newton, partner and the co-founder of the party, he studies law at UC Santa Cruz. I asked him to look up every law pertaining to the use of guns in California, especially in relations with law enforcement officers."

"Pigs," Little Bobby said.

"Now I know you've worked with a couple of brothers, a couple of sisters in this company." He nodded to Nikki, who nodded back to him. "And I know one of your people, Paul, Paul Madison. He's working now with the Panthers' former minister of Culture, Ed Bullins. And that's all right. Mister Bullins and company, they want to work in our own community, exclusively with our own people. They have every right to do that."

We sat transfixed, listening to this man. He spoke in strong, definitive tones, without pauses. He carried anger in his voice, but he was clearly not angry with us.

"So why am I here?" He didn't wait for an answer.

"As I said, we've seen your work. We saw you march with a sign that spoke to all those middle-class white people at the parade. The people in the bands and on the floats and — most important — to the people on the sidewalk.

"We know your heads are in the right place. We saw how you can travel light. So we're here to talk about combining forces. You may already know about the effort we make to reach out to the white community. And all people. People of all colors and ethnicities. We are not separatists. I believe that the exclusion of black power separates us. Isolates us, because black power implies black economic power. You would have to establish a separate but equal and parallel black economy. If you study economy, you know you cannot extricate yourself from an economic system. You gotta interact with it."

"Damn straight," Vinny said.

"Ho Chi Minh says we all swim in the same sea," Tommy said.

"Any separation of the black radical movement from the white radical movement is arrogant and self-defeating. It plays into all that old Machiavellian shit — divide and conquer. We fight on two fronts — racism and capitalism. The two are intertwined and we've got to destroy both. We can do that together."

The company sat breathless, waiting for the next line. We wanted to hear more from this man. I got it. Vinny knew about the Black Panther program. He reached out.

He wanted to bring theater, not agitprop, but theater for the people. The Minstrel Show spoke to white people about their own racism. Now he wanted to connect with the black community. So he invited Bobby Seale over. And Bobby Seale had come.

Olivia spoke up. "We talk about racism."

"We've seen that."

"And you speak to police brutality," I said. "With armed self-defense."

"We do."

"And our latest show, *L'Amant Militaire*, whacked Vietnam."

"Hold on," Seale said. "Thing is… we want you to talk about other things. Not about Vietnam. Not about self-defense. Not about police brutality."

"Soo what do we talk about?" Donna asked.

"We want you to talk about housing. Education. And we don't need you to teach it. We need you to represent our demands."

Little Bobby spoke up. "We believe that if the white landlords won't give the black community decent housing, then we should liberate the housing." He sounded sincere, excited; nobody flinched at his recitation.

"We want to teach our people about themselves, their history," Little Bobby continued. "If a man…"

"Or a woman," Nikki said.

Little Bobby paused. He looked at Nikki and grinned. "Or a woman or a girl…"

"If a girl does not have knowledge of himself — herself — where he comes from history…"

"You see," Nikki said. "History. His story!"

"Okay, okay," young Bobby said, grinning. "Whoooeee, girl…"

"What'd you call me?" Nikki said, laughing.

The whole room broke up. Laughter of release, relief.

Little Bobby smiled a sweet smile. "I get it. If a woman don't stand equal with her people and the world, she don't stand a chance."

Nikki pointed at Little Bobby with approval.

"And what I say to the brothers — and the sisters," young Bobby rocked on. "If you want to be in a gang, why not be part of a gang that's taking on the police and the US government. The biggest bullies on the block."

The company broke out in applause. Everyone stood, talking to each other, asking further questions of Big Bobby Seale and Little Bobby Hutton until they walked out the door. I wished we had music to play. It would have been good.

Kim returned in the late afternoon. She'd been to North Beach, eaten abalone, gotten buzzed on espressos, read Diane di Prima's poetry at City Lights. She had walked through Chinatown and smelled of sandalwood incense.

She found me. She was flushed. "Had a great time. North Beach is a trip. But I don't want to go back to that house," she said.

"Funny," I said. "Neither do I."

Kim sighed. "I guess I'll go back to Iowa."

"You don't have to do that. If you don't want to." I felt unburdened and detached from whatever Kim wanted to do. I didn't want to go back to the Digger house and neither did she.

Before the Black Panthers arrived, Spider, Jeffree, and Donna had returned from a construction site with sheets of liberated plywood and 1 x 4 pine for the puppet stage. Kim and I helped them carry the materials up the long stairway from the alley.

We sat down in the shop. Spider had brought back a six-pack of Rainier and we sat drinking the cold, sharp ale.

"How's your new place?" I asked Spider and Donna.

"It's fantastic!" Tommy said.

"Way up in the hills," Donna said. "The whole place smells of eucalyptus. It's quiet and still kind of wild. There's houses below us, but not beside us."

"Sounds wonderful," Kim said.

"We paid one helluva price for it," Spider said.

"Meaning?" Kim asked.

"We wouldn't have it if we hadn't needed a lawyer," Donna said.

"And we wouldn't have needed a lawyer if I hadn't gotten busted," Spider said. "But I did."

No one wanted to get busted, even in California. In Mexico, drug offenses were scary heavy and the whole justice food chain was corrupt.

"Mexican prisons are a combination of jail, whorehouses, gambling halls, and bodegas," Donna said. "For a price, you can get anything you want in jail. And the inmates are close to their jailers. Half of them are each other's cousins. Of course, Spider wasn't anybody's cousin, but I met a lot of cousins getting him out."

"My hero," Spider said. "I bought a joint from a snitch."

I guessed Spider was one heck of a craftsman but a not wholly together person.

"I like to say Spider provided us with an exotic interlude to our cross-country adventure," Donna said.

Spider squirmed, but I could tell these two people felt okay about each other in a way I hadn't yet experienced.

"So where are you guys staying?" Donna asked.

"I came out to see Richard," Kim said.

"Oh! I get it," Donna said. "And Richard is not available."

Kim just snorted. "Surprise! There's a sucker born every…"

You're no sucker. Got yourself out of the cold…"

"Ate amazing abalone. You don't get much of that in St. Louis."

"So why don't you guys stay with us?" Donna covered us both with a glance. She had a way of acting as if she knew what was going on. What she saw wasn't much of a mystery. Kim sat very close to me. I was leery of the whole combination. I felt as if she was Richard's. *Richard's what?* I thought. *Prairie fling? Roadhouse hooker? A replacement?* I'd spent more time with Kim than he had. Besides, the idea that Kim belonged to anybody felt smarmy.

"We have room," Donna said.

Tommy shifted in his chair, uneasy. I guessed he wanted to claim Spider and Donna as his own.

"That way, you can avoid any difficult situation with the party in question." Spider cracked another beer. "I see you've got your gear."

"My what?" Kim asked.

"Your suitcase," Donna said.

Kim and I climbed into the back seat of Spider and Donna's Karmann Ghia alongside Tommy.

"Plenty of room, plenty of room," he chanted.

"So is this your lifeboat?" I asked.

"Yep," Donna said. "We swing it on davits from the back of the Night Tripper when we're far away at sea."

We crossed to Oakland on the Bay Bridge underpass through the fluorescent Treasure Island tunnel. I saw Bobby Seale and Bobby Hutton reflected in the windshield, Big Bobby and Little Bobby sitting across from us in the studio, talking about the life and death of existence as black men in America. Amerika.

We stopped at the Safeway on Ashby before we began the winding climb into the Oakland hills, past the shacks and shingles of East Oakland, flying high over the police and the poverty, and the work to be done. That night, secure in Spider and Donna's borrowed bungalow below the eucalyptus grove, we fried up hamburger, sautéed onions and shredded cheese, refried beans, and warmed corn tortillas. We built messy tacos afire with hot sauce and jalapeño peppers. We drank more ale and smoked weed and revisited the conversation we'd had with the Panthers. It seemed as if we'd been given an awesome responsibility and marveled that Bobby Seale, the chairman of the Black Panther Party, had singled us out as allies in the struggle that they had taken on, not only for themselves, not only for black America, but for all of us. In Babylon. In Amerika. In the belly of the beast.

"Tommy," Donna said. "Why don't you crash on the couch for the night?"

Tommy felt dissed. He'd established a beachhead in the Night Tripper and he wanted to hold it. I knew Tommy better than I thought.

Spider showed us to the bus. There were two sleeping spaces. He made sure both were comfortable. Once we had settled into our separate bunks, Kim said, "Wow. It sounds as if you guys had quite a day while I strolled through North Beach, nursing my hurt feelings."

"You did the right thing," I said. "You're making the best out of a bad trip and that takes…"

"Takes what," Kim said.

"Guts and ingenuity," I said.

"Thank you," she said. I heard her sigh. "I guess all roads lead somewhere."

"And yours led you to a Digger commune, a trip to North Beach, and a school bus high in the hills of Oakland, perched under a eucalyptus grove."

"And a visit to a warehouse where a bunch of lunatics are mixing politics and art to seize the time," she said.

I raised up on one elbow, Kim raised up on hers. She opened the quilt. The night light shone on her white body and the dark triangle at the base of her belly. I slipped across the aisle to join her.

22

ANGELS AND WOLVES

The next day, Richard showed up on a motorcycle with a couple of Hells Angels. The alley below the studio windows rocked with the big-barreled combustion of Harley engines. The cacophony drowned out any chance of talk in the studio and drove us to the windows. Below, Richard, backed a chopper up against the wall. Two other riders followed suit, the trio of flatulent percussions ripping up and down the rev range, making as much racket as possible to punctuate the simple process of parking the bikes in the alley.

"I don't want to talk to him," Kim said.

"I know just the place," Donna said. "Let's go."

Kim leapt up and grabbed her bag off the theater seat beside her.

Donna led Kim to the far corner of the studio, where a

tall costume closet lurked under a stack of black flats and a rolled-up canvas backdrop from an earlier *commedia* show. She tilted the flats forward, I pulled the painted canvas roll outward, Olivia opened the double doors to the closet, and Kim stepped in.

"We won't forget you," I said.

Heavy boots stomped up the stairs.

We slid back and took our seats. Richard and two large, jean-jacketed men filled the entryway. They smelled of motor oil and road dust. Richard appraised the room. "Hello, people," he boomed.

Vinny and Olivia sat implacable.

Donna and Spider stood up.

"You can't come in here," I said.

"I can go wherever I want," Richard said.

"Free city, right?" Olivia said with pointed sarcasm.

"One percent," Richard said.

What's up," Vinny asked.

"Can we talk in private?" Richard said.

"We can talk right here," Olivia said.

"Okay," Richard said. "If that's what makes you feel right."

"That's what makes me feel right," Olivia said.

Spider and Donna looked as if they hadn't seen much that surprised them, including the entrance of three leather-clad road boys.

"Nice bikes," Spider said.

"Thanks," Richard said. "This is Bunchy."

The taller Angel took off his sunglasses as a nod to civility. "How are you doing?"

"And this is Velocity," he said and pointed to the second Angel, a young, chubby red-faced blond with squinty eyes and a goofy smile.

"Nice place you got here," Velocity said.

"We wanted to say 'hello,'" Richard said. "And I wanted to apologize for the way I said 'goodbye.' I probably didn't realize how hard it was for me to quit the Troupe."

"I see," Olivia said. "So all that animosity… that probably wasn't really about the truck."

"Or a manifesto on private property," Vinny said.

Richard laughed. "No, probably not," he said. His eyes fell on a paper bag with Chinese calligraphy that sat on an empty chair. He walked over. "Hmmmm. Sandalwood. Incense. Chinatown. Tourist shit." He raised his eyes and looked around the room. His eyes fell on me. "Has Kim been here?"

"No," I said.

"You haven't seen her."

"Not since the other night."

"Bullshit. You know exactly where she is, don't you."

"Who's Kim?" Olivia asked.

Donna and Spider shifted in their seats. "I bought all that Chinatown stuff for my nieces," Donna said.

"You get one of those finger traps in there?" Velocity asked. "You know, the ones where if you stick your fingers in, you're fucked?"

Donna had no idea what was in the bag. "No," she said. "I missed those."

Richard walked over to me. "You guys got together after I left the other night."

"How's that your business?" I asked.

"You know all about Kim and me," Richard said.

Bunchy laughed and walked to the window, ostensibly to check on the bikes.

"Relationships of ownership are invalid here," I said, quoting Bob Dylan.

A muffled pounding banged out of the closet at the back of the room. "Let me out!"

Donna rose and walked to the back of the room.

Richard stood there.

"You keep prisoners here?" Velocity asked.

"What the hell is going on?" Bunchy said.

Donna shoved aside the stacked flats and opened the door.

Kim burst out. "Who the hell do you think you are!" she shouted across the room. She walked toward Richard. "No, never mind who you think you are. I don't know and I don't care." She walked right up to him, looking straight upward.

Richard backed up.

"More important, what do you think I am? Your thing? Your squeeze? Your slash?"

I got up. Vinny got up. Bunchy came back across the room.

Donna crossed back, and Spider joined her.

"Ride 'em, cowgirl," Velocity said.

"Whooeee!" Bunchy shouted.

Richard seemed to soften. "I came to apologize to these people," he said. "I didn't know you were here."

"Well, I didn't know you had a long-term girlfriend. You forgot to mention that when you invited me out here. You may think this is the free-love capital of the world, but I'm not a part of it."

"Hey, Richard," Vinny said. "Thanks for dropping by."

"Yeah," Olivia said. "And thanks for the apology. I'd forgotten how sensitive you really are."

Richard turned to Bunchy and Velocity. "Let's go, guys." The trio of bikers trooped across the studio floor. The back of Billy and Velocity's jackets were decorated with large, embroidered colors: HELLS ANGELS — Oakland, California.

"Holy shit!" Tommy said. "You guys are Hells Angels."

"Nice company you're keeping," Olivia said.

"I came to apologize," Richard said.

I was sure he'd had a suspicion that Kim had left with me. He knew where to find me. But it seemed clear that his appearance at the studio was as far as he wanted to pursue Kim... or me. What surprised me was the solidarity the Troupers showed when confronted with Richard's attempt at bodily possession.

"Nice meetin' you guys." Velocity grinned, revealing a comic gap where his front teeth used to shine. We heard the trio clomp down the stairs, Richard's heavy voice. A few seconds later, the Harleys roared to life and rumbled down the alleyway into another world. We all applauded Kim.

Back in Oakland, Kim and I sat in Spider and Donna's Night Tripper bus and talked long into the night. What had begun as an acceptance of Kim as Richard's visitor — had turned to fascination… and attachment. My usual "I don't give a damn" bravado stopped bouncing off the surface of the pond and sank like a stone. The times were changing, or I was changing. I found out that Kim wasn't. Not toward me. She'd been honest and warm from the night Richard left her at the Digger house. Beyond that, I'd begun to ask stupid questions, the self-related variety.

"You're kind. You're sweet," she said. "You're cute, smart, and funny… and a little young."

"Why," I asked. "How old are you?

"You really don't know anything about me, do you?"

"Well, you don't know anything about me, either."

"Whatever," she said. "This isn't a contest."

"I know you come from Iowa."

"Wrong." She laughed. "I come from St. Louis."

"Yikes," I said. "Never been there."

"So what else?"

"Pretty sure you're a student," I said.

"How about that I'm a teacher?"

"Wow," I said. "You don't look a minute over undergraduate age."

"Not sure that's a compliment or what."

"What?"

"Never mind," she said. "I'm a graduate student. And I teach."

"You're sure as hell not anybody's schoolmarm."

"I'm going for my doctoral in the English department. And I teach undergrads."

Kim got up and padded down the corridor to the Night Tripper's tiny bathroom.

I watched her return, easy in her nudity. I lay there ogling her, grinning.

She shook her head and laughed. "Which are you — man or dog?"

"So, I guess you wouldn't want to stay. I had it in my head that I would ask you to stay for a while."

"You are a dog." She slid back into bed. "Last I checked, I'm not out on loan."

"Ouch."

"Oh relax," she said. "Don't take everything so seriously. You want me to stay? How? As if I had nothing else to do?"

"As if I really like you. I'd assumed... I mean you came out to see Richard."

"For spring break... and ready to bail at any moment."

"Oh right!" I'd lost track of schooltime.

"See? Assumptions are usually a sign of mutt thinking. If you weren't so smart, sweet, and funny…"

"And what if I wasn't all those things?"

"I'd say you were a young, enthusiastic golden retriever. Bowwow."

I felt lousy. We hadn't talked about our lives. We'd been so full of the mess at the Digger household, the full agenda at the Troupe, the confrontation with Richard, crashing with Spider and Donna, we'd never really stopped to breathe. And beyond Kim's experience at the Troupe, we'd had our collective mind blown by the visit from the Panthers.

"But you're not what I'd call a dog." Kim brought me back to her time-space coordinates. "Because of all those things," she said and stroked my cheek.

Later, as a spring moon cleared the eucalyptus treetops and slid toward the Golden Gate Bridge, we finished our conversation.

"So I can't persuade you to stay for a while longer?" I asked.

"No, you can't. You have a life, I've seen that. And a very exciting and meaningful life."

"And a lonely life," I said.

"And now you learned I have a life, too."

"Yeah," I said. "Imagine that."

"I don't have to imagine it. I live it."

We kissed each other in the moonlight, barely brushing lips. "You know," Kim said. "Your life? You should begin to write it down."

"Someday, maybe," I said. The prospect of writing seemed odd. I couldn't figure how I would decelerate out of the here and now to write anything down.

"G'night." Kim turned her back to me. Soon she began breathing calm, light, and steady.

23

THE FIRE THIS TIME

The next night, I drove Kim to the airport in Spider and Donna's Karmann Ghia. The lights from oncoming traffic cut through the cold night. Silence kept us company. We were exiting each other's lives as quickly as we had entered them; we didn't have much to say. The traffic thickened out of town, four lanes moving slow.

A spasm ghosted through my chest. *I'm gonna miss her,* I thought. I hardly knew her, but I loved her soft, wry humor as much as I loved the smell of her body. *Easy come, maybe, but not so easy go.* Hadn't been so easy coming either — the westward blitz in Richard's Volvo, the frigid winter stop in Iowa, the mess at the Digger household, the flight to the Oakland Hills, Black Panthers, Hells Angels, circumstantial intimacy, and now, goodbye.

Kim sat silent. The airport lay stretched out before us.

I exited the freeway and began the downhill crossing to the terminals.

"You can just drop me off."

I didn't want to be alone. "No. Let's park and I'll join you."

"You have money for parking? They charge an arm and a leg."

"Oh." I hadn't flown for a long, long time. Not since I was a kid.

"Here." She handed me a five and rested her hand lightly on my forearm. "I can't believe this stuff is all happening at once."

"What stuff?" I asked.

"All of it. Richard, the war, what you guys are doing. What's going down on campuses."

I parked. We walked into the terminal and sat down at the gate where her flight was scheduled to leave. Quiet had settled on the big room, a Sunday night, travelers returning home to their jobs, their lives.

"Usually when I leave a place," Kim said, "I tell people I'm going earlier than I really do, so I don't have to say goodbye."

"You don't have to say goodbye."

Kim ignored me. "Then I lie around, read magazines, and relish being alone and on my own."

"And now?"

"I'm glad you're here," she said. "Even if it's to say goodbye."

The loudspeaker called her flight. She rose.

"Maybe it's just 'so long,'" I said. "For now." I was really laying it on.

"Don't do that," she said.

We stood up. Kim put her arms around me. We held each other tight. Surprisingly tight, surprisingly still. Finally, we kissed. Then she pushed away and walked to the gate. I waited for her to look back, but she didn't. She nodded and smiled at the gate attendant, handed him her ticket, and walked out onto the tarmac.

At the studio, we began to talk about how the Gutter Puppets would work. We had to be portable. We had to be fast-moving — easy to set up, easy to strike.

"I was thinking about something like this." Spider laid out a large sketch pad and opened pages filled with quick, sure strokes of a soft pencil. He'd designed a hinged tri-angle of plywood — a frontispiece with two wings that would travel flat and open out when you stood it up like a phone booth. He'd drawn Punch and Judy whacking each other in a proscenium with a sill that served as a forward thrust or a shelf, depending on puppet needs.

The puppets had to be simple, sturdy, and be able to project strong images, like *commedia* figures.

"I hate to sound simple-minded," Donna said.

"Simple. Good." Vinny said.

"I'm thinking sock puppets," she said.

"You come all the way from Bread and Puppet?" I asked. "Sock puppets?"

"Flamboyant yet pragmatic," Spider explained.

Emmett took their side. "None of us have been immersed in the labyrinthian chambers of puppetry," he said, stroking his beard. "Which can get as complicated, hierarchical, and baroque as any other discipline, I'm gonna bet."

"So what do we know?" Lenore asked. "I'm down with sock puppets."

"Yeah, whatever works," Olivia said.

"Speaking of whatever works," I said, "we don't have a fucking story yet. We don't even have characters."

"Now we're talking," Vinny said. "Characters and story are gonna limit our limitless possibilities."

"Then the puppets can tell me," Spider said, "about where they want to live."

"Well, heck," Olivia said. "First thing we gotta do is a show about the Panthers."

"Only not about the Panthers," Nikki said. "About what they want. All that stuff Little Bobby was talking about."

"Yeah," Vinny said. "Where's that ten-point program? They don't want us to do the obvious stuff."

"Police brutality, Vietnam cannon fodder…"

"They want us to talk about housing, education."

We read the ten-point Panther program out loud, cho-rally. Rhythms and fills began to break out —

Forty acres and a mule. Broken promise on an overdue debt.

Germans confess to murdered Jews — how do you make amends for six million?

When does whitey confess to black people — 50 kid-napped and murdered slaves.

Racist landlords rent obscenity for homes.

We want to build our own decent homes.

Real education fosters self-knowledge. We began to stamp and clap, putting the lines to tempo.

Downstairs, the door shrieked open. Footsteps tore up the long staircase and a figure ran into the room, a messenger in motorcycle boots and a blue jean jacket. He bent over, catching breath, then stood.

"They killed Martin Luther King."

Each of us sat or stood alone in shock. I grasped after King, desperate to find him, anything, a fragment, but he had disappeared. I scanned my interior for a glimpse, an image, a blotch, a Rorschach inkblot. I couldn't find his face. The round features, the moustache. I heard his voice. The measured comfort of his voice. The music of it. The lilt, the rise and fall. A small wooden church in a grove, the turpentine smell of hot sun on pine woods, sounds of gospel, his voice, spoken gospel song. Voice, his voice. Words, his words. Deliberate, considered, spoken slow, no need to rush, all the time in the world. He held his audience still. I sat captive, pulling back his words and phrases, sung, thought shaping his words, phrase by phrase, his voice redounding in my ears.

Go tell it on the mountain. Over the hills and far away. The arc of history, his words.

If you allow me to live a few years in the second half of this 20th century. Allow me to live. The world is all messed up, you see. The nation is sick, trouble is all around. Now that's a strange statement but I see God working.

When King spoke of god, it felt right. Not the stomach wrenching "no" I usually felt when people referred to The God, with a capital "G." I felt Martin Luther King's god, the god of protest, of resistance, of good trouble, of peace. Martin's god was right here, right now, but he was gone. Eerily, his voice rolled out of the radio, melodious, his last sermon to the garbagemen of Memphis, Memphis, named after a city in ancient Egypt.

Something is happening in our world and the masses are rising up. We want to be free. Survival forces us to grapple. We are a poor

*people. Nonviolence or nonexistence. Our right-
ful place in this world. We are determined to be
people. Pharaoh cannot hold slavery if he cannot
divide the tribes of Israel.*

The Old Testament. All this made sense, unlike the
New Testament hymns of my childhood, with their meaningless verses.

*We march to put the issue where it is supposed
to be. No stopping point short of victory. In that
majestic struggle there. Ain't gonna let nobody
turn me around. A fire no water could put out,
even before the fire hoses. We will transform Bull
Conner into a steer.*

Ain't gonna let nobody turn me around. Gone. Never
again.

*Collectively we are richer than all the nations
of the world. That's power. God sent us by
here. Make the first item on your agenda.
Withdrawing economic support from you. Not
to buy Coca-Cola in Memphis.*

I broke the silence. James Baldwin broke the silence.
"The fire next time."

"The fire this time," Nikki said. "I need to be with my

people." She snatched up her voluminous African woven bag and walked out of the room.

"Where will you go?" I asked.

"I'm going where the cold winds blow," Nikki said. "Gonna weep, gonna sigh, gonna moan, gonna cry." She walked to the stairway. "Gonna dance in my good-time clothes." She turned. "And you motherfuckers better be ready when I get back."

Nikki's departure felt ominous. We needed her authority, but she had none. We drove back to Oakland, looking through glass at the few others on the bridge. What did the others feel, behind those windshields and painted doors? Feeling white in the car with white Donna and white Spider. White with Tommy and Jeffree. Nikki had gone to mourn with her own. Without her, I felt lost, disoriented in a white wasteland.

Over the gray bridge, over the gray bay. Where will we go? What will we do? *What is to be done?* Vladimir Lenin, gone so long. This nation. How will we live through this? Will they kill us all? Them and us? A strange time, all the otherness of childhood, growing up white in white New England, racist Boston so close by. I wanted black. The black of what I knew, Lead Belly, Howlin' Wolf, Muddy Waters, the blues. High in the hills, sequestered, claustrophobic, the five of us trapped. Who would we join? How would we link to the world of them? The others. Those people. Oh gawd. What then?

The cities began to go up. Washington, D.C., block

after block in darkened Eastern Standard hours. The fire this time. How much loss can we take? Anger hung heavy in the air, weighed down with immeasurable sadness. Waves of sense memory, TV images, sound fragments, all the times we heard him speak, watched him. I had seen him alive, five long years before in Washington, D.C., with the red-haired girl in the Rambler. We had broken our silent, obsessive return East, had felt our way into D.C. with the busses and the signs — "March for Jobs and Freedom." We had abandoned the car and stumbled into a calm and powerful mass of people, a world of people, singing and crying and listening to the Reverend Martin Luther King, cooling our feet along the reflective pool. Now he's gone and nothing fit, nothing made sense.

High in the Oakland hills, we flipped on the cruddy TV and crowded around the gray light, holding one another. Loss and shock and anger morphed into epithets and analysis. Fucking FBI did it. Fucking Mafia did it with the FBI. Like Kennedy with the CIA. There was no question here, only one shooter, not like that bullshit the Warren Commission brought out about Kennedy offed by one misfit snitch — Oswald. Shit, we knew dozens of Oswalds by then, guys who didn't know what side they were on. This guy set up by the people who killed Kennedy from so many trained rifles. No, this was already different. One shot and King is dead. They played parts of the speech he made the day before, saying we don't have to argue with anybody. We don't have to go around acting bad with our words.

He was stuck between Gandhi and Malcolm X. And Martin again.

"We don't need any bricks and bottles," he said. *Allow me to live just a few years in the second half of the 20th century, I will be happy.* But they killed him, and the bricks and bottles began to fly.

Helplessness milled around for an hour. Then rage flared and leapt into a whirling dervish, flying though the April night in Washington and Baltimore and Chicago, hurling bottles topped with flaming, gas-soaked rags, shattering windows, the fire rising, people trapped and dying in the smoke, gunfire, trucks full of guardsmen, military men, no weekend soldiers, these, with their barbed wire and bayonets.

I went numb.

I didn't know what to feel, how to feel. I stepped outside the stunned household and let the eucalyptus scent caress me. I climbed the steps in the quiet night while the East Bay lights blinked and glistened below and boarded the Night Tripper. I slept the sleep of the dead.

The next morning, we crossed back into the city, silent, only coffee to begin our day. Cities had burned overnight, a reprise of the anger from the previous year, carrying sense memories of the burnt-out, wet-ash smell of the tour — Detroit, Newark. Only Oakland and San Francisco remained calm. Who knew why? Maybe people held on to King's final words. *We don't need any bricks and bottles. We don't need any Molotov cocktails.* In the light of last year's uprisings, the preacher's words seemed incongruous. Out of context. Back at the studio, dismay swam among our collective thoughts and emotions like minnows, darting here and there, directionless. Theater? Puppets? We had lost a colossus.

24

LITTLE BOBBY HUTTON

Two days later, the Oakland cops killed Little Bobby Hutton. Nikki returned to the studio. She looked exhausted, fragmented, torn apart, as if she had been rendered by a cruel cubist. There'd been more violence, more loss. But now, her anger focused on the men, the young Panthers. They'd heard MLK's last speech. But they'd also listened to Malcolm X. They'd listened to Stokely Carmichael. Now they were all up in it, looking for violent restitution.

No more rocks and bottles? No Molotov cocktails? Hell, the youngbloods said. Where did that get the Reverend King? Eldridge Cleaver had vacillated, manic. Nikki's pain and anger carried a cynical edge. "Eldridge says he tried to talk sense into them," she said. "Shit. Youngbloods. Maybe he did try. But then he turned around and helped them plan an ambush. They're all talking no more peaceful protest. No more turn the other cheek. No more of that molasses-slow boycott bullshit."

Oakland had not gone up in flames, partly because the Panthers went door to door urging people to be cool. "But the Oakland pigs," Nikki said. Most of them live out in the suburbs anyway, not in Oakland. They act like an invading army. And if you're black, they know they can kill you and get away with murder.

"Hell," I said. "We didn't need to set *L'Amant Militaire* in Italy. We coulda done Oakland."

"So they went out," Nikki said. "Two or three car-loads. They went out to hunt Oakland pigs. A 'preemptive strike,' Eldridge called it. Shit. They didn't know what they were doing. They didn't have Fidel along for the ride. And Eldridge is no Che Guevara."

The Oakland cops scattered them, pinned down an unlucky few, and called in reinforcements. Eldridge and Little Bobby wound up trapped in a house. "The cops claimed it caught fire from bullets, but that was bullshit," Nikki said. Eldridge wanted Bobby to give up, go out naked, arms held high. Bobby had refused the indignity. "Another naked black man on the auction block? No way. Not for Little Bobby. He came out hands raised with his pants on. They shot him dead on the front steps." Nikki shook with rage. "These dumbass young guys with no leader, just macho-man Cleaver." He had been injured but not arrested. He claimed the cops had ambushed the

Panthers. "My heart is broken," she said. "And these lies. How can you lie about such a thing? To your own people!"

She looked around the room. "You all are coming to Bobby's funeral with me."

"We can't do that," Vinny said.

"Oh yes you can," Nikki said.

"Nobody's gonna want to see us there," Lenore said.

"I am your connection. You remember what Big Bobby said. There's no room for rifts. I want you there. You gotta be there. You're gonna be there."

So we went back to Oakland, armed with hearts and minds and our theater, holding the image of young Bobby Hutton in his stingy brim and sunglasses, sitting in our studio, reading off the Panther Ten-Point Program, so hopeful. The funeral was for family and friends, but afterward, people came out to Lake Merritt, a local park. White people, families with kids. They went and the police couldn't decide whether to stand in plain view or hide. The Panthers spoke on the back of a flatbed truck. Eldridge Cleaver was nowhere to be seen. Later we'd find he was on his way to Cuba.

Marlon Brando climbed up out of the crowd. I thought it was weird, having this celebrated white guy up there. I'd seen Brando in every film he'd done. He was an icon, first of the theater, then of film. He was everybody's bad boy but mine. I always thought he was corny, his acting over-the-top. His bad-boy act worked in the theater, but on film, he came off as melodramatic, from *A Streetcar Named*

Desire to *The Wild Ones*. And the last picture I saw Brando in, *One-Eyed Jacks*, made me laugh. I'd seen it stoned at the Brattle Theatre back in Cambridge, light years before, and all I could ask was, "Who are all these Hollywood boys acting bad for? But now, here he was, standing up on that truck surrounded by Panther black leather, sunglasses, and berets; for the first time he looked like a real human being.

Nobody introduced him. "We just came back from Bobby Hutton's funeral," he said. "I'm not gonna stand up here and make a speech. You've been listening to white people for 400 years." People listened. "I haven't been in your place. I haven't suffered the way you've suffered. And somehow, that's gotta be translated to the white community. Now! Time's running out for everybody. That's enough." He left the truck bed, grim-jawed and silent.

I turned to Vinny, sitting on the grass next to Olivia. "'Translate it to the white community.' That's what Bobby was talking about."

And there he was now, Bobby Seale, who'd sat in our office with Little Bobby Hutton a week before, standing up on that truck bed, looking grim and pissed off, smoking a cigarette. Another young Panther stepped forward and launched into a story about a thirsty man and a stream. The people listened as the Panthers stood beside the storyteller, implacable, only 10 days after the murder of Martin Luther King.

"A man came along at the bottom of a mountain," the young Panther began. "He was searching out a clear stream of water. He was thirsty. Very, very thirsty. Now, when the man found the spring of water, it was muddy. It was filthy. Then another man explained to the black man that the stream is dirty because at the top of the stream, at the top of the hill, there's a hog in the stream. There's a hog muddying it all up."

Another Panther stepped forward. "That stream is freedom," he said. "Black people want their freedom. Martin Luther King in his own way. Malcolm X in his own way. Marcus Garvey in his own way."

Traffic moved smoothly on the nearby boulevard. Children ran on the grass. The sun shone as if nothing had happened.

The Panther continued. "W.E.B. Du Bois, Nat Turner, Mister Patrice Lumumba over there in the Congo. Mister Ho Chi Minh over there in bloody Vietnam. Fidel Castro down in Cuba. All these people are trying to get the hog out of the stream. Not just for you and me. For everybody."

I could hear a rhythm. A tempo. A chorus. I turned to Olivia. "There's our story," I said. "Our bridge to whitey."

Kathleen Cleaver, Eldridge's wife, the daughter of a foreign service officer who had come of age in poverty-stricken nations and who had attended a Quaker school in Philadelphia, spoke to MLK's final speech and the Panthers' mission. "We're not here to debate nonviolence or violence. We're here to celebrate a young man who put his life on the line to practice his right to self-defense. He died like a warrior for black liberation. In the name of brotherhood and survival, remember Little Bobby Hutton."

"'Brotherhood?'" Nikki asked. "Can't she talk about sisterhood in the same breath with the brothers."

"So only young men can die as warriors?" I asked Nikki.

"That's what the girl said," Nikki replied, never taking her eyes off Kathleen Cleaver. "But I don't like it."

Bobby Seale stepped up to the microphone. He was trying to make the best out of Little Bobby's loss. "Bobby Hutton was my little brother," he said. "Seventeen years old. He joined the Panthers to police the police. Little Bobby may have been shot down, but he lives to represent the next wave. He lives to represent our youth. Bobby Hutton is gonna carry forward the vision of the party because the Black Panther Party refuses to let you get slaughtered. We do not make nonviolent protest without making sure we defend ourselves."

As we left, Bobby Seale motioned us behind the flat-bed truck. Olivia embraced him.

Bobby wasn't embarrassed by the show of affection.

"We won't let him disappear," Vinny said.

Bobby handed Vinny a rolled-up collection of prints on thick poster paper. "Here," he said. "These prints, they're all drawn by Emory. Emory Douglas. He's our minister of culture, these days. You might be able to use these prints — show people how we live."

We unrolled the drawing — strong, impressionistic

portraits of black men and women of all ages, some armed, some young and handsome, some old and worn. Donna looked over my shoulder. "Wow," she said. "These are powerful."

"Emory's a powerful man," Bobby said.

"I've seen his stuff in the Black Panther paper," Lenore said. "He talks about all of it. Even the breakfast program."

"Maybe these will give you ideas," Bobby said.

Back at the studio, we moved quickly. We tacked up the silk-screened images that Bobby had given us. I sat down to write up the story about a thirsty little black panther, a stream, a hog, and a big black panther. Donna disappeared into the shop and pulled the cover off the sewing machine. Spider and Jeffree set up sawhorses to cut plywood sheets for the puppet stage. Together, we rocked in time to conjure up the art, to give voice to our sadness and rage, to hold high the lost, to dignify our loss, to celebrate Martin and remember Little Bobby, to bend the arc of history toward justice.

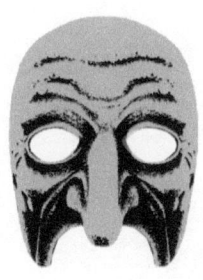

25

NIKKI AND THE UPSTREAM HOG

Vinny put me together with Nikki. He told us to draft scripts for the Black Panther puppet shows. Come up with characters, story ideas, rough out scripts. Short, beginning, middle, end. The Troupe would perform them at demos and in the parks, hit-and-run pieces that we could perform anywhere and be gone before the cops discovered we didn't have a permit. Nikki and I sat shoulder to shoulder at a table in the corner of the studio and got to work.

At Little Bobby's memorial, we'd heard the Panthers tell the story of the thirsty man and the hog in the stream. True to our discovery at Little Bobby's memorial, we chose that story as the basis for our first script.

"Okay," Nikki said. "We know the story. How are we going to tell it onstage?"

"We need a narrator," I said. "And characters. And those same characters are gonna need to appear in all these shows."

"Puppets."

"Yeah!" I said. "Free at last. No actors' egos, no equity rules, no costume complaints. Do the show, stuff the players in a box, and head for the next gig."

"Hey," Nikki said. "I'm an actor."

"Me, too," I said. "But that don't mean I have to eat with them, do I?"

"Okay, wise guy. Puppets. Characters. How about two black panthers?" Nikki asked. "A big black panther and a little black panther. The big panther can tell the story and the little panther…"

"Yeah, in honor of Little Bobby Hutton…"

"He can come bopping along, get into trouble, all that."

"Yes!" I said.

"The teacher and the student."

Donna and Spider were cutting and drilling plywood in the shop, building a portable puppet stage, "Punch and Judy"–style. They put Tommy to work painting.

"Want coffee?" I asked Nikki.

"I'm good," she said. "Stoked on the process."

I headed for the big, nasty, aluminum coffee urn that lurked in the office. Behind closed doors, Vinny and Olivia sat hunched together on the busted couch. Juris, the long-haired Swedish dramaturg from Berkeley, huddled with them. I hadn't seen him come in. They stopped talking when I burst through the doors. "Everything all right?" I asked.

"What's ever all right?" Olivia said.

The room felt electric, shock electric.

"Okay! I'm gonna leave you all to it." I hustled out with the coffee. It seemed odd to me. Most meetings at the Troupe were open. People came and went. The three of them seemed cloistered, secretive.

"Wow," I told Nikki. "I just walked into a very strange case of bad vibes."

"What about?"

"Probably the new show."

"*Turandot.*"

"Aka *Congress of the Whitewashers*. The Swedish guy was there," I said. "Adding his two cents' worth. He makes me nervous." I was curious about Brecht. I had talked about his play with Vinny and Olivia over Chinese food. I wanted to be part of the process.

"We better move our butts," Nikki said. "Those guys are gonna have a puppet stage built and we won't have anything to show them."

I refocused on the job at hand. "That upstream hog story is an allegory, right?"

"Yeah," Nikki said. "I guess so!"

"So, let's do it like a fairy tale," I said. "You know, 'Once upon a time...'"

Nikki stepped in. "A little black panther was walking along under the hot sun."

"And boy, did he get thirsty. The sun beat down on his little black pelt."

"Mm-hmm." Nikki nodded. "He said…"

"…I sure am thirsty." I completed the line.

"Yeah, cool!" Nikki said. "Narrator narrates, puppets act it out."

"Back and forth, back and forth. Tell the story, then show it. Don't let the audience forget it's a puppet show," I said. "Little black panther came to a stream. The water looked cool and delicious."

"Mm-hmm. That water sure looks cool and delicious," Nikki said. "He took a sip."

"Wait a minute," I said. "How we gonna show the stream?"

"It could be a character," Nikki said. "Everything is alive, right?"

"Yeah, sure. But how many puppeteers can we squeeze into this puppet booth?"

"Hey, Donna," Nikki shouted. "How many people in the booth?"

"Two," Donna shouted back from the shop. "Three in a pinch."

"We need a stream," I said.

"And a hog," Nikki yelled. "We need a moveable hog."

"One stream and one moveable hog, comin' up," Donna hollered over the clatter of Spider's jigsaw.

Nikki settled back. She slung one knee in her clasped hands. "It's an old hog," she said. "Four hundred years old.

Old as slavery. Old as capitalism. Just as ugly, too."

"Yeah!" I said. "Slavery and capitalism. Sidekicks. You think that's a coincidence?"

"There are no coincidences." Nikki continued. Her voice took on a distant, trancelike quality. "The hog is a capitalist hog. An old capitalist hog. And that hog wants to expand the hog trough."

"Like the Dutch. Sailing the ocean seas to build new troughs. Africa. The West Indies. Manhattan!"

"The hog needs labor. And he's gotta pay for labor. And that money melts away. When the hog pays people wages, who knows where they'll spend them? They might even use them to buy some other hog's junk."

Nikki was rocking out. I scribbled furiously, getting her stream on paper.

"We need people to work for free." I took on the hog's voice.

"'Good idea,' the hog thought." Nikki continued. "Slavery wasn't new. First, whitey…"

"Who's whitey here?" I asked.

"The Dutch and English," Nikki said. "Whitey tried to kidnap the Africans, but the Africans kicked whitey's ass. So, whitey built forts on the coast and let the Muslim salt traders and black compradors capture the Africans and bring them to the coast."

"What's a comprador?" I asked.

"You know," Nikki said.

"Yeah, but the audience doesn't."

"Got it," Nikki said. "We could make a sign. Have it pop up on cue."

"Saying what?" I asked.

"You know, something like…"

Nikki grabbed a sketch pad and a magic marker and scribbled:

COMPRADOR

OPPRESSED PERSON

SUCKS UP TO OPPRESSORS

RATS OUT OWN PEOPLE

"…that kinda thing."

"But wait a minute," I said "Compradors. Are we gonna have a big and a little black panther go this deep?"

"Dunno," I said. "Depends. Let's see how much time we have."

Nikki continued her recall trance. "So whitey put the African slaves on ships. The slaves were black and the hogs were pink. No way to mistake who was who."

"It's gotta be a pink hog," I yelled back to Donna.

"So it suited the hog to be racist," I said. "Capitalism loves a stacked deck."

"And 400 years later, he's fucking up this nice, clean stream with all his bullshit."

"Hog shit."

"So how are we gonna get the hog outta the stream?" she asked.

"I dunno."

"Maybe big and little black panther don't know either."

"Yeah. Maybe we open this up," I said. "To the audience."

"Isn't that a cop-out?" Nikki asked.

The office door burst open, and Olivia stormed out. Without a word to anyone, she swept up her coat and bag and clacked down the long stairway to the street. A moment later, Vinny and Juris emerged shoulder to shoulder, muttering and gesticulating to each other.

I looked at Nikki and shrugged. "So I guess the *Whitewashers' Congress* trio didn't get along so well, first time out."

"Maybe there'll be room for you to help with the writing," she said.

"Wow," I said. "Do ya think?" This play excited me. It had the potential to talk back to all the spin the media had put on the war. Listen to any returning G.I. You knew in the first two weeks you were in Vietnam. You weren't fighting for freedom, Mom, or apple pie. You were killing people. Or getting killed. And I was sitting in this room partly because a bunch of old white guys gave a draft-age Harvard grad a break.

And the guys who had to go? I owed them. I had to believe in the power of art. I had to believe I was fighting back. And if I had any say at all, I was about to push *The Whitewashers' Congress* into the struggle.

Vinny stopped at the stairway and nodded at Nikki and me. "Let's get a report on the puppet shows tomorrow. After workout. And we should call a rehearsal for the marching band, too. Tomorrow."

"'Night, Vinny," people shouted in a chorus from the studio shop and the rehearsal floor. Vinny and Juris clumped down the stairs.

Nikki watched them go with a question mark for an expression. "What the heck happened with Olivia?" she asked.

I shrugged. "He's the director. Before she's a company member, Olivia is his girlfriend."

"Girlfriend?" Nikki said.

"Okay, companion on the road of life," I said.

"The girlfriend part didn't look so happy."

"She wants to be heard."

"And seen," Nikki said.

"Vinny is the director. On the road, he's the director. In the studio, he's the director."

"Yeah, so?"

"So whatever Vinny wants…"

"Say no more," Nikki said.

Spider and Donna wanted to call it a day. Nikki and I wanted to keep working. Tommy wanted to see Janis Joplin at the Straight Theater. He and Jeffree disappeared into the fog. The remaining quartet piled into Donna's Karmann Ghia, drove back over the bridge, and turned up Ashby. We motored past the sheltered world of the Berkeley campus to the house where Spider and Donna were crashing, thanks to the lawyer who had sprung Spider from a Mexican jail months earlier. The little bungalow huddled down the hill from the Night Tripper, Spider and Donna's well-appointed gypsy bus.

Spider cooked up a potful of pasta and a red sauce. "You gotta slice the garlic paper thin, like this, with a razor blade," he said. Donna tossed a salad from out of the bottomless depths of the refrigerator. A bottle of wine materialized on the table. Nikki and I read the notes and volleyed scraps of narration and dialogue back and forth. Over pasta, we talked to Spider and Donna about how to build the hog and the stream.

"What about a hog like a pink piggy bank?" Donna said. "He's a capitalist hog, right?"

"And while he's onstage, a hand keeps dropping down and shoves another coin in the slot," Spider said. "I can make that happen."

"Cool," Nikki said. "What about the stream?"

Donna sketched out a corkscrew roller painted blue with oscillating white lines that could be clamped on the front of the puppet stage. A free puppeteer's hand could reach around and turn the crank, giving the impression of flowing water.

"It's an old vaudeville trick," Spider said. "Rolling waves."

"And the sign will be easy," Donna said.

We were excited. We wrote up a draft of "The Upstream Hog" that night over the bottle of wine and read it out loud.

When we finished working, I drove Nikki home. She lived in East Oakland. Black Oakland. On the way home, The Who's new tune "Magic Bus" came on the radio.

"You didn't invite me up into your magic bus," she said.

"Did you want to spend the night up there?"

"No. I didn't. I simply expected it, that's all."

"Why? I mean, you could have."

"That's where you live, isn't it?"

Her face shone in the streetlights. For the first time, I saw freckles.

"Do you expect that from guys? An invitation?"

"Yeah, pretty much."

"But we work together."

"Yes, we do."

"And we've already been through a lot together. Martin Luther King gone. Little Bobby Hutton murdered."

Nikki sighed. "Yeah. Right here in the 'hood. Our own Little Black Panther." She looked out the window. "Now take a look at where I live, Mister Charlie."

"What? Where? Why'd you call me that?"

"Just kidding," Nikki said. "Just fucking kidding." She sounded tired. "Pull over. I'm home."

I was on the broad, bright-lit strip of MacArthur Blvd, but the side streets looked shabby and narrow, crowded with row houses. On MacArthur, every other building featured a liquor store or a check-cashing joint. "Where do you live? I don't see any apartments."

"Right up this street." She put her hand on the door.

"It's late. Shouldn't I...?"

"It's cool. I'm just a black girl in the 'hood. The brothers all know me. Say it loud, comrade. I'm black and I'm proud." She put her hand on my arm. "Thanks for the ride. It's good to be working with you." Nikki bounced out of the car before I could say stop, let me take you to your door.

I watched Nikki walk off into the darkness. Maybe she didn't want me to see where she lived. Why not? Nikki didn't seem like one to shy away from her own reality.

Then I was alone, a white boy in the 'hood. I pulled out into the sparse, late-night flow on MacArthur Blvd. Red light filled the Karmann Ghia interior. A loudspeaker squawked. "Pull to the side. Pull over. Now!"

Shit. I wasn't carrying, but who knew what a search of the Karmann Ghia would turn up? I pulled over.

The mass of a cop's uniformed belly, badges, straps, and gun belt covered the window. He tapped on the glass.

I rolled down the window.

"So you like dark meat."

"What?"

"Dark meat. That hooker you dropped off."

"What? Are you kidding? We work together."

The cop laughed. "You tryin' to tell me you're her pimp?"

"No. No. You got it wrong."

"Oh yeah, I bet I do." The cop hitched up his belt. "Look," he said. "I don't give a shit what you do."

A second cop car pulled in ahead of me, light flashing. The interrogator pig's sidekick came up to the other side.

"What's her name?" he asked. "Where's she live?"

"I don't know," I said. "She wouldn't let me drop her off at her house."

"Okay. Gimme her name."

"Why do you need to know?"

"What's her name." A command, not a question.

Before I could answer, two cops in the front car leapt out and hustled down the street after Nikki. I couldn't see where she'd gone. My pig's partner blocked the view from the passenger-side window.

"Let's see your license and registration."

I pulled out my license.

The pig looked at it. "You from Massachusetts? This your car?"

"It belongs to other people I work with. I borrowed it to take her home." I put my hands on the steering wheel. "I'm gonna reach in the glove compartment. Look for the registration. So don't shoot me, okay?"

"You trying to be funny?"

"No. I don't want to get shot."

"Keep it up, kid."

The glove compartment was a mess. I found a grease-stained envelope and handed it to the cop.

The cop looked at the registration.

"You're all from Massachusetts, huh. They all look like you?"

"What do you mean?"

"Like girls. With the hair and all. We got enough of them already, without you people comin' out from Massa-fucking-choosetts."

"What do you do, working with this girl?" the other cop asked.

"We work in a theater company. In San Francisco."

"So what are you doing in Oakland?"

"We live here."

"This sounds like bullshit to me. You're from Massachusetts, you work with this colored girl…"

The two other pigs crossed into view through the windshield. They had Nikki handcuffed between them.

"Where are you taking her?"

"Look, you don't need to worry about it."

"Yeah, I do. She's a friend and a colleague of mine."

"A 'colleague,' huh? You got a way with words, professor."

The two pigs pushed Nikki into the back seat of the other squad car.

"Where are they taking her?"

"If I was you, I'd stop asking questions. Now get out of here before I charge you with solicitation."

"But she isn't…"

He threw the license and registration back through my window. "Shut the fuck up and get the fuck outta here."

Adrenaline shot through me. Rage wouldn't get me anywhere, and I couldn't just leave. Maybe if I waited, they'd drive past me, so I could follow them.

"Outta here!" the cop barked from his car.

I started the Karmann Ghia and took off. A block down the street I pulled over in front of a truck to hide the Karmann Ghia from view.

There was a pay phone on the corner, but I couldn't leave the car. I didn't want to lose them. They had to be heading for a precinct station, wherever that might be. I'd have to call when I got there. I was going to need help to spring Nikki.

The two squad cars drove past me. The ruse had worked. Neither had turned a head except for Nikki. She saw me and turned straight ahead. So near yet so far away.

I pulled out and followed them. They cruised down MacArthur onto Park and headed toward Lake Merritt. They drove through a gate in a cyclone fence and disappeared behind a grim-looking brick-and-stone edifice.

I went in the front door. I was hoping that the cops wouldn't recognize me. It was a weeknight and quiet. I went to the front desk. "I need to bail somebody out."

"Yeah? You a bondsman? Hell, you don't look like no bondsman I ever seen."

"No. You've got a friend of mine here."

"This her?"

The two cops jerked Nikki past the desk, still handcuffed. She looked at me with a cold, unrecognizing stare that showed no connection, an ancient stare, the stare of a black woman in the clutches of two white cops.

"Friend of yours?" The desk sergeant raised his eyebrows.

"Yeah, she is. We work together."

"You a hooker, too? Or a John. You can't be her pimp. And you're not a lawyer. Your hair's too damned long."

"She's not a hooker, dammit."

"Whatever she is or isn't... They'll take her upstairs, take her prints, a mug shot, put her in a holding cell."

"How long will that take?"

"Depends. If it's just a routine takedown, an hour, two. It's quiet here. If she's a newbie..."

"A what?"

"No priors. She may get out with a citation. Phone's over there."

"Thanks."

The sergeant didn't register the sarcasm.

I pulled the phone-booth door closed. Inside, my heart beating, I wondered how I would have fared if I'd been black. At my age, I'd already have known the routine. As it was, I didn't know shit about getting booked or arraigned. I was standing in the middle of a different world. Hands shaking, I dug into my jeans, found some quarters and dimes. A sleepy Spider picked up the phone on about the 10th ring.

I told him what had happened. I could barely believe it myself.

Scuffling and shuffling noises led to Donna's voice. "We'll call Gordon," she said.

"Now?" It was past midnight.

"He's a lawyer. But I have a feeling this isn't going to

happen until morning." The phone went quiet. "So they busted her and let you go."

"Yeah. Surprised?"

"No," Donna said. "Not surprised."

"I'll stay here until I hear back from you."

"Okay." Donna was quiet, calm. She sighed. "Talk soon."

She hung up. I sat in the lobby and watched the late-night traffic roll through the precinct station. A drunk told the desk sergeant where to shove it. Two real hookers came in, short skirts and wigs. They seemed to know the arresting officers and the banter was angry but full of practiced humor. A busty woman in a tattered cardigan came in, frantic and in tears, asking after her boy. *Oh, the sadness. How does anybody stand it,* I thought. *Why should anybody stand it? Cruelty. Practiced cruelty.*

The phone in the booth rang. "Come on home," Donna said. "We'll go back for the arraignment in the morning."

"What if they let her out?"

"Gordon doesn't think they will."

"She doesn't have a record."

"You don't know that. Besides, she's black."

"This doesn't sound good."

"None of this sounds good," Donna said.

I hung up the phone. Checked again with the desk sergeant.

"I'll see," he said. "If you're not a pimp, a john, or a lawyer, then what the hell are you?"

"An actor," I said.

"Oh yeah? My nephew wants to be an actor. Ever been on TV?"

"No," I said. The sergeant gave me a look like I was a nobody and humped his fat ass up the stairs.

The place fell quiet, the ceiling creaking with footsteps above. I hoped one pair was Nikki's.

The desk sergeant wheezed back down the stairs. "Come back in the morning," he said. "And I'll look for you on TV."

No chance for tonight. Another lesson learned. One world for color; another for white.

I drove back to our eucalyptus domain in the hills, numbed by the layered differences in treatment Nikki and I had experienced. I lay awake for the rest of the night, running the movie of Nikki's arrest on my mind screen, cursing myself for not standing guard at the precinct. She had been kidnapped on the strength of a profile — a black woman stepping out of a white man's car. She'd been pursued, captured, manhandled, humiliated, and abducted. I had been stopped, chided, cajoled, challenged, and released untouched. She had been threatened, numbered, and caged without recourse. I had been allowed to question, demand, inquire, and seek assistance. How could such differences explode from the simple act of a person opening a car door in a certain neighborhood, at a certain hour? Was Nikki just any black girl or any woman or any Negro? Was I all white boys, all white men? What made her vulnerable and me immune? I knew, but I did not understand.

By the time we returned bleary-eyed to the precinct station, Gordon, the man who sprung Spider from a Mexican prison, had freed Nikki from an Oakland jail. Gordon was a chubby young man in his 30s, curly-haired and mustached, one loose shirttail revealing a trace of a frog-white belly. He carried the jovial attitude of a person who had done the right thing. A bedraggled Nikki stood at his side looking defiant. She carried the same glazed protective shield she had worn the night before, when she passed me in the precinct station on the way upstairs to be booked.

"Come on, Gordon," Donna said. "We're all in this together."

"Cut the crap," Gordon said. "Not one of you has a pot to piss in or a law degree to swing around. Stand down. I'm supporting the arts."

Nikki stared at Gordon as if he was a Martian. "Thanks," she said and turned to Donna. "Can we get out of here?"

After we said goodbye to the jovial Gordon, Nikki and I climbed into the back seat of the Karmann Ghia. "Do you want to go home?" Donna asked. "Clean up?"

"Hell, no," Nikki said. "I'm not having much luck with white people driving me home."

"I hear that," Spider said.

"Do you?" Nikki said. She sighed. "Thanks for bailing me out."

"We didn't do it," Donna said. "Gordon got there ahead of us."

"Could I take a shower at your place?" Nikki asked.

"Sure," Donna said.

"I need to wash some upstream hog offa me."

26

SLEEPING WITH THE ENEMY

We didn't go into the studio that day. Nikki showered. Spider and Donna left us alone, and we loafed around the Night Tripper after everyone else took off. We didn't plan to land alone together in the Night Tripper. At first, we lay side by side on top of the quilt like a couple of cadavers. Nikki fell asleep in the morning sunlight, but within minutes she began to mumble, whimper, and toss. After I covered her with the quilt, she calmed down and we dozed. An hour later we woke hot and restricted and kicked off our clothes. I'd never entwined with a black body, and she'd never seen a naked white man. I felt white-belly ugly compared to her delicious, brown color.

All morning, Nikki flashed from cold and angry to bewildered and numb, to frightened and vulnerable and back again. I felt enveloped in a fast-moving Atlantic

317

storm, the atmosphere from her emotions changing in seconds from bruised purple to lightning bright to butter-yellow warmth. She clung to me; she pushed me away.

"Doesn't this white skin mess you up?" I asked her. "After what happened?"

"Yeah," Nikki said. "But I'm trying to cogitate on it before I run out of here screaming. It's a good thing you smell good."

She dozed off again. I traipsed down the outdoor steps to the bungalow's kitchen and brewed coffee, hoping the simple ritual would steady me in the aftermath of last night's tumult. When my heart stopped pounding, I brought the coffee pot back up to the bus with a couple of porcelain mugs. After we finished the coffee, we loafed around longer. We dressed and — cranked on caffeine — tumbled down to the house and babbled about puppet shows while I scrambled eggs and toasted the long end of a baguette.

That afternoon we sat at the kitchen table and pulled out the drawings Bobby Seale had given us. They were pen and ink lithographs that Douglas Emory had drawn for the Black Panther newspaper. The illustrations were ragged, angry, the work of a skilled artist boiling down his rage into tableaux.

We worked hard. Neither of us took time to think or talk about the night before, although my mind roared with cops and Oakland streetlights and troubled sleep against Nikki's warm body. We studied Emory's drawings. We wanted to represent the tableaux Emory had cast with his drawings but — without the puppets — our options were limited. We began to work around Emory's images and lines.

A young woman with a kerchief in her hair stands in her kitchen and sprays roaches with a hand pump filled with DDT. "Rats and roaches in my apartment," she says. "I spray DDT where my kids eat."

A skinny old woman in a housedress sits in a straight-backed chair, pocketbook in hand, waiting for somebody. A bare light bulb hangs by its frayed power cord over her shoulder. "I live on the third floor. I can barely walk. No elevator, no hallway lights."

A man in a work jacket and boots stands on the edge of a vacant lot littered with broken bottles and splintered boards. "My children have no place to play."

We soaked in Emory's stark figures, felt a rhythm come into our words. We wanted more time together to write and lounge on the back deck of the Oakland bungalow.

We worked together, worked well. The more we worked, the more we enjoyed each other's bodies. "I'm sleeping with the enemy," she'd say and nuzzle me. Nikki was like every girl I knew and like nobody I ever met before. She was a woman, but back then, I would have called her a girl, maybe even a Negro girl. She looked different, smelled different, tasted different. She talked, acted, and invented with me like everybody we knew who lived on the brink of the apocalypse — a horror of a war, equality shot down in the streets.

Nikki couldn't sit still. She pushed toward a revolution that would allow her to contribute her talent, skills, and fury to the battle. I watched her cross the gap that began with recovery from arrest and stretched back to the capture of her ancestors and their compressed imprisonment in the dank hull of a tossing, stinking-wet slave ship, survivors thrust naked into public view in a strange land where pink men spoke in tongues and tore her family ancestors apart like legs ripped off a roasted bird.

The phone rang. It was Donna.

"You guys still alive over there?"

Nikki held up the receiver. Donna's voice sounded calm, warm, and gentle.

"Sure," Nikki said, looking at me. "We're working on the puppet scripts. How's the stage coming?"

"It marches," Donna said. "When are you guys coming in?"

We took the hint. It was time to report to the studio.

Forward momentum can be persuasive. Donna and Spider had finished the stage. They designed and built it as a hit-and-run guerrilla weapon. Detach the front proscenium and pull a couple of pins and the stage collapsed into a flat, lightweight triptych of quarter-inch plywood, brightly painted.

Nikki and I sat down with the ensemble to present our work. The script about the upstream hog worked beautifully. Nikki and I had already developed a workable tempo between us that was fast, funny, and impactful.

The housing show was more difficult. Our wordplay knocked people out, but we had no way to capture and translate the power of Emory's drawings. Donna came up with the idea to reproduce Douglas Emory's tableaux on large poster boards and have a third actor stand beside the stage and flip through them while we chanted and sang the script. "Bread and Puppet Theater–style," she explained. Everybody loved the work. Nikki and I collected plenty of laughter, applause, and support. And every eye glinted with innuendo.

27

THE HOME FRONT

William Kunstler, the civil rights lawyer who would defend the Chicago Seven, described our resistance by saying that the Vietnam War had redounded to the home front. We who did not deploy to fight the war and those who did, were, in Dylan's words, bringing it all back home. That made perfect sense to us — we rocked in time to the rhythm of 1968. In the distorted reflection of the war in Vietnam, our 20th-century civil war rolled across America — beating down black and brown Americans, soaking students with rage and despair, sending kids to kill and be killed, kids too young to vote.

William Kunstler was right. The war redounded to the home front. Weed and LSD redounded into heroin from Bangkok and methamphetamines from Bakersfield. Murder in villages redounded to murderous cults in

Hollywood. National guardsmen drove jeeps armed with 50-caliber machine guns and barbed-wire bumpers through the downtown Chicago streets. In Vietnam, American kids our age locked and loaded their M16s and snaked into villages. In San Francisco, families from Middle America locked doors and closed windows and cruised down Haight Street, gawking at the destitute kids. Tourists in station wagons looked hermetically sealed behind safety glass, as if they had landed on another planet and couldn't breathe the air.

The Democratic Convention would thrust mealy-mouthed Hubert Humphrey into battle with the Republican crook from Orange County. In Vietnam, carpet bombing resumed from B-52s flying too high to be seen or heard from the villages below. Drunken, closet-gay J. Edgar Hoover launched COINTELPRO to target leaders in the civil rights and antiwar movements. The pigs would riot in Chicago, Berkeley, Oakland, San Francisco, Detroit, Newark, New York, and L.A. Nixon's silent majority refused to stay silent any longer. The war savaged Vietnam and Vietnam savaged America. Resistance gathered momentum like a rolling stone.

The Troupe knew it was time to bring it all back home. After the Cracker Barrel Minstrel Show, we overcame the onus of the Calgary bust that had quashed the New York trip the year before. We didn't have Dick Gregory or the Town Hall booked anymore, but we'd hit the road and stirred up trouble on campuses with *L'Amant Militaire*.

Growing tighter with every show, the Troupe skipped from campus to campus across Amerika. We ricocheted and spiraled through New York's theater scene. We formed liaisons, garnered awards, and returned home via the nation's winter highways. Back in San Francisco, we exited our own resurrection. We fought on against an entrenched system, despite fatigue, clashes, fragmentations, and loss. Our leaders left. New faces appeared.

Bobby Seale and Little Bobby Hutton had enlisted us as dramatic envoys to the white world. In the next breath, a racist murdered Martin Luther King and two days later, the cops killed Bobby Hutton in a shootout. We slipped between fire fights in occupied Oakland to mourn our newfound friend and grapple with our assignment — to revive a murdered Bobby Hutton with a pair of black velvet sock puppets.

We checked our arsenal. The raucous commedia of *L'Amant Militaire* had dissolved as with all theater productions into thin air. We had assembled a marching band and three Black Panther puppet shows. A good beginning, but we needed heavy artillery. We had sat, just the three of us, in Chinatown over beer, tea, moo goo gai pan, and rice and conjured Brecht's *Turandot* aka *The Congress of the Whitewashers*. We had a copy of Brecht's version, but it was unfinished.

I went to the library to research *Congress*. It felt good to sit in the reading room at the long, polished tables and card catalogs. I didn't have a professor to answer to and no preppie competitors. It was easy to access books at the city library. At Harvard's world-famous, double-grand Widener Library, you had to fill out request slips. A despondent student would fetch the books you requested from the stacks. It could take a half-hour for them to return. At the other library in the Yard, Lamont, the stacks were open to students. Male students. Women weren't allowed in Lamont. Too much distraction for the young gentlemen, they claimed.

I had accepted gender apartheid in those days. I was too entitled to allow inequity to cross my mind. I only knew one Radcliffe girl who commented on the males-only exclusion of Lamont, and she was a very self-assured writer who volunteered to work in the theater, where she had been relegated to second-class citizenship. In those days, you could always find a way to keep a good woman down.

By comparison, the San Francisco Public Library felt civilized and the information accessible. They even had those low brass lamps with the green glass shades, for chrissakes. I worked alone, accompanied only by my curiosity, scholarship, and the conversation I'd had with Olivia and Vinny in that fogbound Chinatown restaurant with the bossy waiter.

The ancient story of Turandot, the principal character in *Congress* had been kicked around the world, beginning with a 12th-century Persian poet named Nizami who told the tale of an Asian princess and the men who wanted to marry her. Four hundred years later, a young Venetian traveler obsessed with Islam and Sufi dervishes translated Nizami's tale and brought it back to Italy. A century later, a fierce Italian playwright named Carlo Gozzi adapted the story into a *dell'arte* drama.

Next, *Sturm und Drang* dramatist Friedrich Schiller, who wrote *William Tell* and played around with wealthy men's wives, wrote a version. His *Turandot* was staged by Goethe in Weimar Germany in 1802. It became a big hit. In 1920, Puccini wrote a Turandot opera. That was probably the best-known version of this story.

I couldn't stop digging into the history that surrounded Turandot and the fantastical royal court of the mythical Asian emperor who was her father. The world had shaped each treatment of the story as it would shape ours. In the 18th Century, Gozzi had been recruited into the Italian army. When he returned to civilian life, he set out to preserve traditional Italian theater, to rescue it from brash innovators like Carlo Goldoni, who had written *L'Amant Militaire*. Gozzi was obsessed with the growing bourgeoisie in Italy. There were supposed to be rich people and poor people with nobody in between. He wrote to expose upstart bourgeois playwrights. I imagined that Gozzi had been recruited by the Spaniards, like poor Harlequino in

L'Amant and didn't like his sucker's role in the war with Spain. He had become a bitter old reactionary, determined to preserve the old ways.

Frederich Schiller was radical for his time, a romantic revolutionary, like William Blake and Lord Byron or the Spanish painter Goya. Puccini, already wealthy and famous by the 1920s, had become pals with the Italian fascists, including Mussolini. Not surprisingly, he was a misogynist. He cast Turandot as a stereotypical ice princess, fond of executing her subjects, including her suitors. Finally, I came across a Russian theater artist named Yevgeny Bagrationovich Vakhtangov.

In the Soviet Union, during the brief but hip avant-garde revolution, before Stalin brought the hammer down, Vakhtangov did a modern version of Turandot, using Gozzi's script. Vakhtangov came out of the Moscow Art Theatre, where Stanislavski had developed new naturalistic acting techniques. Brecht saw the production, Lee Strasberg from the Actors Studio in New York saw the production. Vakhtankov's version was radical, exploding with wild Bolshevik design work, avant-garde, cubist, and totally cool.

Vakhtangov had studied with Stanislavski; he sounded like one of us. His Turandot used masks, music, dance, abstract, avant-garde sets. And like Stanislavski, the Soviet troupe worked long and hard before rehearsals began, looking at the play's text and the motivations of its characters. I wanted to do the same with our version. It must have taken guts to bring Gozzi's 18th-century *commedia* into contemporary Russian times. I liked the sound of this guy, but he died in 1922, the same year that he staged *Turandot* in Moscow.

Then came Brecht. He wrote his *Turandot* about intellectual corruption, to expose the fragmenting socialist thinkers who had fought among themselves while Hitler grabbed power. Unlike the earlier versions of the story, Brecht concentrated more on the whitewashers than he did on the character of the princess.

I didn't want our version of the play to trash the American New Left the way Brecht had dumped on the fragmenting Weimar socialists. The Germans had fought among themselves and failed, but our left wing was building coalitions like the Troupe was doing with the Black Panthers. The New Left's fragmentation would come later, but now, we were uniting while the media played spoiler, diminishing the power of resistance, and delivering military-industrial doublespeak to a Vietnam war-weary America.

Brecht's *Congress of the Whitewashers* takes place in an imaginary Chinese empire immersed in a strike by cloth-makers and clothing manufacturers. The empire's naked poor protest the emperor's lies. No cotton? Everybody knows the growing season had been excellent. But screw the naked people. The emperor has too much cotton. He won't sell; the price is too low. He begins to lie. The crops were terrible, he claims. We have no cotton. To disguise his big lie, the emperor hires professors and media intellectuals. He tells his courtiers to repeat the lie. The crop was terrible, they claimed. "We have no cotton." The emperor orders his intellectuals to invent reasons why the cotton market should be so dry when there was so much cotton grown. The winning thinker will win the hand of his daughter.

After several days in a research trance, I surfaced, hot with ideas, excited about building our own version of *The Whitewashers Congress*, a version for now. Brecht had focused on intellectual corruption. In our world, Brecht's play would expose the media's Vietnam distortions, celebrate the torn nation's protests, and ape the hollow impotence of our own Congress. I brought my research and ideas to Vinny. "When can we get started?" I asked.

He stretched back in his desk chair.

"Soon, kid, very soon," Vinny said. "We're working on it."

"Who, you and Olivia? Is that Swedish guy working with you?" I didn't wait for an answer. "Listen, I know how we can stage *Congress* in the present. At least I got an idea after all this research."

"Cool," he said. "How goes the Gutter Puppets? Have they rebelled? Cut their own strings, morphed into clenched fists?" I left without answers. It seemed as if Vinny had gone fuzzy on the topic. I suspected that he and Olivia were not getting along. I hoped their battles wouldn't encroach on the new play and my hopes for its message.

28

GUTTER PUPPETS HIT THE QUAD

We had two Gutter Puppet scripts and the Panther breakfast show in the oven. We were planning to work out the kinks in the parks, but we got a call from San Francisco State University. The campus chapter of SDS heard about us from other chapters on the tour, and the Black Student Union had learned about the puppet shows from the Panthers. At the planning meeting on campus, Nikki and I were tagged as an item. Nobody gave a damn except to grin at us as if we were a couple of cute puppies.

"Don't know if I like being made a thing of," Nikki said after the meeting. We sat in the student dining hall, drinking coffee.

"These guys don't care," I said.

"No, but what about the other side?"

"What other side?"

"White people."

"Ain't I white?" I said.

"Straight people. Young Americans for Freedom. The cops."

"Oh right," I said. "Them. We'll be safe onstage." I laughed. "Especially in a puppet booth."

"Yeah, I guess." Nikki said. "But that doesn't stop me from thinking about it. We're not always onstage, y'know."

"Ain't showbiz great?"

"It's okay," she said. "I like being next to you."

"I'm honored," I said, and meant it. I had come a long way from Lucky and Putnam Avenue. We felt special, Nikki and me. We carried no wounds, at least not from each other. The pain resided outside of us. Inside each of us, yes, pain, anger, loneliness, but together, we felt warm and languid. "I feel like we just had sex, only all the time."

Nikki looked up. "You're sitting in the middle of a meeting, and you feel like you're getting laid?" she asked.

"Kinda."

"I find that hard to believe."

"Why?"

She shrugged. "Plenty of reasons."

"Because it's harder for you to get into the mood?"

"Sure," she said. "You're a guy. You can shoot it off anytime."

"Maybe with a little more practice," I said, "you can shoot it off anytime, too." I leaned across the table and kissed her.

"I can't practice being white," Nikki said.

I didn't have an answer for that. "Let's go back to Oakland," I said. "We can beat the commute."

"And practice being boys and girls together," Nikki said.

"Yeah!" I said. "Like birds of a feather."

"So you're the dove and I'm the crow."

"Crows are jokesters. They laugh at the world."

"I'm sure that'll happen any day now."

"That's what we're here for…right?"

Nikki reached over and caressed my face. I couldn't fly with her wings, but I could love our differences.

With a date set for a Gutter Puppets opening at SF State, we began rehearsing, learning how to use the puppets and the stage. And props. The only way a panther puppet could wield a prop was in its jaws. We had a red "Punch and Judy" bat for improvised moments. We had the stream machine for "Upstream Hog," and Emory Douglas's powerful prints transferred to heavy composition board for "The Apartment Dwellers." Spider had built a stand to hold the prints and we could flip each portrait as called for in the story — the mother spraying DDT, an old woman sitting helpless, a father on his children's vacant-lot playground, a guerrilla man and woman wielding guns side by side.

The band had practiced R&B riffs from tunes like "The Midnight Hour," "Stand by Me," and "Soul Man." They were simple to play and could begin and end on cues from the puppets. Everybody had a good time playing and I began to call the noise they made "music." So off we went to the San Francisco State campus. Even during summer school, students were demonstrating. The Black Student Union wanted a black studies program to teach the real story of slavery in the Americas and how it shaped the nation. The real story of slavery. The story of Vietnam. Without whitewash.

Showtime. We marched onto the outdoor stage across from the SF State student union. We'd already set up the puppet stage, and I had recruited Tommy to guard it. He resented getting the shit work and showed it.

"What's the big deal?" I said. "Somebody's gotta hold down the fort while we march in."

"Yeah, but I know all the street beats and tunes."

"So does everybody else." I left him there to stew in his helmet and Mummers' rags.

We marched onstage and stood in a line to play "The Star-Spangled Banner," only our version contained screams at the rockets' red glare. We smashed a watermelon on the stage for the bombs bursting in air. SDS and the BSU had attracted a crowd, even during summer school.

Through the puppet proscenium, I caught an undercover cop floating at the back of the crowd, cramped in a stiff new jean jacket and aviation sunglasses. Easy to spot.

After we finished our version of the national anthem, the band jumped into "Soul Man." Nikki and I crept into the puppet stage where we'd set out the panther puppets and props. The band pulled to a full stop. We put our free arm around each other's waist as rehearsed.

Lenore stepped up. "Ladeez and gentlemen," she hollered. "The San Francisco Mime-a-da Troup-a presents…"

In chorus, the whole band stepped forward. "'The Gutter Puppets,' performing 'Upstream Hog.'"

"Dedicated to the memory of Black Panther Little Bobby Hutton."

"Once upon a time…," I began

Nikki thrust her puppet out the proscenium. "A little black panther was walking along under the hot sun."

"And boy, did he get thirsty," I shouted. "The sun beat down on his glossy black pelt."

"Mm-hmm." Nikki nodded. "He said…"

"…I sure am thirsty."

"Soon," Nikki said, "the little black panther came to a stream."

"The water looked cool and delicious."

"That water sure looks cool and delicious," little black panther said. The show went smoothly. Nikki and I stood hip by hip and shouted out our well-practiced lines. The drummers hit rim shots at the right time, the band played short riffs on cue, and we were done. The gathered students cheered and whistled, black and white together. Behind them, the undercover spook floated, checking out the audience before he exited the courtyard. *We must be doing something right*, I thought. *We caught the attention of The Man.*

We moved into "The Apartment Dwellers," and the simple show became an instant knockout. Our slum-dwelling characters came alive with Emory Douglas's portraits, all blown up colorful and stretched tall onto the flip signs that Donna and Spider had built.

Halfway through the show, a brace of campus cops and two uncomfortable guys in white shirts, sport coats, and ties appeared.

"They gotta be college brass," Nikki said.

"Oh yeah," the SDS kid said. "And campus pigs. They won't do nothin'."

Nikki and I stayed in character, talking to the cops through the proscenium in the guise of the panther puppets. The scene must have been ridiculous — two uniformed cops talking to a pair of puppets with a trio of suits standing off to one side like a doo-wop chorus.

"Do you have a permit to perform here?"

The two panther puppets turned to each other. "I dunno."

"Do we have a permit?"

"Hmmm, I dunno." The puppets looked around. Little black panther came back up with the red "Punch and Judy" bat. "Is this it?"

The crowd roared.

"You can't perform here without a permit."

"Oh, yessir," big black panther said. "We permit ourselves to play here."

More laughter.

One of the suits walked up to the microphone that stood off to the side. "Who invited these people?"

"These people? Those people?" little black panther asked. "You mean the ones that don't look like you?"

"Hey!" big black panther shouted. "What's the difference between a black panther and a white professor?"

"I dunno," little black panther replied. "What's the difference between a black panther and a white professor?"

Nikki and I were improvising off the top of the situation as if we were on rails.

"The world!" we shouted together.

The timing was perfect. When you time a punch line right, the laugh hits you like a punch, only it feels good. We were both on top of it.

The two organizers, a guy from SDS and another from the Black Student Union walked up to the stage. They presented the suits with a giant scroll of paper.

Nikki slapped me a high five with her free hand.

I kissed her sweaty cheek. It was hot in the puppet booth.

"This is not an official university document," the head admin said.

"Lessee," the Black Student Union kid said. "Is there an official university document that says we're not gonna teach black history?" He couldn't suppress a guffaw. "The real black history?"

"Lessee," said the SDS kid to the white shirts and

neckties. "Do you people... *you people* have an official university document that says if some poor chump pulls two "Ds" he goes on a kill list for the draft board?"

The crowd cracked up. Laughter, applause, whoops.

"Ladies and Gentlemen," I shouted over the rising cheers and jeers. "Students for a Democratic Society, the Black Student Union, and the San Francisco Mime Troupe present..."

Jeffree and Lenore gave us a loud roll.

"A bust!!!"

Inspired, the band began to play the infectious R&B beats we'd created, and the horns played the riff to "Soul Man" — tonic, three minor, four, five, four, three minor, tonic. The crowd recognized the familiar riff and shouted, "I'm a soul man!"

Students poured onstage and began to dance. They carried signs.

ROTC SUCKS

BOMBING FOR PEACE = FUCKING FOR VIRGINITY

FUCK THE ARMY

A file of university cops pushed their way through the crowd

"At least they aren't in Tac Squad gear," I said.

The band played on.

The cops filed onstage. Tommy, Donna, and Spider helped us strike the puppet show. The strike worked like a charm. We retreated guerrilla-style as quickly as we had appeared. The students shouted, "We'll be in touch," and poof! We packed the stage, drums, and horns into the van while the rest of us shed our ragged costumes and walked casually off campus to our "personnel carriers" — an orange VW, the Karman Ghia, and Emmett's faded-blue Valiant with the fake spare tire on the trunk. We motored off while the afternoon fog closed over the campus demonstration and those hired to break it up.

Although the show had been interrupted, we felt victorious. The guys from SDS and the Black Student Union were euphoric. "That's the first time since last spring that we got a rise out of the administration," they said.

"And they showed their true colors," Donna said.

"I guess you guys made a big splash."

That night, Nikki and I rolled around in the Night Tripper bus. We were learning each other — how we fit together. In the quiet of our denouement, I thought of Suzanne in Madison. But that exchange had felt one-sided, what I had wanted, not what my partner wanted. But that had been nine months ago, a gestation period in life and an eternity during wartime. Now, with Nikki, I asked, "Were you with me?"

She looked at me. "Does the earth go around the sun? I never once felt we were out of step." She kissed me and I blushed from head to toe.

29

SHUT IT DOWN

Encouraged by the response to our first performance, we forged ahead with the Gutter Puppets. Nikki and I wrote a breakfast show. Little black panther learns how to cook for kids who go to school hungry. Donna built two black panther sock puppets who could eat. She built a stack of pancakes, a chicken that could lay a pile of bright yellow scrambled eggs, and plastic glasses of painted milk. The band sounded like a band. Vinny kept himself, too busy to join us on trumpet, but the rest of the quasi-musicians began to revel in their ensemble sound.

We ferried the puppets and the Gorilla Band to parks from touristy North Beach to little parks in the Mission District and the projects in Hunters Point. People loved the shows and when Bobby Seale showed up to speak, our authenticity was complete. People laughed at the shows and the band kicked ass in the most unorthodox manner. Nikki and I were delirious. We felt as if we had built this little guerrilla platoon out of our combined energy and that the Troupe had embraced our efforts and furthered them. Turandot and *Congress of the Whitewashers* seemed to have disappeared in limbo.

SF State was coming alive. The Black Student Union had united with Chicano, Native American, and Asian students to become the Third World Liberation Front. The push for black studies expanded into a call for ethnic studies. They invited the Gutter Puppets back. We had to seize the time. They scheduled a rally in the quad. At our planning meeting, we learned that students here and at Cal Berkeley were redefining universities as factories and themselves as workers. They would go on strike and shut down the factory.

Cool. We added "On Strike — Shut It Down" to the marching-band signs and paraded on campus for the rally. SDS and the Third World Liberation Front had been granted a permit for the gathering, but the administration felt threatened.

As we marched in, Tommy noticed squad cars lined up at the far edge of a campus parking lot. "Who are those guys?" he asked.

I had seen these cop clusters before, in the Haight when they had swept through the Sunday afternoon fog and descended on a helpless herd of hippies. When the signal came down, each of those cars would vomit four San Francisco city cops dressed in tactical gear.

"City pigs can march on campus?" Lenore asked. "Is this city property or state property? It is San Francisco State University, isn't it?"

"Hey, pigs!" Tommy shouted. "We're gonna do a show! Come and watch. You might learn something!"

Squad-car doors flew open and fully loaded Tac Squad guys unfolded.

"Shut him up," one of the SDS guys said. "We got a rally to hold. Let 'em lurk over there. We got a permit." We shut him up, but Tommy had lit a fuse. The SF Tac Squad lined up three deep at one end of the main drive. Cops at both ends and the center of the lines carried stubby guns that barked tear-gas grenades. They waited for the word while the SDS and Black Liberation leaders spoke.

The faculty was polarizing, too. The world was still raw from the murder of Martin Luther King and the revelation that black and brown soldiers, many drafted off this campus, were dying in disproportionate numbers in Vietnam. The speaker, a professor, eyed the cops as he spoke. "They can't shut us up," he said, pointing to the cops. "We know from our brothers and sisters, students and faculty alike, all cross the country, campus demonstrations and disturbances are not going to end."

The little crowd cheered.

"Because the issues at stake, including Vietnam and racist America is not going to end. And this campus is not an ivory tower," he shouted. "This campus is a part of the real world — a microcosm of society."

Fists raised, the crowd roared. The Tac Squad trotted down the drive toward the rally. The lead pig line waded into the rally crowd and the students. Nobody was swinging clubs yet, but the crowd, now angry, turned to fight back. Another volley of tear gas floated on the wind from the beach. As the stinging wisps flowed past us, Nikki and I huddled onstage in the flimsy plywood puppet booth, surrounded by ragtag musicians and a bunch of horns. I had learned my lesson well at Madison. "Let's get the hell outta here!" I shouted.

"We haven't even done the show," Tommy said, holding up his "STRIKE" sign.

"We're getting out," I said. "Now!" The Troupers got it. We folded up the puppet stage and fought off the cops with funky second line New Orleans street beats and raggedy horn licks blown loud. Tommy kept hollering. "Fuck the army! Fuck the pigs!"

With one hand on the puppet stage, I grabbed Tommy's collar and dragged him down the back stairs of the outdoor pavilion. "Whose side are you on?" I growled. "Engage and retreat. Engage and retreat." We tumbled down the steps and walked, not ran, toward the gate, drums, trumpets, tuba, Mummers costumes rattling, banging and flapping in the tear-gas fog. Behind us we could hear shouts of rage, screams. Breathless, we tossed the stage, props, the instruments onto the flatbed, and the band dispersed. We retreated guerrilla-style, but the battle had been joined. The storm clouds gathered. It was a time of war. That night, Nikki and I translated our adrenaline into lovemaking beneath the eucalyptus, alone together in the Night Tripper bus.

30

GIMME SHELTER

After the morning workout, Vinny sat us down on the dance floor while he paced. He'd been grouchy all morning, a real downer after the power and ecstasy we felt after our Gutter Puppet guerrilla action. Nikki and I felt tight, and I couldn't help but compare the morning's perfunctory session to the exhilarating Troupe workouts Vinny had led when I first joined the company two years and an eternity earlier.

"So you guys had to go to State." Vinny was furious.

"We were invited," I said.

"And you almost got busted," Vinny said.

"No we didn't," Jeffree said. "We retreated, like a good guerrilla band should."

"Not the way I heard it."

"Where'd you hear different?" I asked.

"A little bird told me," Vinny said.

I knew who the little bird was. Tommy was sitting next to Vinny. Olivia sat on the floor, opposite Vinny.

"That's funny," I said. "Because the little bird chirped the loudest when we left."

"If it had been up to the little bird, we would have all been busted," Lenore said.

"Hey," Tommy objected. "I got caught up in the moment."

So Tommy was worming his way into Vinny's field of vision. I had seen him work behind the scenes in Cambridge with directors at the Loeb and professors at Adams House. Stealth seemed at once uncharacteristic of the gregarious Tommy and basic to his sense of survival.

"Fine," Lenore said. "And what about afterward."

"I was just telling it like it is," Tommy said.

"Cut the crap, you guys," Olivia said.

"We need to be able to go back to that campus," Vinny said.

"Sure we do," I said. "And we will."

"Hell, man," Lenore said. "We're all about Gutter Puppets and Gorilla Bands."

"Yeah, well that's great," Vinny said. "And you'll be ready to deploy as puppets and gorillas when we need that. But right now, we just committed to a festival."

The circle of Troupers reacted. "A what?" "With who?" "Where?"

"A radical theater festival," Vinny said. "On the SF State campus."

"Cool," I said. "So shows like yesterday, they'll give great advance notice."

"Yeah, if you stay in one piece."

Olivia sat silent, as she had so often.

"We haven't heard anything about that," Donna said.

"I just finalized it," Vinny said.

"And this is the first time we've heard about it?" Tommy said.

"You know now."

"A festival means a bunch of theaters, right?" Nikki said. "Who's coming."

"Us. Teatro Campesino. Bread and Puppet Theater."

Vinny had been talking to Luis Valdez, head of Teatro Campesino, a farmworkers' agitprop theater from the Central Valley, and to Peter Schumann, the head of Bread and Puppet Theater. We had met them in New York. Very beat, very European, very radical in a stark, minimalist way.

"And what are we going to do?" I asked.

"*Congress of the Whitewashers*," Olivia said. It was the first time she had spoken in the meeting.

Vinny glared at her.

Olivia sat back. She'd dropped a bomb and seemed to enjoy the role of bombardier.

"Jesus! When?"

"In the fall," Vinny said.

"When in the fall?" Donna asked.

"October."

"And we're already booked?"

"Yeah. So we better get going and stop fucking around with puppet shows," Vinny said.

"Wait a minute," Nikki said. "The puppet shows were your idea!"

"There's a time for everything," Vinny said.

"And now's the time to start building a show." Olivia seemed to enjoy the chaos.

"That's ridiculous," I said.

"We've already got a script," Vinny said.

Olivia laughed. Sardonic.

Vinny glared at her and picked up a pile of scripts. "Read these." He passed them out. "Everybody. I've done rewrites. We meet tomorrow for a table reading."

"Don't we need to talk about the focus?" I asked. "The way we talked about it in Chinatown. Exposing the media."

"And a different way to portray Turandot," Olivia added.

I hadn't seen Vinny spring a surprise before. I wondered what rewriting he had done — and with whom. Behind closed doors.

Then the call came: did we want to come to Chicago in August, during the Democratic Convention? They wanted us to perform *L'Amant Militaire* at a giant antiwar demonstration organized by the MOBE, an umbrella organization of antiwar groups. They were planning marches that would end outside the Chicago convention center and they wanted us to do shows in the parks, many of them in black neighborhoods during the days of the convention.

We also got a call from the Youth International Party — Jerry Rubin and Abbie Hoffman's anarchy machine. They wanted us to bring street theater to Chicago to create circus chaos in the middle of the Democratic Convention. Vinny didn't tell us about the call from Abbie Hoffman and Jerry Rubin, the head Yippies. We learned of both Chicago calls from Lenore, who had seen Vinny reject the offers. She felt it was hypocritical that Vinny kept the news from us. "He wants a collective," Lenore said. "But he wants to lead it."

I called the Yippie office back. They spoke with stoned ambiguity. "You could do some kind of freaked-out floating lotus, electric rocker, acid-test opera, a ritual, or a moveable drama or whatever. You know, rock us with some hip, joyful anti-establishment sweet-Jesus improvs."

They sounded like they'd stepped out of Jack Kerouac's *On the Road*. They didn't know what the Troupe was all about, but it sounded like fun, and boy, were we popular. The Black Panthers wanted us. The Mobilization to end the War in Vietnam, "The Mobe," wanted us. The Yippies wanted us.

We pitched the idea to Vinny.

"Jesus! You guys and your damned Gutter Puppets."

He leaned back in his chair. "The work is here," he said. "Hoffman and Rubin and those guys… They got plenty of momentum on their own."

"We got really good results at State," I said. "We bring our own momentum with us."

"You can bring the same momentum to *Congress of the Whitewashers*," Vinny said and turned to Nikki. "And I want you to play Turandot."

Nikki stiffened. "I can't do that," she said. "It isn't fair to Olivia."

"Olivia doesn't understand the part," Vinny said.

"Maybe you don't understand the part," I said.

"This feels like you're using me," Nikki said.

"To get back at Olivia," I said.

"For what? What am I getting back at her for?"

"For calling you out," I said.

"Calling me out?" Vinny laughed. "What does that mean?"

"You tell me," Nikki said.

"Hey! Who the hell do you think you are?" I'd never seen Vinny quite as unhinged.

"A woman, looking at the situation another woman is in."

"Great," he said. "Now we're all setting our own compasses. For you, the world turns around gender. So good for you. For me, it's history."

"And for me, it's using history to talk about now," I said. "Now is corporate. Now is violence. Now is cruel.

Now is sexist and sadistic. It sure as hell isn't about squabbling intellectuals."

"Suit yourself," Vinny said. "Whatever life and the theater are 'about'..."

"Life and the theater are the same thing," I said. "You taught me that."

"Cut the crap," Vinny said. "It's time to get to get *Congress* up and running. Read the script." He turned to Nikki. "And think about what I just said." He picked up the phone to make a call.

Nikki and I took the cue. We exited the studio and walked down Market to the waterfront. We climbed through the cyclone fence of an abandoned pier and sat on the dock. The Bay Bridge arched over us, a great, gray dragon with a snakelike spine that pierced Treasure Island and disappeared into the tule mist floating into the city from the East Bay. We sat silent for a long time.

"I feel like I just got kicked out of the house."

"I feel like I just got molested," Nikki said. "Like by my uncle or somebody."

"Wow," I said. "That's laying it on the line." I put my arm around her shoulder.

"Damn! What's happening?" Nikki leaned into me. It felt good, even with the world gone weird around us.

We sat in the first cold drops of afternoon fog, listening to the traffic clack-clack over the expansion joints in the bridge above.

"Now what do we do?" Nikki asked.

"Get the hell outta here."

"Yeah? Like where?"

"I dunno," I said. "Like out of this net. I feel like one of those gladiators that gets caught in a web and stabbed to death."

"Jesus!"

"No, Spartacus."

Nikki looked at me and laughed. "Shit man, you ain't oily enough to be no Spartacus. I'm talking about Vinny. What do we do about him!"

"Hell, I dunno," I said. "I've never seen him like this. He can get pretty dark, but wow…" I told Nikki about the night in Madison when Vinny had come on to Suzanne.

"Who's Suzanne?" Nikki asked.

"Somebody I met on the road," I said.

"So what about her?"

"Vinny started flirting with her. It felt malicious, like he was trying to show me who was boss. Of course, after that, he said he was 'just kidding.'"

"That's a tell," Nikki said. "Usually 'just kidding' means the opposite."

"Yeah, well, he wasn't kidding just now."

"No kidding," Nikki said.

"Ha ha."

"At least one of us is laughing." Nikki stood up. "Look," she said. "I've had plenty of guys come on to me. Besides, he was offering me a part. I've had that happen before, too."

"But this was different," I said. "Casting you as Turandot would drive a wedge right through the middle of the company. Olivia would probably leave."

"I know." Nikki sighed. "I bet Vinny knows that. What an asshole."

Vinny's proposition was nasty but perceptive. Nikki had a speed to her, a fluidity, and, although she restrained it, a zaniness. Underneath it lay the steely rage of the oppressed that I had seen when the pigs pushed her into that squad car, when they paraded her handcuffed through the precinct station. She would make a powerful Turandot, a woman who knew the reality of her power, who had developed the silliness expected of her sex as a ruse, and despite her youth, had already forged the tools she would need to rule. It was a shocking revelation, but Vinny was a shocker. And he had set up a battle.

"I'm gonna tell him that was uncool. Hell, Nikki, he's not God and you're not his piece of ass."

"He runs the company."

"Hell, girl, he started the company." The fog rolled in. "But right now, he feels like a guy who needs to be stone-walled." I looked out at the gray bay, the cranes and docks of the Oakland navy yard, the gray shapes of the cruisers and destroyers, the resurrected Liberty ships, all bound for Vietnam. "It's just, right now, I hate the guy."

"We've got more important things to do than let Daddy push us around," Nikki said. "I already told him 'no.' And you're the only survivor of the tour besides those two. You've gotta keep your hand in to rewrite *Congress*. You've got great ideas. It'll work out. We'll work it out." Nikki sat back down and put her arms around me. "Gimme shelter," she said.

"Oh yeah," I said. *"War, children, It's just a shot away, It's just a shot away."*

That night, sequestered in the Oakland hills, we lay together in the darkened bus, and felt the bond that conflict can bring to intimacy. We'd already been through a lot, the two of us, and we knew we were going to move forward.

"Love, sister
It's just a kiss away
It's just a kiss away
Kiss away, kiss away."

Nikki kissed me. I could feel her smile and I let the music move me against her, black against white, sun against moon, day against night.

31

CONGRESS OF THE WHITEWASHERS

Back in Oakland, we gathered in the kitchen to read the script. Even Spider and Donna read parts. When we had finished, I tossed the script on the table. "Damn," I said. "Vinny's gone and changed directions." When we met at the Chinese restaurant, we had talked about how the networks gaslit the Vietnam War. That's what intrigued me about *Congress of the Whitewashers*. It was all about gaslighting — there's plenty of cotton, there is no cotton. We're winning the war. We need more troops. The cotton crop was good but it's missing, we need more time, we need to pull out. We all got a kick out of *that* innuendo. A perfect analogy. We were fucking Vietnam, but nobody got kissed. Doves in the Senate, hawks in the House, Congress in Washington, Congress of the Whitewashers, déjà vu all over again. And now Vinny wanted to use the play to talk about academia.

"He must have been talking to that Berkeley prof, Juris," Lenore said.

"And Ivan." They wanted to explore factionalism among intellectuals. Sure, infighting broke the German left wing in the 1920s, just when it was needed the most. But that was then. Now, Vinny wanted to criticize the American Left for fragmenting while I saw it uniting.

Later that night, the light of a rising moon flickered through the eucalyptus grove behind the Night Tripper. The shadows swayed across the quilt that covered Nikki and me.

"Vinny's in a big hurry," Nikki said. "That festival's got him wound up."

"I think he and Juris have been cooking the rewrites together. Of course, Juris wants to drag the play through academia and Vinny wishes he'd gone to college."

"Yeah, but we've gotta live with this play," Nikki said. "We've gotta perform it. And I don't think a play about academic dishonesty is really gonna grab people."

"I'm supposed to meet with Vinny and Olivia for a *Congress* meeting tomorrow. I'm gonna push for a shift back to the media and Vietnam."

Nikki kissed me on the cheek. "You'll do good," she said. "You got a say in how this should go. You're an O.G. now.

"What's an O.G.?" I asked.

"Original gangster," she said.

I loved that idea. An O.G., a survivor. I kissed Nikki. She smelled sweet. "I'm ready for that," I said. "But I want to make sure we're all at the studio. It's time to open things up."

The next day, I joined Vinny and Olivia to work on *Congress*. I felt out of place in the embattled circle, especially after Vinny's freaky turnaround about the premise behind *Congress* and his divisive proposition to Nikki. But I was ready to push back. I had done the research. I liked *Congress of the Whitewashers*. Brecht had never finished the script. Parts had been written by others, usually the women who made up his consort of intellectual and libidinous courtesans. Because the play was unfinished, we had plenty of wiggle room and *Congress* had comic potential, the best dramatic form for relating critical ideas to an audience. *Congress* should begin with a laugh and end with a clenched fist.

Vinny and Olivia must have already been at each other. A thunderstorm hung in the space. Vinny sat behind his desk like an angry god, arms folded. Olivia paced, shooting lightning bolts into the room. The air crackled. Juris Svenson, the Berkeley prof sat head down, writing on a yellow pad. Ivan was there, too. I was surprised. I thought he had disappeared with the Diggers, but he seemed to occupy a perennial place in the Troupe. The place felt like the eye of a hurricane.

"We read the script last night," I began. "I thought we were gonna use the play to talk about the corporate news media and Vietnam. Not about the left wing in Germany."

"Bad thinking and left-wing factionalism," Vinny said. "That was Brecht's intention."

"That's one direction we could go. But look... right now, we're working with the Black Panthers — thanks to you, Vinny. And they want to work with us. What about the Rainbow Coalition. Isn't that unity? And what about the tour last fall?"

"What about it?" Vinny asked.

"Come on, man," I said. "On tour, we watched those schools unite over Vietnam. They were holding teach-ins together, right?"

"Yeah, so?"

"Yeah, so unity. They sure as hell put out a different story than what CBS was selling."

"Faculties are battling over the issue of Vietnam," Juris said, his accent thickening. "I'm watching it happen right before my eyes."

"Maybe in Berkeley. But out at SF State, faculty and students, they're pulling together. No whitewash. The kids are working across color lines and professors are joining them."

"To do what?" Vinny asked.

"Hell, man, to obliterate the racism. To bust ivory towers like Cal. Daddy Warbucks comes to academia. They suck up military research contracts and rat out wobbly students to their draft boards."

"They're still doing that?" Olivia asked.

"Sure," I said, surprised. "You know…"

Olivia had been with us on tour. She heard students talk about getting drafted right out of the lecture halls. Maybe she'd only been there in body.

"Students know what's happening," I said. "The media just blurs the situation. Let's talk about that." *Damn. I had a better perspective on the play and the times than my mentors.*

"To hell with CBS," Vinny said. "And NBC, too. We're about to watch the New Left shatter into pieces. That's what Brecht was talking about. That's what we're gonna talk about."

"We all read the play last night," I said. "Like you told us to do. Let's see what other people have to say about this." I opened the door to the studio. "Hey, comrades," I yelled. I wanted the word to ramp up the scene. "We need to talk!"

People filed in and took seats on the busted-out couch and the ragged easy chairs.

"Oh Jesus," Vinny said.

"Well," I said. "This is a collective… right?"

Juris twisted his mustache. Ivan looked at Vinny.

"So we're collecting," Tommy grinned. The guy had his moments.

Olivia flashed a devilish grin and laughed.

Vinny shifted in his chair. "The Left needs to pull its head out of its ass. Brecht said it best." He picked up the script. "Right here."

"Okay," I said. "So, Brecht wanted to criticize the Left. Armed with hindsight. He wrote *Congress* about the past. His past. That was there. That was then. This is here and this is now."

"But remember," Juris said, "the German Left made a fatal mistake."

"Oh gawd," Olivia said. "And what was that fatal mistake, herr doctor professor? Please enlighten us."

Juris ignored the sarcasm. "The German Left sabotaged itself rather than uniting to join mother Russia in her infant Revolution. They couldn't think straight. You think the American Left is thinking straight?"

"Oh, come on," Spider said. "Who wants to watch a comedy about the German Communist Party?"

That got a sarcastic hoot out of Vinny.

"Look at the play," I said. "Don't be so literal. The emperor's intellectuals are trying to explain why there was no cotton. The emperor's warehouses are full. Right? Now look at *The New York Times*. Look at the networks. They're all broadcasting the bullshit the hawks put out there. 'Light at the end of the tunnel,' my ass. How many troops should we send to Vietnam? How much cotton is too much cotton? It's a perfect fit."

"How many troops can dance on the head of a pin?" Lenore said. "Hell, man. We shouldn't have anybody over there."

"Look at what just happened with the Tet Offensive," I said. "The fucking Viet Cong took over half of South

Vietnam. Like in *Congress of the Whitewashers*, the storming of the palace by the naked poor. This is talking right to the U.S. in Vietnam."

"You want to talk about foreign wars when we have real contradictions right here at home," Juris said. "Academia is split into fragments."

"Oh bummer, bummer, bummer," Donna said. "You guys sound like a bunch of Cassandras."

"And like Cassandra, we're not to be believed, is that it?" Juris said.

"Oh, get off it," Lenore said.

"The war is redounding to the home front, baby," Tommy said. "Dig it."

Olivia spoke up. "I've been thinking about Turandot."

Nikki and I braced for more thunder and lightning. We hadn't spoken to Olivia since he tried to recruit Nikki for the role. Clearly, neither had Vinny.

Olivia waved the script in the air. "Brecht's Turandot — another trite female written by a guy who didn't understand women. And…," Olivia said, "…by a guy who let women do his writing while he took the credit."

The women sat quietly, watching Vinny. And Juris. And Ivan.

The independent women in my world flashed across my mind — Lucky in Cambridge, Suzanne in Madison, Shirley Clarke in New York, Kim, Donna, Lenore, and now Nikki. But Olivia wasn't finished. She'd done her homework.

"Turandot should be smart. She should be a good-looking woman who knows the power of her beauty — and her brains. She's conjured up her own master plan."

"Nonsense," Juris said. "Brecht portrayed Turandot as a sapiosexual."

"What the hell is that?" Lenore asked.

"She's turned on by intelligence," Ivan said.

"Brecht was a horny old bastard," Olivia said. "He wanted to sexualize Turandot's intelligence. To diminish her. But that doesn't mean she has to suck academic dick."

The women whooped.

"Sure, she's smart," Olivia continued. "She knows all about her father's hired bullshitters…"

"Just like our network bullshitters," Donna said. "All men. Chet Huntley, David Brinkley, Walter Cronkite…"

"The most trusted men in the news," Spider laughed. "What a joke."

Olivia wasn't to be distracted. "Turandot has a plan," she said. "Knowing the world she lives in — male-chauvinist, pig-assed China — she needs a front man. He'd have to be intelligent, handsome, and shrewd enough to partner with Turandot and succeed her father on the throne."

"Just like our news anchors," Nikki said. "You're my daddy, Mister Cronkite, sir. Anything you say must be right. Right?"

"Turandot convinces her father to sponsor a contest," Olivia said. "To find the Tui who can come up with the best explanation for the missing cotton. Turandot will promise her hand in marriage to the winner. Whether or not she goes with him is up to her, of course."

"Right on!" The women all applauded.

"With the right words and the right front guy, she could bring the sympathy she feels for the poor people in her father's kingdom."

"That's a helluva long way from Brecht's script," Vinny said.

"Brecht is just another old white guy," Olivia said. "We need to bring him up to date. A feminist Turandot is the best way to do that."

"Really?" Vinny cracked up at that idea.

"Yeah, really," Olivia said. "Old white guy."

"Are you gonna do the rewrites?" Vinny asked.

"We're going to do them," Nikki said. "Character by character, scene by scene."

"We can do that," I said. "Right, Ivan?" I remembered the first day in the studio when I asked who had written *L'Amant Militaire*. Ivan had insisted that everybody had written it. I knew that creative consensus was an oxymoron, but I wanted to get my ideas across and to do that, I needed a hand in the rewrites. "We'll write it on the rehearsal stage. Together."

Olivia laughed and jerked a thumb at Vinny. "He'll never go for that," she said. "You're all for collectives, so long as you run 'em, right, Vinny?"

"We've already got a script," Vinny said. "We don't have time for this bullshit."

"We don't have time for *your* bullshit," Olivia snapped.

"Jesus, Olivia," Vinny pleaded. "Save it for later, will ya?"

"No! That'll just turn into another one of our fights. Where's that gonna get us? This not about me and you, Vinny. This is about the company and the theater we put onstage." She swept her arm around the assembled Troupe. "What we do and say affects everybody. So everybody should have a hand in development."

Juris got up. "I'm sorry, but this meeting has begun to feel counterproductive."

"So leave," Olivia said. "You're not a member of the company."

"Oh, for chrissakes," Vinny said.

"We can talk later," Juris said to Vinny.

"So you men can straighten things out on your own. In a sane and rational basis," Olivia snapped. "Get the real work done, right, Juris?"

"Something like that," Juris said.

"Wrong, Juris." Olivia's anger flared for everyone to see. I knew its origins; I'd been with her on tour. She believed in the company, but she found Vinny intolerable, his constant sarcasm, his infidelities, his intellectual pals. She was tired of Vinny's knee-jerk habit of fighting back with insults.

Tommy busted in. "We're all going to be part of this. We don't want to just do puppet shows and a marching band. We want a hand in shaping the script. And what about our political mission?" Tommy didn't know squat about the history of the Troupe or how its politics had developed. He'd barely been onstage with the Troupe. "Mao says the art's gotta support the politics," he said.

"So now you're spouting Chairman Mao." Vinny laughed.

"We should all read *The Little Red Book*," Tommy said and held Mao's small, red bible aloft. "And Mao says that art must reflect the reality of the workers and the peasants."

"Which are you, Tommy?" Vinny asked. "A worker or a peasant?"

"And what are intellectuals to you?" Juris asked. "Aren't you a Harvard graduate?"

"Hell, no, man. I dumped out of that pit. I'm a worker. We're the workers," Tommy said. "And professors are bloodsuckers. Besides, this play is set in China. During a revolution."

"What revolution?" Juris asked.

"The script says naked people are storming the empire's citadels," Tommy said. "They want to liberate the cotton from the emperor's warehouses. That's a revolution, isn't it?"

"That's preposterous," Juris said.

"Juris," Olivia said. "I thought you were leaving."

"Do you think we're all stupid?" Tommy continued, "We're doing a Chinese play. What better time to study the Chinese Revolution?"

Vinny laughed that high-pitched laugh. "It's a German play, you moron."

"It's our play," Tommy shouted. "It's an American play. For a people's theater, and we have the right to write it."

Vinny was seething. He was ready to take his anger out. On somebody.

Juris growled and tortured his mustache again.

Ivan looked intently at Vinny. He wanted to look conspiratorial. He came off with his mouth open, at a loss for words.

Olivia sat with her arms folded and a wicked look on her face. "And you," she said, turning to Vinny. "You can't see past Brecht's Neanderthal portrait of Turandot. That's not going to work. We live in 1968, not 1933. Women don't giggle and stare at the ground anymore. We're not your Geishas."

Vinny laughed. "What do Geishas have to do with a Chinese princess?"

"More than you'll ever know," Olivia said.

"No no no," Vinny said. He was angry now. "Tell me about it. We got a production to mount, not write the history of bound feet."

"Oh, fuck you," Olivia said. "And bound feet are just the point."

Lenore spoke up. "You guys are all good talking about the left wing in Germany back in 1930 or 1950 or sometime. We live different. Look at the women around you." She pointed to Donna, to Olivia, to Nikki. "You think we spend our lives tee-heeing for stupid men and their dirty little jokes? You think we flirt our way through life?" She turned to Vinny. "Did we flirt with you to get into the Troupe?"

Vinny laughed, but it was a nervous laugh. "We're doing a piece of theater," he said. "Not a documentary on women's lib."

"'Women's lib?'" The usually calm Donna surfaced. "That's a network word. It's bullshit. We already liberated our own damn selves. This is feminism."

"And we've already got a script," Vinny shouted.

"Okay, Mister Director," Olivia said. "Look at your precious script. Open your fucking eyes. Look at this woman," she said. "Turandot. Who she can be! Her strength. Her wit. Her power." She turned to Juris and Ivan. "All you guys. Look at her, she's standing right there in front of you. You've sure as hell ogled her and the rest of us plenty enough. I can testify to that."

The women laughed; the men shifted in their seats.

"Can't you see it? She's smart. She's a strategist." Olivia looked directly at Juris. "She's just hustling a bunch of horny old professors to come up with their bullshit answers."

"Oh please," Juris said.

"Sure, she knows the power of her beauty. That doesn't mean she's gotta be a giddy girly moron. She also can have the intelligence to hold a master plan in secrecy."

"That's not in the script," Vinny said.

"Oh right," Olivia said. "I noticed how sacrosanct

Goldoni's words were, when you took the knife to *L'Amant Militaire*."

"With the right words," Donna said, "Turandot can bring the empathy she feels for the people to the palace."

"And the empire's dependence on poverty and labor for its wealth and power," Tommy said.

"She could be a revolutionary," Nikki said. "Look at the Panther women."

"But she's a princess," Vinny said. "The Panther women are warriors."

"I can't think of any women monarchs who wanted to rule with beneficence," Juris said.

"Try Cleopatra," Nikki said. "She had a plan, too."

"And Oshun," Donna said.

"Who's Oshun?" Nikki asked.

"She's a Santeria goddess. She's the earth mother, ruler of water."

"From where?" Nikki leaned forward.

"Come on," Vinny said.

"From Africa," Donna said. "She came from Mali and Nigeria with the slave trade, and she lives now in Haiti and Cuba. Even in New Orleans."

"Wow." Nikki looked straight at Juris. "I bet she has a beneficent plan, professor."

"And so does her Creole counterpart in New Orleans."

"Who?"

"Marie Laveau," Donna answered. "A practicing voodoo healer who acted as courtesan to New Orleans wealthiest men and set up her own underground railway to help women escape to California."

"Afro Cuban?"

"Creole. French, American black, and Yoruban blood, Nigeria, all tied up in an elegant body with the heart, spirit, and skills of a medicine woman."

"Like Joan of Arc," Lenore said.

"Joan of Arc was a lunatic," Juris said. "A mad woman."

"All women are lunatics," Olivia said. "You guys have driven us crazy."

"And then you burnt us at the stake," Nikki said.

"And killed our cats," Lenore said.

"And left the rats," Donna said.

"And the rats gave you all bubonic plague," Nikki said.

"Kaaarma!" Lenore taunted.

"This is ridiculous," Vinny said. "There's a festival coming up. And we already have a script."

"Change it," Olivia said. "Change her. Women are changing. Turandot's gotta change."

"Go to hell," Vinny said.

"Oh, go fuck yourself, Vinny," Olivia said. "You can listen to the women around you, or you can model her on those little grad-school honeys you like to fuck. But don't look at me to play a giggling little suck-up."

"I'm not looking at you," Vinny said. "Nikki. Are you ready to play Turandot?"

"Uh-uh." Nikki rose. "No way. Strike two, Vinny. You think I'm gonna scab for you?"

Quiet descended into deadly silence.

Olivia pinned Vinny with her lightning eyes. "What does 'strike two' mean?"

"Screw this," Vinny said and walked out.

32

VENCEREMOS

We had come a long way. We studied mime and adapted *commedia dell'arte*'s bawdy, class-conscious style to the chaotic, hard-working life we lived — a theater full of bourgeois bandits pushing back against an Amerika at war. We cranked out sweaty, profane comedies about the flaming disaster in Vietnam, about living and dying while black, about craven power, callous wealth, and cruel poverty.

We had hooked up with Students for a Democratic Society, the savvy sprawling, student movement that spanned the USA. Everyplace we took our shows, campus radicals surrounded us with exuberant, pissed-off protestors who we embraced with sleazy resistance comedy. Campuses exploded. We didn't instigate the revolution but were sure as hell a part of it. Something had skewed. I didn't trust Vinny's obstinance. Up until now, his insistence on the right way and the wrong way had worked. Now, in the face of this new company, he seemed dictatorial.

Maybe it began with Tommy and his *Little Red Book*. Probably it was an idea whose time had come, as Victor Hugo once wrote. The romantic French revolutionary envisioned a day when battlefields would disappear, and ideas would run the world. The world wasn't ready, but he seized the time. We seized the time. Mao told us that literature and art grow out of people's lives. There is no art for art's sake. Even the claim that art is just art is a political act.

Mao's cultural revolution hung in the embattled atmosphere like the northern lights — bright, ethereal, multicolored, and shifty, more complex and fraught with contradiction than we could ever have imagined. The Panthers studied Mao and sold copies of *The Little Red Book* on street corners. Mao's revolution crept into minority factions of radical students. We felt buoyed by Mao's ubiquitous slogan — "Women hold up half the sky."

Along the way, we had begun to lose the heartbeat that drove the Troupe. What did we know of the terror that emerged inside the cultural revolution in China? Armed with our own ingenuity and the inspiration of Mao's Red Guard, our unholy cadre of actors was fast leaving theater behind. Class struggle and self-criticism took their place beside lust, laughter, and impulse. We gained control but lost vision, direction, skill, and experience. Although the Troupe mounted new work, its style became broader, less complex.

Vinny wanted us to push through that stage. He stayed on as director, but he disappeared for days. His attention had shifted to academic pursuits. Olivia moved out of Vinny's apartment but continued to work with him, splitting her focus between the Troupe and the school that Vinny was setting up. She showed up for rehearsals looking haggard and angry. Nikki and the other women gathered to give her courage and support, but, as in New York, it seemed as if Olivia had reached her limit and shut down. *Congress of the Whitewashers* struggled into life, but without the lascivious charisma or energy of *L'Amant Militaire*, or even the Gutter Puppets. In keeping with Brecht's fantasyland of an ancient Chinese empire, Vinny wanted me to generate Chinese opera music with authentic Chinese instruments — drums and gongs, a scratchy banjo-type instrument played with a bow and a harsh-sounding double-reed horn. I had a tough time getting into the task.

Nikki and I soldiered on. Cosmic glue held us together. The festival loomed in the future. The more the stress, the more we kept each other strong and in balance. When up was down, we managed to spin the down to up. Best of all, we enjoyed each other's company, alone together at the end of the day. Our words, moves, and smells grew more familiar, trustworthy, and intriguing. Gallery doors opened into a museum of us, fresh paintings appearing in each new room. As with our bodies, our conversations deepened.

"You say you know how inequality works. But how can you?"

"I can feel it, I'd say."

"No. You can think about it. You can't feel it because you don't live under it."

"Okay, then, I have sympathy."

"I have sympathy when I step on a snail," she'd say.

"So your sympathy has limits. And you're a woman."

"A black woman. Like when those cops jumped me. You were sympathetic."

"That was empathy. I was angry and afraid."

"For me. Not for you."

She was right. I hadn't been afraid for my life, on the street or in the precinct. I wasn't covering my fear with a steel mask the way Nikki had.

"You weren't afraid about those pigs," Nikki said. "You were afraid of what they would do to me."

"That's right."

"Not what they would do to you."

"No. But I've been afraid of cops."

"Afraid for your life?"

"No. Hey, look, I'm not blind. I can see the difference. And that's about race."

"Race doesn't even exist," she said. "It's a phony distinction. No biology behind it. Just power. Power and control."

"I get it. We've got other fish to fry. Smaller fish, but at least we can catch the little bastards."

"What are you talking about?" she'd ask.

"Yeah. We can't erase 400 years of white people beating up on black people."

Nikki laughed. "Do tell, white boy."

"But we can shape our own lives."

"We can?" Nikki could frown deep. The phony innocent.

"That's what we're trying to do here, isn't it?"

"Sure," Nikki would say. "You and me. Alone together. With the world clamoring outside our window."

"Yeah. But let's just say the political work starts with the personal. You know, use personal stuff to establish a beachhead. We're lucky enough to…"

"'Lucky?'"

"We've got each other. And we can talk. I'm no cop, and I didn't rape or lynch anybody."

"So you say."

"Hell, yeah, I do say it. And you can believe it. I thought back to the nameless girl in Detroit. Do I go there? Or lie? Or recognize that episode for what it was. Gratuitous and harmful but not rape. Hell, I wasn't sure, so I lied. "So in this realm, I'm one half of an equation here. Give me that."

"'Give' you?" Nikki asked. "That you and I are equal? You want me to ah… 'give' you that? What are you going to 'give' me back?"

Silence.

"Me," I said.

Nikki stroked my cheek. "Dear sweet thing."

I laughed. "Okay, then. My knee-jerk responses as a man."

"Such as?"

"Interruptions."

"You've already given me that."

"More interruptions."

"Cool," Nikki said. "You're lucky you don't come first…"

"'Lucky?'" I thought back to my early blundering attempts at sexual pleasure. I had learned — slowly. "Got nothing to do with luck. That takes skill, practice, savoir faire."

"Hell, man, you smell good, that's all."

"Thanks. So no giving you anything. What can I give up to make us equal?"

"I don't want you to give up anything," Nikki would say. "I want you to see my power. But I don't think you can do that."

"I see your power. I wouldn't be with you if I didn't."

"White men don't give up power. Men don't give up power. Nobody gives up power."

"I will. I'm yours. But you already know that."

"In some ways. In others, you can't. Gifts have limits."

"Like what?"

Silence.

"Did you know that every time you look at a woman… let's say a stranger."

"Okay. What about her?"

"That woman has to conduct a risk-assessment."

"What do you mean?"

"She's gotta size you up the way an animal would. How big are you? Could you overpower her? What's your intent, even if it's just the result of your eyes meeting. Where are you standing? Where is she standing? Or sitting? How can she escape if she must? How can she interact with you if, for some reason, she would want to."

"Why would she want to? Because she's attracted to me?"

"You wish. But, okay. Let's say she thinks you're cute. Maybe she needs a job. Probably you own that job. Deep down, somewhere, she's asking 'How can I connect without being hurt?' How can I get what I want without putting out — one way or another.'"

"I dunno. No. Wrong. I do know. Because…"

"Because you've got the power. And she doesn't."

The dialogue was seductive. Nikki and I gradually stretched out our time away from the studio until we began arriving late to rehearsals and meetings. We worked on *Congress* with the others and stuck together as the contradictions broadened. Simplify the story? Get with the people? Or lay out all the complexities of the play as Brecht wrote it, how Vinny's alienated intellectuals clashed with my network liars. My mouth went dry, my voice shook, but I held out for my ideas.

Away from the studio, Nikki and I had become our own laboratory. We both carried the gift of gab and Nikki was teaching me how to fight, not to kill, but to communicate. She taught me how to peel back the layers of the onion, revealing the sweet kernel of reality, but only after so many tears had been shed. The power inequity was huge, the product of millennia. We survived together only because we could sit alone, face to face, and punch it out. The outside world became impossible to deal with while we were parrying power clashes in the Troupe and one-on-one. After rehearsals, we closed ourselves into the Night Tripper and sat there, facing each other, cross-legged, alone together.

Sometimes the work was so directionless and strained at the studio that Oakland and the Night Tripper became an island where we sat in exhausted silence. I wanted to stay with Nikki, but the magic of the Troupe was fading for me. Rehearsals became a drag, a word-by-word battle for possession of the play. We sought a crazy kind of refuge in the personal. You could wrestle with personal politics. With what was happening out in the world, sometimes it got to be too much. One night after a particularly frustrating, confused rehearsal, we retreated to the Night Tripper.

"Hey, I've got an idea," Nikki said.

I was drowsing, half asleep. "Whazzat?"

"Let's go someplace where you'd be in the minority."

"Yeah? Like where? Africa? Join the revolution in Angola?"

"No. Someplace where they already had a revolution."

"The revolution never stops."

"Yeah," Nikki said. "But it'd be good to be someplace where we weren't on the fringe of a maybe-so, maybe-not revolution."

"You want a place where I'd be in the minority as a white guy."

"Right."

"And someplace where we could be part of a revolution that's already happening."

"And someplace where women are treated as equals."

"And someplace where I could play music that wasn't for a marching band."

"Uh-huh."

"A place where we'd have to defy the man to get there."

"Uh-huh."

"Where the living was cheap."

"And we wouldn't be freaks."

I thought back to the students in Lansing, yearning to get out of the cold, to cut cane in Cuba. They would defy the blockade.

We knew without saying it. We could leave the Troupe, join the new society that was struggling to emerge on the large Caribbean Island to the south of us. We had plenty we could bring with us. Nikki's imagination and dance. My way with words and music. Our stagecraft.

I thought back to the night Jackie DeJohnette took us up to the Palladium and the rhythm and taste of black Cuba came across in the drums, in the horns, in the jazz, and the songs in Spanish. Havana. The revolution now 10 years old. Our politics. And I hadn't realized how much I missed playing music. I don't mean music on a Chinese one-stringed instrument. I mean music from my guitar, my voice. With others. In a city the size of New York with a culture as old as slavery. Havana.

We talked to Spider and Donna. She knew a lot about voodoo and Santeria and the gods and goddesses that peopled Cuban life. Santeria was as surreptitious as the revolution had been for centuries in Cuba. The Cuban people, the black Cuban people, took on the saints of their colonizers, the Catholics, but beneath each saint's name, lay an orisha with his or her own power, the power of Yoruba, the power of Africa.

Nikki was fascinated. She wanted to learn more about this revolutionary religion. "How do we get there?" she asked. "Don't we have a blockade around the island?"

"Yeah," Spider said. "And it's just gotten worse since the Bay of Pigs."

"The Cuban missile crisis," Nikki said. "I was just a kid, but everybody was freaking out about nuclear holocaust."

"There's a bunch of people going to Cuba from SDS," I said. "When we were in Michigan, a bunch of kids were talking about going down to cut sugar cane, to help the revolution. I know the first group went already. They should know."

"Some of them are going by boat from Canada. Others are headed for Mexico City and, from there, flying to Havana.

Mexico City. I thought about Frieda Kahlo and Diego Rivera. I thought about the thousand-year-old lagoons and the wars fought there against Cortez and the Spaniards.

I thought about Tina Modotti, actress and photographer who had her Cuban lover shot off her arm in Mexico City by agents of Cuba's dictator. I thought about the exiled romantic Trotsky who got his head hammered by a Spanish communist who infiltrated his household and murdered Stalin's enemy. Mexico City, Soviet Russia, Spain, Cuba, all flowed together in a rich musical broth. "We could get to Mexico City easy enough, right?" I asked. "So from there, we can get to Havana."

Donna and Spider loved the idea. No American theater had visited Cuba since the revolution. And before that, Havana was about sugar cane and United Fruit, gambling and whores, Frank Sinatra, Sammy Davis and the Rat Pack, a mob scene.

Nikki was 100 percent on the way. Her confrontation with Vinny over Turandot had turned her head. She was an on or off woman, and now, as far as she was concerned, Vinny and the San Francisco Mime Troupe was off.

I was torn. For all my enthusiasm about Cuba and the music I had heard and the romance of Havana and a real revolution, kicking and growing, I owed allegiance to Vinny and the Troupe for all I had learned, for the messages we had delivered across our war-torn nation. I had watched the Mime Troupe family rise and fall with the departure of my early mentors, and rise again as we brought new actors in, began the Gorilla Band and the Gutter Puppets. I had been excited about the possible theater festival, but Vinny had shot down the idea of Nikki and I going to Chicago to work with the Yippies. I didn't put much stock in Jerry Rubin or even Abbie Hoffman, but Chicago's convention protest sounded big and broad and I had soured on Vinny's despotic response to any outside ideas about the play's direction.

I had no real connection to a Cuban adventure the way Nikki did. Yes, I could learn about the music, I could live there and find my own way while Nikki followed her curiosity. Would that be so bad? What would it be like to follow another person, a woman, on her journey? Would I have to make it my vision? My journey? Or could I see where Nikki's impulse took us both? Isn't that what we were trying to do? Alongside our arguments about *Congress of the Whitewashers* came the character of Turandot. Whose woman she would be? The male director's or the women in the company?

We sat cross-legged facing each other and launched into one of our Night Tripper talks. Smuggling ourselves into Cuba would take us straight into the heart of sex and color — with roles reversed. Nikki would be in a majority-black population and I'd probably be mistaken for a German tourist. We hadn't had anything to do with Cuba's revolution, but we would be swimming in Nikki's ocean, not mine. If they accepted our offer of theater and I kept my head above water, we'd be dancing a new dance. By the end of our Night Tripper talk, we were going to Cuba.

Nikki and I braced ourselves and climbed the studio stairs to talk with Vinny. We laid out our arguments. Well, I laid out our arguments. Since Vinny started casting threats and promises, Nikki often fell uncharacteristically quiet in his presence. Between the direction *Congress* was taking, the sudden appearance of the Chinese Cultural Revolution in our midst, the mess over casting Turandot, and — most important — our need to figure out our own lives, individually and together, we couldn't stay with the Troupe. We told Vinny of our plans for Cuba and our rationale. To separate race from gender in a neutral environment, check out the music and theater there, and just get outta town.

"Who knows?" I said. "Maybe someday the Troupe could come down to perform in Havana."

Vinny sat and listened. He was surprisingly quiet. "This is what I hoped for," he said. "That people like you would leave the Troupe and — armed with what you had learned — you'd go elsewhere. Wasn't it Che Guevara who said 'Let there be two, three, or many Vietnams?' So go. Let there be two, three, many Mime Troupes. Go to Cuba. Check out the scene. You're both people with a deep sense of theater and its connection to the rest of the world. There's more to the stage, more to life than *commedia* in San Francisco."

"Right!" Nikki said.

"On the other hand," Vinny said, "either of you guys speak Spanish?"

We were both taken aback. "A little," Nikki said.

"You ever hear Cubans speak Spanish?" he asked.

"No."

"I dunno," Nikki said. "Why?"

"Because," Vinny said. "Cuban Spanish isn't really a language."

"What do you mean?" I asked.

"It's machine-gun fire. *Rápido, cabrón. Muy rápido. Sin racionalidad. Loco.*"

"Okay. But we can learn."

"Sure you can," Vinny said. "But we need you here. There's work to be done. Not on your personal lives. You'll work those out. But personal stuff — it's not like it's a mini version of what's going on in the world. The battle between you guys. It's not like today's version of slave labor in America or a firefight in Vietnam."

"But this whole company is messed up with personal conflict," Nikki said. "Look at you and Olivia."

"Okay," Vinny said. "We're a mess. But we're sticking together. And do you think our personal battles are worth a damn compared to what we're trying to say onstage? Here. Right here. Beginning in this studio, with you…" Vinny looked straight into my eyes. He turned. "And with you, Nikki."

"Me."

"Yeah, with you. Do you think I went out on a limb to

cast you as Turandot to cause trouble?"

"Felt that way to me," Nikki said.

"Bullshit. You have a crazy fluidity, and you're wacky. You make off-the-wall choices. Sometimes they don't work. But sometimes they do."

"Thanks."

"I know, I know." Vinny stood. "Terrible sexist thing to do. But underneath the wacky, stagey actress, you've got that rage…"

"Black-people rage."

"If you want to call it that. Women's rage, too. Oppressed rage."

"I'm still not doing it."

"I'm not asking you to. But I'm asking you to stay. Both of you. We need you guys. You can keep us from sending the professors out into the street or the doctors onto the farms."

"What are you saying?" I asked. But I knew. He was referring to our own cultural revolution. Mao's *Little Red Book*, so far away from China.

"They're not going to listen to me," Vinny said.

"No, because your idea about the play is like, to put it politely, a faction of what the company wants to do. Nice choice."

"Yeah, dummy," Vinny said. "And I'm the chump they want to send off to the boondocks."

"Yeah," Nikki said. "I get it. The 'get with the people' faction."

"Look, I'm leaving anyway. I got a school to run. You know that. But they'll listen to you. Getting with the people doesn't mean getting stupid. It means telling the truth, even if it's a complicated truth."

Nikki shook her head. She looked at me. I saw Havana shimmer in the heat. "I dunno…"

"You can figure out shit on the personal level," Vinny said. "But people's personal lives — that's different. The personal — as you guys like to call it — sets up a fake comparison to the political world, to histories of masses and of centuries, whatever. A fake comparison to the world we're trying to set up with *Congress*. We got a festival to do. We got the show to do."

Nikki and I looked at each other. A kaleidoscope of thoughts and emotions whirled between us. We felt sadness, the loss of our escape dream, the loss of looking for ourselves and each other. We felt moved by Vinny's sincerity and excitement of shaping the show. And without uttering a further word, we knew we would stay to grow a thousand flowers from our hearts and minds.

The End

ABOUT THE AUTHOR

Charles Degelman is a writer, actor, and educator based in Los Angeles. He lives with his companion on the road of life, writer Susan Rubin, and three cats. After graduating, he left academia to become an antiwar activist, political theater artist, musician, communard, carpenter, hard-rock miner, and itinerant gypsy trucker. When the dust settled, he returned to his first love, writing.

www.ingramcontent.com/pod-product-compliance
Lightning Source LLC
Chambersburg PA
CBHW060243030726
47493CB00025B/1590